The Killer Among Us

A Novel

George Beck

NOIR
NATION

NOIR NATION

Acknowledgements

Thank you to my parents, George and Francine Beck, for teaching me the importance of hard work and for encouraging me to complete this book. Thanks to Terry Vaughan for taking the time to read through my drafts and offer suggestions. Thanks to my fellow writers and friends who spent many hours chatting about crime fiction and my book. Thanks to my late grandfather, Gerald Beck, and late aunt, Alice Mathias, who both shared old stories and memories, which in turn provoked my research interests in American cultural history. Thank you to my publisher Noir Nation Books. Editor Diane Vacca's sharp eyes and Eddie Vega's immense creative talent helped make this book shine.

George Beck

For my son Jordan Gerald Beck

Far better is it to dare mighty things, to win glorious triumphs, even though checkered by failure... than to rank with those poor spirits who neither enjoy nor suffer much, because they live in a gray twilight that knows not victory nor defeat.

—Theodore Roosevelt

PART ONE

Some Grudges Never Die

I

Mike could never forget the afternoon he'd caught his father and a much younger Abigail Stillman in the back room.

"Now look at her," he thought, every time she came into his shop. A damn rich old crone who probably never spent a single moment thinking about what she had done.

Because of her, his father was dead, and his father's younger brother had taken over the shop. But when Mike was seventeen, his young uncle had died of alcohol poisoning, liver all shot to hell, and he himself had been stuck with the damn butcher shop—a far cry from boyhood dreams of becoming a professional baseball player. Not that he would have made the bigs regardless, though he had a hell of an arm. But one thing was for sure: If it hadn't been for Abigail Stillman, he might've had a chance to find out.

"What do you want, Mrs. Stillman?" he asked in polite though seething anger.

She bent down and peered through the glass front of the meat case, eying each cut. It was always the chop on the bottom she bought, having him move them around, and he always had to be right on the nickel when it came to weighing the ground beef—not an ounce over this way or that.

She smelled like damn dead flowers and wore too much face powder and way too much lipstick. Frail as a bird, too.

But back on that fateful evening when Mike caught his old man and her on the butcher block, her skirt hiked up to her waist, his squat powerful father levered between her legs, his trousers down around his ankles so that his bare hams were exposed, Abigail Stillman had been a looker. Even Mike had to

1

admit that much. Buxom with lots of red hair, and wore those big hats like movie starlets and tight dresses so that the sexuality seemed to drip off her and every man in town had private thoughts about the judge's wife.

Lots of whispers had flown about how the old man must have promised her the moon and stars if she'd marry him, too, because why else would a woman like Abigail Stillman marry a man over twice her age?

Now there she stood, looking old and frail herself, picking out some chops, being her usual picky self, when Mike was hoping to close up, go home, and listen to the Cardinals on the Philco.

He wanted to say, "Hurry up, you old bitch."

But there was something about rich people you didn't speak your mind to, something about their unspoken commanding presence that could still intimidate. He stood there watching her, the old memories worse every time she came in, thoughts that he couldn't shake.

It was because of her the judge had his father killed. Mike learned about it later, after his father was buried.

"I know I did wrong, Mikey. I screwed up big time. Jeez, will you ever forgive me?"

"Hell, no," Mike said. "Hell, no." How could he? You don't when your old man had died from a gunshot wound to the belly.

She might as well have put a gun to both his parents' heads and pulled the trigger. Without his father, his uncle had been no solace, spent every penny on booze. They'd fallen on hard times, and his mother had done what women fear the most. She sold herself.

"Let me see that one," Abigail said. "No, not that one, the other one. No! That one right there..."

Mike wondered if she'd ever complained when his father was screwing her.

She'd even opened her eyes and looked directly at Mike that time and never said a thing, simply smiled, as if she wanted him to see it, his father and her together like that, as if she took some delight in it.

"No, damn it, the other one!" she complained as he fingered the chops on the tray.

The game would be about over by the time he got home at this rate. Dizzy Dean was pitching against the Cubs in Chicago that afternoon. More than anything, Mike wanted to hear something far, far away from Palisades Park, New Jersey.

Like everyone else in a country fallen into financial ruin, it seemed, he wanted a kind of avoidance from reality, a couple of hours of escape into another world where people cheered and a game was played on green grass, and the world wasn't full of brown dust and soup lines.

Everything about Abigail Stillman churned up bad feelings in him. All his life he'd been taught to be subservient: "Remember, kid, the customer is always right!"

He recalled running out of the shop that evening and hiding in the alley until they came out together, his old man and Abigail, her skirt back down now, a lumpy package wrapped in brown butcher paper under her arm. He had given her steaks, no doubt.

They'd kissed, and his old man had stepped back inside. Mike had heard the bolt slide home on the back door, gone down the alley, came out on the street, and followed his pop to Flannigan's, where he went inside, Mike knew, to have a couple of beers and solve the world's problems with all the other patrons before going home to supper.

Mike had sat across from him at the table that night and studied him for any hint of shame or regret. He had seen nothing. And when his mother bent and kissed the old man on the mouth, and he patted her rump, Mike had nearly blurted out what he'd seen. Later he had heard the two of them in their bedroom, the sounds a man and wife made and he put the pillow over his ears to try to drown them out.

Something in him had snapped.

Mike came around from behind the counter, checking the street through the plate glass storefront windows. Nothing happening except across the street sat a patrol car in front of the police station in its usual parking spot. A windstorm blew up, and the sweeping dust kept everyone inside. The street was deserted.

"Let me come over and see which one you're pointing to," he said to Mrs. Stillman, and eased his way behind her.

"That one," she said, half turning to look at him.

He caught her small frail neck in the crook of his powerful arm and pulled upward, lifting her off her feet. Her left shoe fell off.

"Old bitch," he snarled.

She struggled, but it was like a small bird struggling in the mouth of a large cat.

The very act of choking her, of dragging her toward the back, was surprisingly gratifying, erotic to have that sort of power over another.

"Don't struggle," he said. "I'm not going to hurt you."

He figured she'd think it was a rape job.

He took her into the same back room where sides of beef hung from meat hooks, cooled by refrigeration and not blocks of ice covered in sawdust and canvas.

He kicked shut the locker room door.

She was limp by then but still breathing, though barely.

He hefted her onto the same large butcher's block where she had been lying that evening like a sexual sacrifice to a man who hadn't even had a fifth-grade education.

He waited until her eyes fluttered open. Her spectacles had fallen off somewhere—like her shoe. He'd find them later.

"What...?" she managed to croak.

"You know how the game is played, Abigail, don't you? Remember what you did here with my old man? How you got him killed?"

She began to tremble, tried to sit up, to scramble away.

He reached out and pinned her down.

"You come in here, ruin my family, don't think nothing about it. Hell, you didn't even come to his funeral—and expect not to pay for your sins?"

Her eyes were startled little things. He almost felt sorry for her.

"See, you ruined us all," he said. "I wanted to play baseball, but no, I had to take over this place. At 37 now, it's too late for me to do anything but butcher meat. It's all I know. You turned me into a butcher, Abigail. Welcome to my world."

He reached for a cleaver.

2

Tucker and Emma Hammond had come to a crossroad and couldn't decide which direction to take. Both were almost too tired to think, to make a decision. Everything they'd done recently had been a complete failure. Emma said they should head east, that there should be a town somewhere along the road. "What's the point?" Tucker said. "We can't catch a break." He wasn't much into optimism just then. He knew he should be, but he wasn't.

It had been three hours since a middle-aged man passed them in his Chevrolet Roadster Pick-up. The man had stopped, said he was in a hurry, but offered them a fresh quart jug of water. They thanked him and watched as he motored south into the heart of New Jersey. The water was warm and had a bitter taste, Tucker was pretty sure the jug had recently been used for rum. The August sun was blistering, and heat waves shimmered up from the roadway.

At the bottom of their hope and feeling down and out, they were so deep into the abyss they couldn't see any way out. They had lost their home, their savings, and everything they had worked for. After his discharge from the service, Tucker had returned home, taken a job as a cop, and married Emma. Sometimes he felt he didn't deserve her, a man like him who'd seen and done the things he'd done.

As they waited on the highway, it seemed not that long ago that, back in Colorado, they had a home and plans for a family. But then the market had crashed, and when it had so had they. Boulder County Police Department couldn't afford to keep Tucker on, nor the ten other officers who all were sacrificed to keep the county from financial shambles.

"I know I've let you down," Tucker said.

"Why would you think that?" Emma said. "You've done your best. Let's keep moving. My sister will take us in."

"We can't possibly walk all the way to Buffalo."

"I know, but we can find a town up the road. I'll get a job waiting tables or something. Maybe you can do the dishes. That will be our beginning. Next will be New York, and then we'll go from there."

Tucker had known a lot worse situations than their current one. And while the war had been over for over a decade, he still recalled certain things he'd gone through. The rats in the trenches always ate the eyes first if they got the chance. They seemed to know when the bombardments would start, and would disappear just before the slaughter began. It was just one of the things that had sickened him about war—seeing rats eating the eyes of the dead who'd fallen and had to be tossed out until the battlefield was cleared enough to call in the medics.

It was a memory he carried around in his head, one he had to force out of his thoughts along with the other things he'd seen in France fighting the Huns. The bullets and barbed wire and mud and cold, the hunger, the stench of men living in trenches. But worst was the gas, how it could blind you or burn your throat so that you couldn't ever speak right, and that's if you were lucky and it didn't burn your lungs so that you ended up in some old folks' home until you died of suffocation.

It hardened even the best men, and some it destroyed, and Tucker felt he was always somewhere in the middle of those two aspects of life—hardened or destroyed.

Thank God for Emma. She had been his saving grace, had reminded him every day of what humanity and kindness and love were, and thoughts of her pushed away thoughts of everything else.

He shivered, and she asked if he was cold, and he turned to look at her, to gaze at that pretty face with its fine, delicate features, and wondered why any man would have ever wanted to hurt her, and then thought of the other man who'd looked upon that face in loving splendor—the last man she'd been with. Not her abusive husband, but the man after him. But he'd promised her and himself he'd never bring it up and he had kept his promise and he kept it now, erasing the thought. She was with him now and what did it matter about her past.

The ceaseless sun indicated east was to the left. Tucker and Emma continued walking on the barren dirt road—nothing more than hardened dry clay with deep cracks, some wide as a shovel handle, and splintered in jagged patterns that ran like veins toward the sun-scorched brush that flanked the road. Their legs were leaden, and the only things that kept them moving was the momentum of the last step and Emma's indefatigable spirit.

Eventually they spotted a steam traction machine that lay rusting in the Jersey summer sun a few yards to the west. Tucker could tell it'd been a long time since that field produced crops.

Then they heard the chug-chug-chug of a car motor. It came from behind them, which was hopeful. It was going their way.

"You hear that?" Emma said, hope risen in her voice.

They turned around; in the distance the silhouette of a car broke the endless empty skyline, the car's dust plume a rooster tail stretching far back and into the cloudless sky.

"He's going our way. Let's ask for a ride," Emma said, wiping the sweat from her brow for the hundredth time with a frayed hankie.

"Not so fast. Let's feel him out first. Everybody's out for something," Tucker said skeptically.

"Here we go again," she muttered. "You have to have faith in people. It was the government that let us down, not the people."

The car approached, a '33 black Ford V8 Model 18, fast, a real hay-burner. The windshield was plastered with dirt and bore bare spots made by hand so the driver could see. They smelled the burning oil before it stopped beside them. It was driven by a tall man in a white butcher's uniform, his jaw sharp and clean. "You folks looking to hitch?" he asked.

If only he had known how badly they needed it. They were nearly to the point of lying down and quitting.

"Where you headed?"

"Palisades Park... It's close to the Hudson River."

"East of here, right?"

"Of course," the driver said.

Tucker looked at Emma, shrugged, and said, "East is where we need to go."

"Okay," Emma agreed.

They squeezed into the stranger's car, and Tucker caught the driver's wandering glance at Emma. It wasn't unusual for men to gawk at her at first sight. The driver stared at her knees as she seated herself; his eyes seemed to drink in the sight of her.

"The name's Mike," the driver said, extending his hand to Tucker.

"Pleasure. I'm Tucker, and this is my wife, Emma," he said, shaking the man's large hand. Tucker sensed something he didn't care for in him—a curtness, like a guy who had a chip on his shoulder and was all the time looking for someone to knock it off. But Tucker thought, what the heck, ten minutes and it wouldn't matter.

"It wouldn't be too much of a guess to say you folks aren't from around here?" the man said.

"Where's here?" Tucker replied.

"Paterson's behind you, we're passing Hackensack."

"How far are we from New York City?"

"Hang on," the driver said. "Up ahead over the ridge, we'll be able to see the peaks of the buildings."

"It's that close?"

"Still a ten-minute car ride, not counting the time for the ferry."

"So you're hauling a load of booze or what?"

The driver snarled, "Why, you the police or something?"

"No."

"Why ask, then?"

"There's a lot of clanging back there."

"Milk cans."

"Milk cans," Tucker repeated, wondering why a butcher would be hauling milk cans.

The driver turned down a narrow roadway and wheeled into Palisades Park, a small hillside town a stone's throw from the Hudson River. Tucker heard the chatter of the automobile's wheels over the cobblestone and trolley tracks as they motored down Broad Avenue, where the community appeared. There were a police and fire station, eateries, clothing stores, a sporting goods store, a bank, law offices, a theatre, and luncheonettes—one called the Betty Lee, with a sign promoting Borden's ice cream. There was a billboard advertising land and homes for sale. Small-town America, Tucker thought as a trolley clanged past. It looked like a welcome place.

"I bet you guys want me to take you straight to a hotel, eh?"

"No, right here is good. Just a lift into town is all we needed."

They got out when the driver stopped in front of the Betty Lee Luncheonette.

"There's a hotel down the roadway," the man said. "Rates are reasonable."

Tucker once again leaned down to thank the man even while privately being glad to be out of his company.

"Thanks again."

"You two ever get the urge to burn a steak, stop by my shop. It's right there," the man said, pointing to a small storefront next to the Betty Lee. "Mike's Butcher Shop."

"We'll certainly do that." Tucker watched the V8 rumble up the street, the cans loudly clanging from the trunk.

"What's the matter, hon?" Emma said.

"Nothing. Just thinking how good being a butcher must pay to be able to drive a car like that."

"Why'd you ask him about the hootch?" Emma asked.

"I guess it slipped... All that clang-clang-clanging."

"You gotta let it go."

"Let what go?"

"You know."

"What do I know?"

Emma sighed. "You gotta stop thinking and acting like a cop."

"I wasn't."

"What if he suspected you were? Then what?"

"But I am not."

"What if he had a gun?"

"He'd have made my day," Tucker snickered.

"But you don't have a gun."
"I don't need one."

3

Maybe it was then that the butcher decided what he truly wanted in life—when he saw the woman with the silky hair and red dress, a real fine woman who could give a man a lot of pleasure. Emma was her name, and of course to have her he'd have to get the other guy out of the way, now, wouldn't he?

But so what?

He made his delivery of illegal booze and then returned to his shop, where he had to load the bloody tarp old lady Stillman was wrapped in. It was dark by then, the sky bleak with dim moonshine and cloud cover. The back area where he parked his V8 had a heavy coating of dust that kicked up in the easterly breeze. It irritated his eyes, and he rubbed them considering how he'd already swept the dust away a dozen times and how, like clockwork, it came back harder and stronger. Tomorrow he'd find the time to broom it again. But for now he had to dispose of old lady Stillman.

The screen door creaked as the butcher set it back on its hinges and eased his way inside his shop. There he found her rolled in the bloody tarp like refuse among his butchering tools. He noticed some of old lady Stillman's bloody silver hair protruding from the end of the tarp. It had been years since that once shining red hair that she loved to flaunt had grayed. With the toe of his boots he pushed against her head and slid her deeper into the tarp, tucking in her hair with his fingers.

The butcher grinned as he hefted the old lady. She felt damp and cool on his shoulder; his strong back managed the weight with ease.

That crazy old bitch had been a lot easier to kill than he'd thought it might be.

But she had gone as easily as if he'd crushed a bird in his hand.

It'd almost been too easy.

And the feeling of reliving it again, there in the room where he'd done it, of putting her on the same butcher block where she'd committed the original sin and doing to her what his father had done to her all those years ago, aroused him. That, and thoughts of the woman who'd just climbed out of his car, and when she had, how he'd caught a glimpse of her pretty leg as far up as to where the stocking was hooked by the garter belt. It had just been a glimpse, a fractured picture, but it had been enough.

He hefted the old lady outside and plopped her in the trunk.

He turned on the ignition and headed for the reeds along the Overpeck Creek. A few minutes later he parked the V8 on a patch of gravel that led to a fishing dock.

The moon was showering on the creek, and he could see a single porch light on a home across the water in Ridgefield Park. He'd spent many summer days in that place, swimming and splashing in the water with the local kids.

He closed the car door and shuffled to the dock, standing at the edge and looking down into the dark water. There were ripples in the water, and the moon's reflection shone back at him. He heard the water splashing along the bank and saw tires and other discarded items pressed into the muddy bank, thanks to a landfill that had once occupied the area. There was a glass jug and a broken fishing net left resting along the bank. In the early morning hours, local sportsmen would arrive and sink their crab cages and cast fishing lines into the creek hoping for a decent catch. Whatever fish and crabs they caught fed their families, and the rest they sold to a local fish market on Broad Avenue. Then they'd go and meet the butcher for their weekly rations of booze. Sometimes, they gladly brought the butcher a basket of blue crabs or a long eel. The butcher didn't care for either, but he knew his accepting it made the men feel comfortable.

The butcher sat at the edge and dangled his boots off the dock. He thought back to that day some twenty-five years before when, on that same dock, he had kissed Rebecca Madison, by all accounts the prettiest girl in town. Many local boys had desired her. But it was him she'd wanted. They had kissed one afternoon out there in the open, and a fisherman had teasingly whistled to them. Rebecca had blushed, and the butcher had, too. But then he'd playfully pushed her into the water and dived in after her, both fully clothed. They'd splashed around in the water and gone home. That had been all that came from that. The butcher shook his head, considering what had brought him the most pleasure that day: pushing her in the water, or kissing her? Both had been equally gratifying.

Enough reminiscing for now, he thought. He sprang up from the dock, walked back up the bank, and opened the trunk. He considered throwing old lady Stillman off the dock and letting her float downstream. But he thought better of it and hefted her deep into the brush, bending back the cattails and reeds. Sixty or so yards later he dumped her and went back to his vehicle. Let the animals eat whatever was left of her.

Thirty minutes later he wheeled the big V8 into the back of his shop and parked and got out and opened the trunk and removed the bloody tarp. He'd hose it down where he'd butchered the meat and fold it neatly and put it away.

Hell of a day.

4

Tucker and Emma walked along Broad Avenue and window-shopped the storefronts. It was already dark out and breezy. They peered inside the plate glass window of the closed Daniel Reeves Store, where they saw stacks of canned food and on the counter, a box of Oh Henry bars. Inside, a square glass case that sat on the edge by the register was filled with boxes of cigars. How nice it'd be to kick back and smoke a fresh cigar, Tucker thought. How nice it'd be if things were different. If he still had his cop job and his house and whatever savings they had amassed.

They continued down the sidewalk and came to another store that was also closed for the evening. It was called the Paris Confectionery Company, an ice cream parlor with a long, sleek counter and chrome-trimmed stools. There were big ice cream mixing machines and signs for sodas, floats, and sundaes. On the front window hung an American flag and a sign for a ballroom dance to be held at the Broad Avenue Theatre. Inside, a man in a white ice cream man's uniform, with a black bow tie and a bright smile, was mopping, the cotton strands sweeping back and forth over the orange tile floor. He caught their glance, winked, and went about mopping. It looked as if he was whistling. "Should we knock on the window?" Emma asked.

"I don't know if I could be a beggar."

"I can understand," Emma said softly.

"Let the man be," Tucker said as they began walking. "He's closed for the day."

"Looks like one heck of a nice feller," Emma said.

"I am sure he's the bee's knees. But, let's keep a low profile for now."

"What would it take really to beg for something to eat?"

"I suppose it wouldn't take much," Tucker groaned. "But at thirty-four, I ain't done it yet."

"We haven't been in this position before."

"True," Tucker considered. "But if you do it once, you'll do it again." He thought a moment then said, "You can live days without food. Less without water. And we drank earlier."

"So what's the point?"

"It's only day one."

"I know."

"Tomorrow I'll find a way to make money and we'll eat and drink. You have to trust me."

"You know I trust you."

They stopped at the intersection of West Central Boulevard and Broad Avenue. They studied the place. South along Broad Avenue they saw vehicles parked along the curb, the cobblestones cut by trolley tracks down the center of the roadway. There were shops strung up from across the municipal building. They saw the Bank of Palisades Park. It was the tallest building in the area and had huge columns three stories high surrounding the main entrance. Next to it was the Borough Hall Barber Shop, a shoemaker, and a store called Van Heertun's, which had a sign protruding from the building indicating Thibaut Wallpaper, paint, and hardware. Emma commented, "This looks like a town one could raise a family in."

"Places like this," he said, "are what make America America."

"We'll, there's definitely enough places to eat," Emma said. "An ice cream float right about now would've been swell."

Tucker smirked. "Tomorrow you can have two floats."

"I know, I know," Emma said. "It's my stomach talking. Don't pay no mind to it."

Moments later they had crossed the street when Emma stopped, saying, "That sign says the Erie Railroad is a few blocks down the hill. That'll take us to Buffalo."

"Says here the Hundred and Twenty-Fifth Street Ferry is somewhere up the hill."

"Look further," Emma said. "It costs thirty-five cents."

"Yeah, and?"

"That makes seventy for the both of us. And how much do we have?"

"Not even enough for that ice cream float." Tucker frowned

before saying, "Maybe we can sneak aboard one of them."

"Not a good idea." Emma glanced at the municipal building, where a police cruiser was parked along the curb, a blue light hung from a soffit in the corner indicating Police. There was a small park on the side of the stationhouse; a long fire station sat behind the rear of the building. "Not with the cops around... Not worth the risk. We'll find a way to make money."

"There might be one more train passing tonight."

Emma looked back at the police cruiser, then checked her Hamilton wristwatch, cream faced with black numbers and a cord band. "I doubt there's another train. It's late."

"Okay," Tucker said. "Then we'll need to find a place to sleep."

"That driver said the hotel is down this way. Must be by the train."

"Emma, we don't have any money."

"You think we can talk to the proprietor?"

"No."

"Why not? I can offer him my watch."

"We're probably not the first to be stranded, Emma."

"But maybe he'll be sympathetic to us."

"Doesn't matter."

"What doesn't matter?"

"A lot of people lost their homes."

Emma tapped Tucker on his shoulder and sheepishly said, "Let's try it at least."

"It ain't worth trying."

"Should we ask the police for help?"

"No."

"I think we should."

"No. Let's walk around."

"Where to?"

"Around."

5

They pushed their aching legs south along Broad Avenue, stopping at the Columbia Avenue intersection. There was a store on the corner with a sign that read Morsemere Pharmacy.

A blue mailbox sat between two tall telephone poles where four cars were parked along the curb. Up ahead they could see a massive apartment building that dominated the area.

The moon was throwing a cold, gray luminosity over the town. The streets were empty, save for a boy who raced by on a red bicycle, holding a fishing pole with a crab cage and rope tied to his handlebars. Seconds later followed another boy on a brown bicycle with also a crab cage and rope tied to his handlebars. He was peddling as fast he could. "Slow down," he called out to the boy on the red bicycle.

They found themselves walking up East Columbia Avenue. "The deli right here looks abandoned. Want to sleep in there?" Tucker asked.

"No."

"If not here, we need to find some place to bunk down for the night."

"Where's that?"

"I don't know."

Her pretty face covered in a sheen of sweat. She mumbled, "I'm exhausted, Tucker, but what choice do we have?"

He looked at the door and then at a broken window above which hung a small rusted sign that read Radisson's Deli. It occupied a two-story red-brick frame building.

They creaked open the door and found an old and dirty oak chair. "How many years since somebody sat in that?" Tucker asked, pointing.

Emma shook her head. "About as many since these windows seen a clean rag. You sure this is a good idea?"

"If we're going to, let's move in and be quiet before somebody catches us."

"Maybe we should sleep out in the reeds along that river we passed earlier."

He smirked. "That'd be fine with me. But you know how you get with critters. Especially snakes. Sounds crazy, but I think this place is better than sleeping in the reeds... No muskrats, either."

"Oh no, Tucker!" Emma gasped. "There's mice in here, too. Let's leave."

"There'll be small compared to muskrats, possums, raccoons, snakes, and other night critters."

"God, no... forget that. I'll take my chances." Emma tiptoed in. The place was filthy, the dust lay thick and heavy on the uneven and buckled parquet flooring. The place smelled old and musty and a dusty calendar on the wall read February of 1924. There was no food or provisions left on the broken shelves. Tucker found a cabinet under the counter where an antiquated and dull chrome till sat lonely and abandoned, its drawer open and empty. He opened the cabinet and found a stockpile of canned food. He grabbed a rusty can of cut beans.

"Is it edible?" Emma asked.

"It's rusted out on the bottom. I doubt it."

Emma's head sank. She rubbed her stomach and looked away.

"But," Tucker said, "If we cook it good and hot it should be fine."

"What else is there?"

"It's all the same. Most of the cans are worse than this one."

"Leave it, Tucker. If we must we know where it is."

"Okay."

"Okay."

"Last resort," Tucker said. "Rust can lock the jaw as hard as cement."

Emma frowned, her voice tired and almost defeated. "It's come to this," she said wearily.

6

Chief Henderson could've shot the dog, but he wanted the rookie to do it.

"What?" the rookie replied, adjusting the policeman's belt that fit loosely around his waist, his uniform neatly pressed, the silver buttons glittering from the sun's reflections. He liked the idea of wearing that uniform.

"Shoot the damn dog." But the kid had never thought being a cop would have him do anything so damn inglorious as gunning down a dog. "Shoot it, and let's wrap this up and go and get something to eat," Henderson said, lighting a Chesterfield.

Henderson wondered if the kid had the mettle to be a lawman, or if he was just another fresh cop who wanted to go around wearing a gun and a badge so he could get more women.

The dog's snarl grew fiercer. It was menacing and attached to a long chain that prevented them from reaching the porch. The rookie officer held out his .38 Smith and placed it into the sight picture. "Go lay down," he shouted to the dog. "Do it now."

The dog continued stripping his teeth, its bark louder and nastier. "Go lay down," the rookie said again.

"Shoot the damn dog, kid," Henderson spat, and adjusted the policeman's hat that sat haphazardly on his head, sweat soaking his brows.

The rookie exhaled and pulled the trigger, hearing the loud pop followed by the harrowing screech the dog let out. It paced in circles briefly before it fell to its side and, within seconds, went limp and lifeless.

"Now, was that hard?" Henderson chuckled.

The rookie, blue eyes looking up at Henderson and feeling a pit in his stomach, muttered, "Easy as pie, I guess."

Now for what they were there for.

Chief Henderson and his rookie officer Frederick had to

execute a warrant. It was early afternoon, the heat climbing to over a hundred degrees when a slight westerly breeze brushed through Chief Henderson's hair. With the dog no longer an obstacle, they approached the porch, Henderson stepping over the dog without even glancing down at it.

They had to arrest old man Charlie Burgess for killing his neighbor's horse after a dispute over where the property line sat. Basically, the old man felt his neighbor's horse's stable encroached on his property and should be moved. The neighbor had a deed with dimensions and proof to show the old man was mistaken. But that didn't stop the old feller from slipping through the wooden fence and soaking the horse's feed with turpentine. When the horse refused to eat it, Burgess had lifted his shaking, wrinkled hand and slit its throat with a large rusty kitchen knife. The neighbor had seen him climbing back through the fence.

Henderson also figured to ask Burgess if he'd seen Abigail Stillman lately. Some of the local seniors had stopped by his office earlier, saying it was strange that old lady Stillman hadn't shown up at Carol Velesco's house for their usual game of cards. Six local women would sit around a card table every Friday and fill each other in on the town gossip. It was well known that Abigail Stillman missed church, local events, and such quite often. But her weekly card game at Carol Velesco's was gospel. Earlier, a quick check of the Stillman house had turned up empty, but nothing he saw had particularly alarmed Chief Henderson. The place was orderly and neat. And since it was well known that, even in her old age, she'd find intimate companionship with old man Burgess, Henderson figured to see if she'd been by recently.

Her disappearance wasn't a priority for Henderson. Truth was, he had disdain for her. As in many small towns, people were tied to each other in one way or another. Old lady Stillman had at one time been Henderson's stepmother, having swindled his dad, an old judge who, even in his dying years, still had a yen for younger women. Two things always made it possible for a much older man to court a younger attractive companion: money and influence. And his dad had both. Lady

Stillman had soaked the old man until he died, having sat there holding the old man's hand as he took his last breath. She'd even forced out cold tears. Henderson recalled that cry as they closed in on Charlie Burgess's porch.

"And so what if she's dead?" Henderson said aloud to himself.

"What if who's dead?" the rookie replied.

"Never mind."

The rookie turned to Henderson. "Old lady Stillman, huh."

Henderson shook his head. "I ain't gonna talk about that now. Let's do what we're here for and get going."

"I've heard stories about her," the rookie said.

"Well, later you're gonna tell me what you heard, and then I'll tell you the truth."

The idea of searching for the Stillman woman turned Henderson's stomach. He spit into the skeleton of a rotting bush. It looked dry enough to spark a fire. Regardless, he still had to investigate the disappearance of his former stepmother.

"Burgess is too old for jail," the rookie said.

"That's for the judge to decide," Henderson replied. "If he thinks he can live his days out in his home, then that'll be what he does."

"I thought you're the judge and jury around here."

Henderson smirked. "True, but this one's gotta be done this way."

"Seems pointless to even arrest the old feller... This ain't no big caper. Let me handle it myself. Soon I'll be flying solo."

"Not so soon," Henderson said. "Don't get all wet. There's still a lot to learn."

"Oh, come on," the rookie said, feeling his oats. "I shot that dog with ease, didn't I?"

Henderson raised a brow.

"This is pretty much pointless," the kid said.

"Maybe you're right, Freddy. But we'll see what the judge says. Probably give him a few days in jail to think about what he did."

7

Officer Frederick knocked on the front door of the dilapidated ranch house in the hilly section of town, Henderson in tow. The east corner of the house had partially collapsed from years of neglect. The yard was overgrown with sun-burnt brush and piled-up garbage. There was a rotting settee that had sunken into the earth. You could hardly tell Charlie Burgess had once been the wealthiest man in town—had all the money in town, and old lady Stillman would've liked to dig her claws into him back then, but he'd been taken. And at that time she was still shagging Henderson's father. Time had passed, though, and Burgess had either lost his money or done a good job hiding it. From what everybody could tell, the man who bought yesterday's bread was now broke.

"Answer the door, Burgess," the rookie called out. "We know you're in there. This won't take long... just need to ask you some questions."

Henderson fingered the handcuffs in his back pocket. Should he put them on an old man? he asked himself, but shook his head. "Maybe you're right, Freddy. Forget it. Hell, he was a leatherneck, that'll be his saving grace. Just talk to him and see if he's seen lady Stillman."

"All right, forget it. I'll serve him the papers, and I'll meet you in the car. No need to take him in. We know where he is."

"Now you're starting to see how things run around here," Henderson said. He turned and walked back to his vehicle, sat in the driver's seat and twisted the cap off his flask. He tilted his head back and let the afternoon sun rush over him, taking a long swallow. It had been a protracted week, and he wanted badly to be home in his favorite chair, filling his belly with whiskey.

It was hot. The sky opened up and the sun scorched the already barren land that yearned for rain. The drought had destroyed the crops and the people who relied on them.

Officer Frederick thumped on the door again, louder. When nobody opened it, he gave it a try. It opened right up and he went in.

Henderson was re-twisting the cap when he heard a gunshot and nearly pissed himself. Then another.

Frederick appeared in the doorway. He was holding himself. His uniform shirt was dark, and Henderson could see blood seeping through the fingers pressed against his belly. He looked scared, stumbled, and fell to the earth like a broken thing.

Henderson leaped from his car and ran toward him where he lay on the ground, kicking his feet into the dirt.

Frederick looked up at Henderson with those baby blue eyes—ones full of the innocence of youth—and his mouth twisted. The rear screen door slammed, but Henderson was so consumed, he didn't hear it.

"Bastard!" Frederick gasped, then closed his eyes and went slack as a fish line when the fish gets off the hook.

Henderson spoke his name. At least he thought he did. But his mouth and throat had gone dry, his teeth grinding. Then there was a great silence. He drew his pistol and crouched low to the earth, half expecting a man to come to the doorway holding a gun, aim at him and shoot him just as he had the boy.

Then a little wind came up out of nowhere and fluttered through Frederick's hair, but that was the only thing that moved.

Henderson looked up at the door, filled with anger at whoever it was who had shot and killed his partner. He charged inside, didn't blade himself at the door or try to conceal his approach. Screw that, he told himself. Screw that. If he too was going to die, he was going to die fighting.

But he didn't have to fight anyone.

Charlie Burgess lay slantwise on a dirty brown sofa just inside the door—a little shelf separating the area from a small kitchen that smelled of frying grease. The old man was bleeding from a wound to his face. Frederick's black revolver lay on the floor by his right foot. Henderson couldn't make sense of it.

Henderson looked closer and became very suspicious.

Charlie Burgess's one eye was partially open, and his hands were knotted into fists. He looked older than his seventy-five years. The blood from a dark bruised wound on his face, just below his left eye, had leaked down across his grizzled cheek and into his open mouth. His teeth were snow white, the sort of dentures you could buy cheap in Harlem. Flies were buzzing around his face, already doing their work.

Henderson touched the man's flesh. It was cool as arctic ice. He swabbed the blood on the old man's face with his index finger. It was dark and crusty. He rubbed it between his fingers. It turned into dust and floated to the floor. It didn't make sense. The old man had been dead at least several hours.

Henderson looked around the house, under the bed, behind every piece of furniture. Nothing. He lifted the latch on the kitchen floor that led to the crawlspace underneath. If someone was hiding, he would have had to be in there. He dropped to his knees, looked down into the hole, and saw the sun coming through the porch planks. "If you're hiding in there, come out now!" he shouted. Nothing moved, and Henderson went back to check on Frederick.

He gagged after that, tripped over the dog's carcass, landing on his hands and knees and retching, but nothing came up.

The hot sun beat through his clothes.

He stroked back the young man's hair and kissed him on the forehead. Not only had he lost him; now he'd have to bury his oldest son.

8

Panting like a wolf, the butcher sitting on the small stone wall at the rear of his house pinched a cigarette between his lips and lit it. He took a long drag and let the smoke fill his lungs. It calmed him down. With a rag he wiped the sweat from his forehead, arms, and neck. It was hotter than usual and he had worked himself up a bit.

He wiped down the warm metal barrel of his Smith & Wesson "N" frame .357, a large double-action revolver with wooden grips. He liked it a lot. Having dropped it twice in the dirt during his frantic run from Charlie Burgess's house, he made certain to run some of the rag around the rim of the barrel and in the small crevices where dirt had filled. You should have seen how old man Burgess had begged him not to shoot him, how he had pleaded for his measly life. The butcher snickered, thinking about how wide the old man's eyes had flared and how whole he had felt when he shot him in the face. More thrilling still had been sitting there with the dead man, talking with him, soaking in the power he had over another human.

But that'd almost gotten him caught. It'd been a close call. He wasn't expecting Chief Henderson and his son that early in the day. The single shot that dropped the dog caught his attention, and it gave him an opportunity he couldn't pass up. A score needed to be settled between Chief Henderson and the butcher. He had been waiting for it since he learned that Henderson's father had the butcher's dad killed. The butcher had known it for quite some time—old lady Stillman, the poison that had ruined them all. She'd paid. Now Henderson would, too.

The butcher didn't know if he had been spotted or was suspected of being there. He had to admit that he was a little nervous. Just do everything the way you normally would, he told himself as he turned the lock on the back door and entered his house. It was getting late on Saturday, and he always rested then before running the illegal booze. He waited until his heart had stopped pounding, then made a sandwich.

His mother came into the kitchen. "Can you make me one, too?" she asked.

"I'm busy now, Nancy."

"It'll only take a second."

He laid his sandwich on a plate, turned toward the parlor. "Glad to see you're motivating yourself to do something."

She held onto the counter and pointed her cane at him. "If you can't do a simple thing to help your sick mother, then you don't have to live here."

"Why should I do anything for you, Nancy?"

"Why do you insist on calling me by my first name?"

The butcher's shoulders rose a fraction of an inch. "It is 'Nancy,' isn't it?"

"No, it's 'Mother,'" she said, curling her lip. "And at times I wish it wasn't."

"Still wishing I wasn't born," the butcher groaned. "That's a good start."

Her hair had grayed a lot over the past year, since she had been struck by a trolley crossing Dean Street in Englewood. The doctor had said she'd been lucky not to lose a leg, or worse. She had also been fortunate that they had a hospital there and had been able to treat her before she bled out. The butcher wouldn't have minded that.

Over the previous year, her health had in fact deteriorated, and she could have used help. But that wasn't going to happen. Not as long as her only option was her son.

"You'll miss me when I'm gone," she called out into the parlor.

"Don't flatter yourself, Nancy," he snapped from the settee, finished his sandwich, and dropped the plate onto a side table. "It's the other way around."

"What are you talking about?"

"Ask Henderson. His son died earlier. He was killed," the butcher said, relishing in the moment.

"Who died, the young boy?"

"No, the older one, the one who just became a cop."

"Oh, my," she gasped. "He was only... what? Like eighteen years old, maybe twenty."

"What difference does that make?"

"Don't be so cold, Michael. This is horrible," she said. "So young."

"At lease he died with dignity, Nancy. Could you say the same for yourself?"

She eased her way into the parlor. "I'm not going to stand here and listen to you berate me like this."

"Don't waste your breath," he said, closing his eyelids. "You know the truth."

"That's enough," she said. "You can leave."

"So can you," he muttered.

She said nothing and turned back into the kitchen. He rolled his neck, got comfortable and drifted off for his usual nap before waking a few hours later and setting out for the open road.

9

The butcher returned just as the sun was rising over the town. Everything was still peaceful and quiet. Everybody in Palisades Park was still sleeping except for the butcher, who although he was pleased with the results of his work during the night, was feeling a deep despair.

He filled the percolator with water and coffee, and set it on the stove. Soon, the aroma of fresh coffee began to fill the house. He found his coffee mug on a hook above the sink and stirred a spoonful of sugar into it, thinking briefly about the money he'd made. It was enough to take a weekend vacation, enough for five people to enjoy a day at the Palisades Amusement Park with a steak dinner. There was a lot of money in illegal booze, if one had a fast car and the nerve. He'd make himself some real dough. He had a funny thought: I should have been a baker, I like making dough so much.

But it wasn't just the money; it was the thrill of it. And of course there was always the impending risk of a good old racketeer shakedown, especially when you were dealing with the big players in Newark and Paterson. In fact, that had happened to a feller named Roger whom Mike had befriended and met often in the wee hours at the loading docks.

Roger never had recovered from the baseball-bat beating he took when he refused to turn over a cut of his profits. Poor feller was now confined to a wheelchair. Every few weeks, Mike dropped by Roger's house and gave his wife an envelope of money to help them get by. He didn't have to, and he never made a big issue of it. He simply saw it as taking care of a fellow and a friend during difficult times. Maybe one day, if he were unfortunate enough to become handicapped, some soul out there would return the courtesy.

But so far, Mike hadn't met any resistance, and he kept his

pistol ready during his runs. He'd be damned if somebody did to him what they'd done to Roger. Let them try, he thought.

Soon he would head off to the butcher shop. But first he had to pay a few bills. He sat at his mother's Victorian writing desk, heavy pine with a black leather inset, a gift from a former customer.

He searched for his checkbook and noticed a letter he'd read many times; he knew it'd be best not to read it again, but he went ahead anyway.

It was addressed to his mother from Charlie Burgess, who had in his time been a boy-lover who'd had his way with young Michael more times than he cared to remember. It made Mike wonder what ever had happened to women staying true to their husbands, even after death. But his mother had been desperate. The death of Mike's father had left them impoverished, and the avenue she had chosen to feed them had been filled with filth and enough hurt and confusion to choke a horse.

His father's older brother had long since severed ties with the butcher and his mother, leaving only the younger uncle to fill the dead father's shoes.

So the younger uncle, in his infinite drunken wisdom, had set up a fight club in a garage out back. Saturday night fights were popular; people from all over the county would place their bets and root for their man, shouting and drinking and smoking heavily. And when the fight was over, his mother would invite some of the men inside and get paid for sex.

As Michael got older, she'd slowed down and often told him the men were her friends and they were stopping by to talk. She'd even gone so far as to post a sign that read Fortune Telling Inside. As if Michel was that naive. But after his mother met Charlie Burgess, he had showered her with enough money to make her stop selling her body. At that time, Charlie still had his money. And lots of it. They'd dated, and in a miniscule way it had legitimized her standing in the community—not much, but, as the years flew by, some forgave her. But not the butcher. Never.

He sipped his coffee and pinched the bridge of his nose, squinting and drifting off. The pressure was knotted tightly between his eyes; it rolled over his head to the base of his neck.

The first memory of Charlie's deviant side was of October 9, 1905, game one of the World Series. Michael had sat in the stands at Columbia Park with Charlie, who had persuaded his mother to allow the two of them to take the road trip to Philadelphia—Michael, nine years old then, his father dead for a little over two years. He had been smiling as he watched the New York Giants defeat the Philadelphia Athletics. All the perils of youth glowed in his eyes. But when the game ended, Charlie had kissed him on the lips, which had confused him beyond belief.

If only it had ended there, he thought. But it hadn't.

Later that day, when they were riding back home in Charlie's fancy stagecoach with plush red leather seats, twilight falling, Charlie had wheeled off into a desolate stretch surrounded by towering corn husks. The sun spirals shining off the chrome trim had still been powerful enough to start a fire in those fields.

Charlie hadn't been nice about it. He'd known what he was doing. When he stroked Michael's hair, the boy had protested, "Sir, why are you doing this?"

"Doing what?" the man had said. "There's nothing wrong with me showing you how much I love you."

"But, mister," Michael had said. "It don't feel good when you touch me."

"It's just love, Michael. We all need to feel it. If your dad was still alive, he would have done this to you, too."

"Daddy never did this, Mister."

"He would have."

"I don't believe you."

"Trust me. He would have."

Charlie had hugged Michael, and he had jabbed his tiny elbow into the man's ribs. "Mister, I said I don't want to do this."

Charlie had shaken off the blow; Michael hadn't been strong enough to even cause a bruise. Charlie'd hugged him again, saying, "Trust me, Michael. This is natural and loving. I'm doing this for you."

Michael had tried to squirm from the man's grip, even screamed with all his might: "Mom! Help!"

There had been a brief moment where it looked like Charlie was reconsidering what he was doing.

But he wasn't.

He had clamped his fingers around Michael's throat and revealed a chrome Buck knife with a long, sharp blade and serrated teeth, Michael terrified and shaking. What could he have done to stop him? Charlie had run the blade along the tiny hairs on the neck of the boy, whose resistance, feeling the warmth of the metal, had collapsed, the wonderment of his youth stolen.

"And if you tell anybody," Charlie had said, "I will kill you."

A car passing outside shook him from his reverie. The butcher felt the broken blue-wax seal and slipped the letter out. It was addressed to his mother. He read it aloud. But when he got to Tell Michael I miss him, too. Send my love, he gritted his teeth. "That bastard," he snapped. "He paid for what he did," he screamed to his mother, who was resting in her bedroom. "He's gone off to where all the other—boy raping palookas go... He's gone to hell, Nancy."

She heard it and let out a gasp. "You killed him?" she called out, her voice shaking.

"We're even now."

"You killed him?"

"He killed me a long time ago."

"Heaven, no!" she shrieked. "What's gotten into you?"

"The devil called his servant back home."

"You're not making sense. Did you kill him?"

"I just gave him a ride, Nancy."

"You drove him where?" she exclaimed, standing now in the formal parlor, scratching her temple.

"To hell."

"You did what?"

"He's burning now," he said, getting up from the desk. "You knew he molested me."

"I've told you a thousand times, if I would have known I would've stopped it."

"No, you wouldn't, Nancy."

"Yes, I would've."

"Did he pay you for me too, huh?"

"You're talking crazy."

"I hope you got more for my young ass than what you got for yourself."

"Quit staring at me like that... I'm sick, Michael."

"You look fine to me."

"My chest is tight, and you're scaring me. Are you drunk?"

"Nope."

"Did you really kill him?"

"I didn't do anything."

"Then who did?"

"He did."

She reached into a closet and retrieved her cane, leaning on it as she walked over to her son. "He committed suicide?"

"No."

"You're not making sense."

"Go back to bed. I'll have him call you tomorrow."

The old lady remained there, though, before her son. She gazed into his cold eyes. "Where did I go wrong with you?" she muttered. "Heaven help us."

"If it's any solace, father is equally responsible."

"What?"

"He was shagging lady Stillman. I caught him one day at the butcher shop."

"You did not. Your father was a good man."

"Good enough to get himself killed for sleeping with Judge Eric Henderson's wife."

She swallowed. "I will not stand here and allow you to speak such nonsense." She dug her cane into the carpet and started for her bedroom.

"And it was Chief Henderson who killed Dad."

"That's nonsense," she said over her shoulder. "All of this is nonsense."

He watched her struggle back into her room. He continued sipping his coffee, thinking back to the first day Charlie had touched him. "You knew Charlie was molesting me!" he shouted. "I hope it was worth the money."

If only, he thought, one of his parents had cared.

10

Early the next morning, Tucker and Emma surveyed the street. The sun was out, and a warm breeze fluttered through Emma's hair. A man was driving a brown truck with a yellow legend on the door that read Palisades Park Lumber & Supply. He was hauling a load of lumber, two orange flags flapping from the overhanging rear load. Six very noisy children were kicking a ball across Broad Avenue while two women watched from a nearby bench, possibly waiting for a trolley that was visible in the distance. Nearly all of them glanced at Tucker and Emma. Fortunately, it wasn't that unusual to see people who appeared beaten down and out of luck those days. The roads and the freight train cars were full of such souls.

The young couple heard a lot of hammering and discovered where it was coming from when they saw a man building a home on West Ruby Avenue, across from a large nursery with some flowers and shrubs. It gave Tucker a hopeful feeling that such a place could still do business in that day and age, that at least some people had money to spend. He and Emma paused there on the corner of Broad and West Ruby, staring down the block as the hammering continued.

Emma pointed up Broad. "Looks like a cop's coming this way."

As the officer drew closer, Tucker took notice of the size of him—six foot six, maybe even six-seven.

Tucker was certain because he reminded him of his former cop partner Leo Cunningham, a one-time collegiate baseball player who had sparkled at Columbia University with the likes of Gehrig. People had feared the big man and looked up to him for leadership, as if there was an unspoken understanding on life that shorter people would never experience, that being tall allowed the eyes to see the world from a privileged perspective. Tucker hadn't necessarily believed that was always true, but when he saw the size of the lawman before him, he couldn't help but think about it.

A man was across the street when the cop called to him, "Boots, get over here."

The man hustled over, looked up at him, he said, "Yes, sir."

"Who did it?" the cop growled. He was square jawed and looked like he spat nails. "Tell me who killed my son."

The man took a step back, hands up. "How would I know, sir? I don't know of such a person."

"Somebody knows!" the cop shouted.

"No, sir, I don't."

"You're no angel, Boots," the cop thundered and, with both hands, struck the man in the chest. He collapsed to the ground, and the cop stood over him. "I still got that open warrant on you."

"What for?"

"That stolen motorcycle."

"It wasn't me."

"Don't lie to me."

"I ain't lying, Chief."

"You taking me for a fool?"

"No, sir, I ain't."

"Well, then?"

"Well then what?"

"You liked the way it rode."

"No, sir. I ain't never rode no Indian."

"Who said anything about an Indian?"

The man shrugged. "So you taking me in, or what?"

"I could."

"I know you could."

"Don't get fresh with me."

"I wasn't, sir."

"Then tell me why I shouldn't haul you in?" the cop said, lifting the man from the ground. "And toss in a good beating on you?"

"Sir, I been staying out of trouble. Yes sir, I've been good."

"You're going to find out for me, Boots."

"I'll try."

"You will."

"Okay... I will."

"Let everyone know," the cop spat, and clenched the man by the shirt collar. "Anybody who knows of him and doesn't tell will be punished severely."

"Yes, sir."

The cop let go. The man scampered to his feet, visibly shaken, and said, "Yes, sir... You'll be the first to know." He curtseyed and quickly whisked himself off, checking back periodically to see if he was being followed.

The cop brushed his hands on his pants and adjusted the policeman's hat that sat high on his forehead. It had a brass badge affixed to it. He appraised the street. There was a heavy, potent smell of cinnamon bread baking, and Tucker could taste it. Turning to Emma, Tucker said, "That cop is on a vengeance trail. He's going to kill someone."

"You think that man knew?"

"I don't know. He looked sincere."

"Maybe he does."

"I doubt it."

Emma gasped, "Should we hitchhike now to that ferry and get across the river into Manhattan? We'll be able to blend in there."

Shouting interrupted their conversation. It was the cop. "Tell me, Johnny," he exclaimed, standing in front of a two-storied brick building with a barber's shop occupying the first floor.

He was scolding a man sitting on a bench outside the barber shop, his uniform creasing and his brass buttons glittering as he throttled the man. Tucker saw something in the man's hand. He looked closer. Maybe a bottle of water. The cop towered before the man and began shouting, "You sit here all day. You had to've seen something."

The man said nothing.

"You hear me, boy?"

The man was wide-eyed and looked mortified. He tried to speak but couldn't. He seemed panicked and confused. With shaking hands, he lifted the bottle to his lips and took a long swallow, gulping. He tried again to speak. Nothing.

In a flash, the cop had ripped the bottle from his hands and smashed it on the sidewalk. The sound of broken glass echoed out in the quiet morning. "You better tell me," the cop said. "I know you see who comes and goes."

Just then the apartment door swung open and a woman came rushing out in a blue dress and white apron. She had a rolling pin in her hand. When she saw the cop, she tossed it on the sidewalk and called to him, "Chief! What's gotten into you?"

He turned to her. "Somebody knows, Susan."

She wrapped an arm around the cop's waist. "Now, darling, we understand how difficult this is for you. But you know Johnny's deaf. If he saw something, I would have told you."

The cop said nothing.

"Are you hungry?" she asked, escorting him toward her door. "Come upstairs. Breakfast is still hot. I'll fix you a plate."

"Molly's got food."

"Come in and sit a while."

"No."

"You need a lift back to the office? My husband will gladly drive you."

"No."

There was a pause, and the woman seemed to be thinking deeply when the cop said, "You hear anything, give a call." He set off down the avenue.

"Let's get out of here," Emma said.

"First we need to find something to eat."

"I think it'd be best to leave, Tucker."

"We need to eat. Then we leave."

"...Okay."

I I

With the police chief out of sight distance, they walked down West Ruby and stopped to watch the man in blue jeans and yellow shirt framing a house and causing all the hammering. There were five homes on that side of the block; behind them were lots of overgrown shrubs resting against the nursery fence. A truck was parked on a dirt patch out front, brimming with supplies, and it looked as if he could use another hand. But Tucker knew that, during those desperate times, people were used to doing everything solo—couldn't afford to hire a hand. Most folks were working for very little, next to nothing. Tucker tasted the salt of his sweat; he noticed Emma's eyes were jaundiced, and that she too sweating profusely. He heard a loud growl. "Was that your stomach?" he asked half aloud.

"...Yes."

"I know you're hungry."

"It's okay."

"I'm sorry, Emma."

"Stop."

"But—"

"Stop."

"It shouldn't have come to this."

"It's temporary. You said that," she said.

"I know."

The rising sun was breaking the plane of the steep hill to the east. It looked bigger and hotter than the day before. She shaded her eyes with one hand. "Go over there."

Just then a scrawny gray cat limped by, and it got Tucker thinking. "What makes you think he'll hire me?" he asked. "There's not even enough food to feed strays."

"He's working alone, right? That stuff looks heavy."

Tucker shrugged. "Maybe he's not working for money."

"Who would build a house for free?"

Tucker sighed. "Okay, a day's pay will provide enough food to fill our stomachs. And—"

"Then we're out of here."

Tucker approached the burly built man. He looked to be in his middle thirties—six feet tall and broad-shouldered, with big arms. Sweat was dripping from the saturated white sweatband he wore above his brows. His shirt was drenched with perspiration. It looked as if the early summer sun was overcoming him. "Sir, could you, uh, use a hand?" Tucker asked sheepishly.

The other turned, wiping sweat from the back of his neck. "Matter of fact, maybe," he said, studying him. "I didn't expect it to be this hot. Had I known, I'd have waited till later... or tomorrow."

"Well, if you let me do the heavy lifting, that should cool you down a bit."

"I could wait."

"Why wait?"

The man lopped the hammer in his apron. "I ain't making a killing here. If you're worth it, I can give you a couple of dollars. But that's it. And I ain't promising anything until I see your work."

"I'm no slouch."

"You good with a couple of dollars?"

"I'm good with that. But considering I am stranded, forget the cash. I'll work for dinner for my wife and me. And if you'd be kind enough to allow us to wash."

"Wife? Where's your wife?"

"Over there." Emma was standing across the street in the shade of a large maple. When the man glanced at her, she nodded.

"Could be worse," the man said. "At least you're not alone."

The man angled a ten-foot two-by-four onto a saw horse and lifted his saw. "I never thought I'd be conducting a street interview. You have any experience, or am I going to waste my time showing you all day?"

Tucker lifted the long end of the wood. "No need for lessons... So do we have a deal?"

The man allowed the wood to fall to the ground. The smell

of the fresh-cut lumber reminded Tucker of Christmas. "Fine," he said, and Tucker shook his hand. "I can tell a working man from his hands," the man said. "Name's Dominic."

"I'm Tucker."

"What brought you here?"

"We lost everything. Our car caught fire. We only have the clothes on our backs."

"You say you lost everything?"

"Everything but each other." Tucker liked him right away. Hearing their hard-luck story, this man—unlike others, who, probably hurting themselves, showed little compassion—had a heart and seemed like an honest man helping another where he could.

"Before you foot the ladder, Tucker, reach inside my truck and get a quart of water for you and your wife."

Tucker nodded, knowing he had not been wrong.

A few minutes later, he had crossed the street, shared the water with Emma, and told her about the promise of food and a bath. She beamed, the color returning to her pretty face. "What shall I do while you work?" she asked.

"Whatever will occupy the time."

She took another long swallow of water and said, "I think I'll go for a stroll. I'll be back later. Impress him."

"Stay clear of that cop," Tucker said. "He looks like trouble."

12

Tucker and his employer worked through lunch, straight to dusk. The sun was casting a long shadow on the eastern side of the house by then, making it dark in the alley between the houses. The day had cooled a bit but not enough to provide the relief anybody needed. Both were saturated in sweat and sawdust. Tucker's shirt had a salt ring where the sweat began to dry. Tucker felt his forehead and knew his temperature was still climbing, that he couldn't sustain a high level of effort for much longer.

He was still hammering on the ladder, though, when Dominic called up from below, "Come down. That's about all we can do today."

Tucker climbed off the ladder and wiped his sleeve across his sweaty brow. "There's just enough sunlight to finish," he said, dizzy.

"Take a break, boy," Dominic said. "You have that faraway look in your eye."

"I'll get through it."

As dizzy and achy as he was, Tucker had the satisfied feeling of having a hard day's work under his belt. It always came with a good effort.

"You want to work the rest of the week?" Dominic asked.

"...What'd ya say?"

"I said I have work for you for the rest of the week."

Tucker's eyes opened wide, and he swallowed the last bit of saliva inside his dry mouth, "Actually," he managed to mutter, "I can work as many days as it takes to buy two train tickets," his voice almost a whisper. "The Erie goes to Buffalo, right?"

"Sure does," Dominic replied. "We better get you something to eat. You're not looking too good."

"I'm fine."

"You burn like an Indian."

41

Tucker felt the soreness of the sunburn on the back of his neck. "That sun was hot today."

Dominic nodded. He took a five-dollar bill from his pocket and stuffed it into Tucker's blue jeans. "You earned it."

"But I thought—"

"You earned it," Dominic repeated. "Where's your wife?"

Tucker knew she had to be somewhere close. "Be right back. Let me find her." He moved shakily down the roadway, feeling a pain that buried deep inside his skull. There was pressure between his eyes that he hadn't had since the war, when he dragged the wounded from the battlefield to the field hospitals. One soldier he'd never forget—a kid named Tommy. He had hoisted him over his shoulder and ran to the dun-colored tent in desperation and fear. He had known Tommy was dead but hadn't been willing to accept it. And when he had laid him on the canvas stretcher and the doctors had rolled him off and replaced him with another soldier, Tucker had been struck by the same great pressure between his eyes that blinded his thoughts, and moments later the pain had turned into a horrible headache that he'd never forget. He was starting to feel it again.

It didn't take long for him to find Emma. She was sitting outside, on the stairs leading to a church with a stone wall around it. Over the main entrance, a sign read Grace Luteran Church. There was also a sign on the lawn advertising for parents to sign their children up for the upcoming summer bible camp.

He was delighted to see her after the long day. He shook off as much of the pain as he could and, stifling a grimace, said, "Finally, we're going to eat. I think I impressed him."

She smiled, offered him her dry lips. "I knew you would."

She looked famished, her cheeks sunken. Regardless of the small mercy and his own pain, a wave of ignominy swept over him.

He grabbed her hand and led her back.

They found Dominic tying his lumber down to his 1928 Chevrolet Stakebed—four large black wheels supporting the green wooden bed and cab, thick black bolts and hinges holding the bed together. It was a powerful truck, made by the best worker in the world, the American working man. Just give him the work, and he'd show you how it should be done.

"My wife, Emma," Tucker said.

"My pleasure," he said, tipping his hat. "She's mighty attractive, Tucker."

Emma smiled. "You do nice work."

"Thanks, ma'am. Your husband's a strong man... Dinner at my place?"

Tucker didn't mind the glance he gave her. It was innocent. They climbed aboard the truck. Dominic cranked the engine, and off they rode, wind blowing through their hair.

"The tracks and cobblestones make the road bumpy," Emma said, clutching the door handle as she noticed the immense crimson sun sitting low on the horizon like a giant orange, the pinkish skyline foretelling another hot day tomorrow.

"I hope you like good home cooking," Dominic said.

Tucker smiled inwardly. Home cooking: Hell, he'd have eaten fried ragweed at that point. By then Tucker's stomach was wrenching with hunger pain; so was hers. It was disheartening, the notion of not belonging, of not being a part of your surroundings, in a real sense a feeling of "matter out of place."

Everybody should have a home, wherever home was.

13

Chief Henderson lifted his head off his desk after a long afternoon nap, a piece of paper stuck to his chin from the drool that had escaped his mouth and pooled onto the leather insert. He peeled off the paper and squinted to read it, his brows narrowing. It was the warrant for Charlie Burgess, its corners frayed, the judge's signature covered with a bloodied fingerprint. He leaned back in the chair, resting his elbow on the bookshelf next to his desk.

The phone rang. "Henderson here," he said, resting the handset of his Western Electric phone against his ear. "Yes, this is him... Hello, Mayor... It ain't deep enough for them boys to drown, Mayor... You say it's got an engine?"

Henderson ran his fingers through his salt-and-pepper hair, thinking briefly about what his job had become. Two boys had been spotted with a motorized six-foot fishing boat on Klaus's pond, and this small boat in that tiny pond had the mayor and residents concerned. "...I'm certain they'll run out of gas soon... Yes, sir. Okay, I'll post more signs later," he added. "...Yes, and I know all about Piraglio's goats. I'll see to it he fixes that broken fence... Anything else, sir? Maybe something about the killer?" There was a hint of disdain in his voice.

With all that was going on, with all the mayhem, Henderson couldn't understand the logic of some people. Yes, an unauthorized motor boat was spinning around a small pond, and goats were slipping out and eating the garbage of neighboring homes. It was all true. But did it really matter? He knew he'd come to the point where policing was more about serving the community and less about protecting it. What's next? he thought. Somebody gonna call and ask me to feed their goldfish while they're out of town?

"You know I'm short-handed right now, mayor. I'll get to it when I can." He slammed down the receiver.

He heard the patrol car outside and saw his last and only cop walking through the door—big, tall Arthur Dankert, a war hero and well respected young man. He was both physically and mentally strong.

"What was that gunfire about on the hill earlier, Dankert? I responded up there and didn't see nothing."

The young patrol officer stood before Henderson, his blue uniform heavily starched and crisp, his boots glossy. He was holding a paper bag. "That was nothing."

"Nothing?"

"Yeah. I just bet Galunci I could hit a can if he tossed it in the air."

Henderson chuckled. "Well, did you?"

"Nah, I lost two bucks on that one."

"Serves you right.... What I tell you about firing your gun over nonsense?"

Dankert grinned, "If I won, I would have bought you dinner."

"What's in the bag?" Henderson asked. "You got something you want to share with me?"

"Two coffees and some sinkers."

"Well, hand 'em over."

Dankert set the bag on Henderson's desk and removed two cups of coffee. "So what's with this old lady Stillman? I'm hearing lots of rumors, but people don't seem all that upset around here."

"What'd you hear?"

"That in her day she was promiscuous and dated lots of men."

"That all?"

"Yeah." Dankert sipped his coffee. "She ever bang you?"

Henderson looked up with a flat glare in his eyes. "Shut the hell up and give me that doughnut if you're not going to eat it."

"Just asking, boss. From what I gather, that's the way she was."

"That'd be kind of sick if I shagged her, huh?"

Dankert offered a confused look. He picked up the bag to remove a doughnut. "Who at one time or another didn't enjoy an older woman?"

"You trying to be funny?"

"Huh?"

"The bitch was in her thirties before I was even born."

"So."

"So that's it, huh, Dankert. For a good cop, you're an idiot," Henderson said. "And you got pretty poor sources."

"...What are you talking about?"

Henderson ripped the bag out of Dankert's hand. "That bitch ruined my father. You think I would sink that low?"

With a confused look on his face, Dankert said, "I ain't suggesting nothing like that boss. Honestly I ain't."

Henderson exhaled. "If you're eventually going to hear the rumors, I prefer you hear the truth from me."

Dankert said nothing.

"After my mother died, my dad started dating lady Stillman, and she soaked him for every last penny."

"But wasn't your dad the judge?"

"Surprisingly for a man of the law, he was blind to her ways, and when he died she got everything."

"Everything? Abigail Stillman got all of your dad's money?" Dankert said. "How'd she manage that?"

"She was half his age—short skirts, low-cut tops, and a devilish waist."

Dankert nodded knowingly. "I heard a long time ago she was caught with Mike the butcher's father, and days later he ended up dead. Any truth to that rumor?"

"Yeah, but my father had nothing to do with that," Henderson lied. "Mike's old man was trash, an alcoholic who probably would have died anyway."

"Women," Dankert sighed.

Henderson let out a deep breath; the smell of booze permeated the room. The sun was slanting in from a window behind the chief's desk where a plant sat on the sill. Out the window, the mayor was talking with a man in a blue suit, white shirt and red bow tie. "Well, forget that. It looks like you'll be out of a job by the end of the week."

Dankert grimaced. "I thought it was going to blow over."

"Remanding Patrolman Walker to the county jail wasn't enough for these bastards." Henderson curled his lip. "I received word earlier that the county's going to charge you with official misconduct."

"Really?"

"Yes."

"Have you talked to the mayor about this?"

"Yeah."

"And?"

"And what?" Henderson said.

"Is he going to put a fight up to keep me?"

"No."

"He's outside now. Bring him in here and we'll ask him to reconsider."

"He's the one who's pushing to remove you."

"That son-of-a-bitch," Dankert snapped. "Does he realize we lost half the department already? With Walker and Freddy gone, it's just us."

Henderson had felt goose bumps when Dankert mentioned Freddy, and he briefly lost his concentration. "Uh, what were we just talking about?"

"Walker."

"What about Walker?"

"The drunk-driving homicide charge."

Henderson rubbed his eyes. "I am fighting for you, Dankert. But they saying you're an accessory."

"How?"

"They said you should've stopped Walker from driving. Said you shouldn't have been in the vehicle. That you were both on duty and in a police cruiser. They said that's official misconduct."

Dankert scratched his chin. "I told Walker it wasn't a good idea to drive the cruiser, and he told me to get in and to shut up. You know this. Why send me up the river, too?"

"Because a father and son were run over, and they're both now dead."

Dankert's brows furrowed. "The boy died? I thought you said he was going to live."

"He died from complications last night, and the county stopped by here before, and they want your head. That man outside talking to the mayor is the boy's uncle."

"I understand. But it was raining, and the wipers were barely working. Walker didn't see them in the street. And I wasn't driving."

"They say it doesn't matter."

"But I wasn't."

"But you were drunk and in the cruiser."

"That's what they say." Dankert stepped in closer. "Is that what you say too?"

"You know I told 'em you weren't. I swore to it. But the family is demanding justice, and the county's saying, if you turn in your badge, you won't see any time."

"It's only what they say. Where's the proof?" Dankert shouted.

"It's not me who has the problem, Dankert." Henderson sprung from his chair. "You lower your tone when speaking to me. I told you, it's them doing the saying."

Dankert snapped, "Well, boss, what about you? You're drunk right now. Is that official misconduct or something?"

Henderson clenched a fist and slammed it on the desk. "Don't worry about me, son," he whispered between clenched teeth. "I'm trying to save your ass. Another word out of you, and I'm going to lay a proper beating on you. Now, get back out there on patrol."

"How are you saving me? I'll be unemployed in a few days. I got a wife and kids."

With a stern finger, Henderson pointed to the door, "Tell Piraglio to put some wire in that fence, and swing by Klaus's pond and tell them kids no boating."

Dankert turned for the door. "There's a killer running loose around here, yes, sir, and we're firing cops," he muttered. "And there's nobody getting hired. More people will die, and then you'll see."

Henderson curled his lip and watched his patrolman walk away.

14

Henderson's door flew open, and in came a panting teenage boy. "Mr. Ferruchi needs help. He sent me here to summon you," the boy called out.

Henderson rose from his desk, grabbed his policeman's hat, and started for the door. As a habit, he felt for his holster and extra bullets. "What's the problem, son?"

The boy, catching his breath, said, "It's Veronica's ex-boyfriend, Carlson. He's talking crazy. Says he's gonna kill himself."

Henderson wanted to say, You mean my dead son's girlfriend, but instead he said. "Where are they now?"

"Down at the Oak House. Mr. Ferruchi said to hurry. Said it was urgent and serious."

Henderson raced to the police cruiser and sped off. As he spun the wheels onto West Central Boulevard, he slammed the accelerator and the rear of the cruiser fishtailed on the dusty pavement. He steadied the cruiser and thundered ahead.

Oak House was a home that Mr. Ferruchi and his wife ran for displaced children who didn't have parents. Seventeen-year-old Veronica was Freddy's girlfriend, and the Carlson boy had dated her a year or so before and wasn't willing to accept that she had moved on.

He slammed the cruiser against the curb and jumped out into the bright early afternoon light. "Come quick!" Mrs. Ferruchi shouted in panic from the front lawn, her hair all tweaked up in rolling pins. She was wearing a beige night gown. "He's in the backyard, and he's talking crazy."

"Who is?"

"Carlson."

Henderson swallowed. "What's he up to now?"

She fell silent, covered her mouth, and continued pointing toward the rear of her house.

Henderson had gotten to know Carlson fairly well—by

all accounts a fine young man who was educated some, athletic, and good looking. They say traits like that will make you the pick of the litter. The poor kid probably didn't see it that way. But, like Veronica, he had no parents and lived in the Oak House across the hall from Veronica and, over the past year, had tried three times to kill himself with a knife. The poor boy was not willing to accept that Veronica had moved on and was happy with Freddy.

Henderson smelled something burning. As he hurried closer to the backyard, he saw a moving torch of flame. That fool kid Carlson had set himself on fire and was running out into the front yard, passing Henderson in a hurry.

Henderson reached for him, but the boy was enveloped in blue gasoline flames. "Run inside and bring me a blanket, Mrs. Ferruchi!" Henderson shouted. "And somebody get me a bucket of water."

By then, Mr. Ferruchi was already running out the side door with a bucket of water. The screen door slammed behind him with a smack that broke the quiet afternoon. With shaking hands he handed the bucket to Henderson. "I'll get another one," he said, and disappeared back into the house. Moments later he was back with another bucket in hand.

"Roll on the ground," Henderson shouted, and doused the boy, but it didn't do much. A couple buckets couldn't douse all that fire. Henderson felt the heat on his skin. Felt his fear.

"You better roll on that ground now, boy," Henderson demanded.

Carlson continued to run in circles.

"Here, Chief," Mrs. Ferruchi gasped, tossing Henderson a blanket, which he spread in front of himself and tackled the boy. They landed on the grass with a loud thud, and Henderson managed to smother the rest of the fire.

The smell of burning flesh so strong, Henderson could smell it still later that night on his clothes and in his hair as he washed.

The boy glanced up at him, his eyes jaundiced, eyelids and eyebrows and hair gone, his lips, too. Henderson wasn't sure how his eyes were still in place. The boy sobbed, "I don't want to die, Carter."

Henderson was taken aback. Why would he call him by his first name?

Henderson looked closer. He nearly gasped at what he saw. For a man who had witnessed lots of men die over the years, even watched his own son choke on his own blood and perish before him, it was something new to him. There were places on the boy's belly where the chief could see his insides and what was left of his lungs. But there was no blood. When the skin burns that badly, it cauterizes and sheets off a body; that much, Henderson knew, was true.

He folded the dead boy's bony, skinless fingers across what was left of his gut and watched him take his last breath. He looked Henderson in the eye as he did.

Then he heard a horrid, squawking scream. He looked behind him to find young Veronica crying her eyes out. But when he stole a glance at her, she had hushed and it appeared she was calming. He didn't understand why at that moment.

Then he knelt over the boy. He was thinking how quickly things got bad. Within only a few days, two young men had died in front of him—the first by another's hand, and this one by his own. Henderson exhaled; what he had seen cut deep into his memory, scarring it forever.

They say time heals all wounds. Some take more time than others. He wished it would be true for Veronica. He hoped she could move on as he would force himself to do and not let what she had just seen affect her. But who knew?

15

"This house was built the same year the train depot was assembled along the Erie Railroad," Dominic declared somewhat proudly.

"When was that?" Tucker asked.

"1887." The other nodded. "It was one of the few homes this high on the hill."

"There's a beautiful view from up here."

Tucker thought about that train and pictured himself and Emma traveling along the countryside to Buffalo. How pleasant that would be. He looked around the formal parlor and rapped on an outer wall. "Built solid," he said.

"That's the way Granddad wanted it. Built to last, and thirty-one years later died right there in the hallway."

"Right there," Tucker said, examining the area. Having been a cop, it reminded him of the many people he had seen dead on their house floors. Cops were typically around during pivotal moments of transition. Either for a birth or a death, they witnessed all of it. In his last few years on the job, it had seemed more people were dying than delivering. But he'd known that wasn't the truth and at times forced himself not to be so cynical. The truth was, more babies were being delivered in newly built hospitals.

"It was what he wanted," Dominic said. "He loved this house. We laid him out over here, and people from far and wide came to pay their respects."

"Sounds like he was a great man."

"That he was," Dominic said.

Gas lamps were still affixed to most walls, some missing where the pipe protruded from the wall with a brass cap. The house had otherwise been fitted out with electrical lighting. There was a large fireplace and a wooden stove that Tucker could see would keep the place warm during the winter months. It was a cozy place, and through the front bay windows lay an unobstructed view of the meadows, the creek, and the remains of a closed landfill.

"Tucker, Emma! Come eat while it's hot," Dominic's wife, Lillie, called into the formal parlor, which was wider than most. The large windows were framed with elegant cream curtains. The walls were decorated in brown flowered-velvet wallpaper that looked like it belonged with the fancy tapestries in the homes of the social elite. Emma commented, "Whoever designed this place has a keen eye for style. The wallpaper's beautiful."

Dominic, sitting on a side chair, turned to her. "You like it, dear? It was left over from a job I worked on in Manhattan. The foreman said I could keep it."

"Looks very nice," Tucker added.

"Stuff like that seems hard to come by," Emma said.

"Lillie and I like contemporary things," Dominic said.

Tucker and Emma rose from the settee and entered the dining room. Dominic followed, and they sat at the table. The anticipation on Tucker's face was obvious.

Lillie was a good hostess, a thick woman about thirty years old with smooth, bronzed skin and a big heart revealed by an ear-to-ear smile and polite voice. Her marcelled hair framed soft features; her purple gown had sunflowers and birds embroidered on it. She served a steaming kettle of chicken-and-potato pepper-corned stew on the table. The steam swept across Tucker's nostrils and sent a feeling of mouth-watering comfort through him. Dominic passed Emma fresh bread and butter. "Thank you, sir," she said.

"Call me, Dominic, Emma. No need to be so formal in this house."

"But, sir—"

"Dominic is fine."

"Very well, Dominic, then." She smiled.

He returned the smile, and they dug in. Tucker was starved, and his shrunken stomach nearly burst at it.

There was a brief moment of silence. Then Tucker asked: "Are things safe around here in town?"

"So you've heard." It was Dominic.

"We saw the chief of police earlier; I think he was drunk— and shouting at people to tell him who killed his son?"

Dominic, who was folding a napkin, sighed. "Lately, things have been scary. Murder doesn't happen often around here. And to make matters worse, last month one of the cops ran over a father and son on Broad Avenue... The father was killed instantly, and the boy died last night. Poor kid suffered."

"Did the cop run over them purposely?"

"No, not at all. It was a car accident. The papers are claiming the cop was drunk, though, and that he was reckless."

"Sad, very sad," Tucker muttered.

"What's sad is that Walker the cop, is a great man. He's crushed about all of it."

"I can understand," Tucker said. "Back home we had an officer die in a motorcycle crash, and the trucker who hit him committed suicide a day later. It was an accident—everything indicated it was. A blind spot on a sharp intersection. But the trucker didn't see it that way, blamed himself, and the following day we found him caught on an outcrop along the river."

Dominic shook his head. "You must've seen a lot in your life."

"I think, after the war, there's nothing much that can shock me."

"Understandable," Dominic murmured. "Understandable... All we can do is pray that the chief catches the killer."

"I truly hope he does," Tucker said. "This is one town I'll never forget."

The young people finished eating and continued socializing with their new friends, a husband and wife who had opened their hearts to strangers in the most desperate of times. A blessing, they knew.

"You have a place to stay?" Lillie wanted to know.

Emma's head sank.

"No," Tucker said. It came out like a croak. The embarrassment of his predicament had settled into a dusty corner of his brain that he'd buried deeply.

"We have a spare bedroom," Lillie said, clearing the plates, "and you're welcome to stay. It's been a long time since we had house guests."

Dominic said, "There are towels in the hallway cabinet."

"We don't want to impose," Emma told her, only half honestly.

"Impose? Not at all. We'd be delighted."

Tucker said, "Thank you for the hospitality."

"So it's settled," Lillie said, winking. "Follow me, then, and I'll take you to your room."

She led them to a small bedroom in the rear. It had a tall twin bed, a chest, and beautiful white curtains with butterfly lace. It smelled a bit musty, but, for them it might as well have been a bridal suite.

When their hosts had left them alone, Tucker and Emma sat side by side on the bed, their legs barely touching the floor. They say you marry a girl most like your mother. Tucker hadn't planned it that way. His mother had been sweet like Emma and she too had experienced the horror of an abusive husband. Like the last man that Emma had been with, Tucker's father had laid a hand on his mother. And seeing that, growing up, the boy had promised himself never to do the same, not once. But when he had returned from the war, his father had died, and his mother lived the rest of her life free from abuse until she died peacefully seven years ago.

"A lot nicer than an abandoned deli, Emma, huh?" Tucker said quietly.

"Why? What wasn't nice about that place?" she asked, a smile playing on her face. This was the kind of talk that had passed between them during the good days, and now it went a long way to picking up their morale.

Tucker returned the smile, his back still aching from the deli's hard floor and the strenuous work. He hugged her. "Yeah, mark that down as the nicest joint we've been thus far. You think they have a postcard we can send to your sister?"

"I am certain they must."

Even in the darkest of times, her smile could brighten his mood.

"You bathe first, Emma. I'm going to set the bed."

Sitting with her and chatting while she took a bath had been another of their old life memories. But he didn't want to act the randy guy in another man's home.

16

The butcher's headlamps were barely visible on the dark asphalt roadway out of Newark. He rolled his neck and let it drop into his shoulders. It was the hour of deepest sleep and, for him, the peace and quiet he longed for. Even the constant clanging of moonshine jugs had a calming rhythm. He opened the window and let the cool breeze run through his hair.

"You did good work tonight, Mike," he said to his reflection in the rearview. "Four trips, and still enough time to eat before preparing the sausage." He was very pleased with himself; the extra money was keeping his shop open and allowing him to live comfortably. It had been over thirty-four years since the founding of the borough and the rapid expansion that had taken place. Years before, an aggressive marketing campaign in Manhattan had brought many new faces to town. Property had been divided up, and the locals had welcomed the newcomers. Those transplants had helped expand their businesses. But when the country fell into financial ruin, Michael's small butcher business had dried up. Running booze through the night helped keep the doors open and the meat fresh.

He dozed off a bit, and when he shifted his eyes back to the roadway, he saw four deer crossing—including a large buck frozen in the glare of his headlights. He hit the brakes as hard as he could and swung the vehicle, fishtailing and striking the buck with his rear quarter panel and bumper. The other deer managed to scamper off. "Sonofabitch," he grunted, gripping the wheel. "I don't need this nonsense now."

He smelled gasoline.

"Damn it," he snapped, seething, killed the engine, got out, and lifted the trunk; the hinges creaked in the tranquil night. All the glass jugs of booze looked intact. But then he found the gallon of gasoline lying on its side, soaking into an emergency bag, a survival kit complete with drinking water, matches, clothes, rope, salted beef jerky, a pair of scissors, a hunting knife, a wool hat, gloves, and a thick wool blanket. He reached in and lifted the bag. Gasoline was dripping from the bottom of it, and the fumes made him dizzy. He found the matches in the bag and threw them into the dry reeds.

Cautiously, he closed the trunk and found the buck lying fifteen feet ahead in the roadway. It was gasping for air, nostrils flaring, eyes broad, grunting in pain. The butcher fished his pistol from his breast pocket and sighted on the animal's chest. "Least I can do," he mumbled to himself, feeling more compassion for the animal than he did for most humans. He was about to pull the trigger when he realized his hands and sleeves were saturated in gasoline. He put the gun away and went back to his trunk to retrieve the rope.

When he returned the buck was gagging and blood was dripping from its ears and mouth. "Easy, feller. It'll all be over in a minute," he said stretching the rope. He adjusted it to fit snuggly around the windpipe and then he pulled it up over his shoulder, like a fireman hoisting a hose. The animal's neck rose with the momentum, and it let out a harrowing bleat that shot across the quiet land before it went peacefully still. In the distance the howl of a lonesome dog shattered the ensuing silence.

The butcher's back strained as he gathered the buck's legs and dragged him off the road. He dragged the front legs a couple of feet, then swung the rear legs past them and continued in this fashion until the carcass rolled into the runoff trench.

He brushed his hands together and continued his journey east, where he pulled into a chrome-paneled diner in Little Ferry that looked like a railroad car, with a sign in the window that read Fresh Coffee. Breakfast Specials.

He wheeled into a spot aside the three cement steps that led to the entrance, his tires crunching on the gravel. He was hungry, and the bottle of hooch he'd gulped down earlier was rolling over in his stomach. He could feel the acid in his throat. A hot cup of coffee would flush it down.

When he walked in, a bell above the door jingled. "Good morning, Michael," said a curly blonde waitress in a black apron with lacy trim.

"Good morning, Tracy."

"I haven't seen you in while. Where you've been?"

"Busy."

She escorted him to the counter, where he sat down on a stool. The place was empty and smelled of the antiseptic a busboy was using to clean the dessert display. Lots of layered cakes, whipped creamed pies, cookies, and brownies sat on a rear counter next to the coffee station. There was a pile of newspapers at the end of the counter. Next to the bathrooms was a coat rack with lots of hangers and no coats. On a shelf above it was a phonebook and a box that had a menu taped to it.

"Same as always, Michael?" she asked.

"Yeah, eggs over easy. No bacon. It's too greasy."

"Watching your figure?" she asked wryly. "Because you shouldn't."

"What's that supposed to mean?" His ego seemed challenged, and he shot her a curious glance.

"A man should be your size," she said, placing a saucer under a coffee mug. "Any smaller and, well, it just won't look right on you." There was honesty in her comment, and he was satisfied.

Michael grinned. "Just feeling a little rebellious tonight."

"I wish my husband felt that way sometimes. Actually, I wish he just felt something. He's so stale. It's been so long, I...." Her voice trailed off, and she simply set the cup of coffee before him and smiled. "It's fresh, darling."

"Smells great. Maybe it's you, Tracy. You should spice things up. Get off the night shift."

She leaned her elbows on the counter coquettishly. "How I wish. But if I did, they'd foreclose on the house. It's not much. But it's a home. This second job is keeping us afloat."

"We all do what we have to. When things turn around, it'll get better."

"Can't get no worse."

"Ain't that the truth."

She stood there holding the coffee pot. "Did you find yourself a lady to settle down with? Get a dog, some kids, and a house with a white picket fence?"

"Actually, I did," Michael grinned.

"Sweet gal?"

"She's a real sweetheart."

"Whattaya call her?"

"Name's Emma."

"She's a keeper, huh."

"It was love at first sight. Do you believe in that?"

"Of course. There was a time I felt that way about Teddy. I guess I still do."

17

The butcher was stirring sugar into his coffee when the bell jangled again, and over his left shoulder he saw Chief Henderson come in with a newspaper tucked under his arm. "Morning, Tracy," the cop drawled.

"Quiet out there, Chief?"

"Nothing worth talking about. Same ol' stuff."

The butcher was sipping his coffee when Henderson asked, "You take a bath in gasoline, Mike?"

Michael put on his best face. With a grin he said, "It's my new cologne."

Henderson grinned back in a conspiratorial way. "The ladies must fancy it," he said with a snicker, brushing his moustache with his thumb and index fingers. "They say it's poison on the skin."

The butcher sniffed the air. "I hit a deer and the spare can tipped over. The whole interior reeks."

With a knowing nod, Henderson said, "They're moving at this hour. I hit one a few years back. Little guy. But it still did a number on the cruiser."

"It was an eight-pointer. Looked healthy. I dragged it over onto the east side of the road. You think the boys at the VA could use some good chow?"

"Where about? By Huyler Street?"

"A little further west. I'd say a hundred yards past the Wrigley's billboard."

"I know exactly where that is. I'll phone the local boys and let them know about it. No need to waste good meat... Looks like it did a number on that vehicle of yours."

"Yeah...." The butcher gestured at Henderson's newspaper. "Say, that Hubbell's got a solid arm. You hear any of the Yankee game yesterday?"

Nothing could distract a person more than baseball talk,

and it did with Henderson, too. "I missed it," Henderson said, holding up the newspaper. "Looks like Boston outscored them 15 to 2."

"That's a lot of runs," Michael added. "Did Ruth or Gehrig play?"

"Both," Henderson said.

"That's a lot of runs," Michael repeated.

But then Henderson asked, "Have you seen old lady Stillman around?"

"Nope."

"When was the last time she came into your shop?"

Chewing on his eggs, Michael said, "I'd say a few weeks ago. I'm surprised she's missing. Think she's dead?"

Henderson said nothing.

"'Cause I doubt she's dead. You know, stuff like that only happens to the good ones."

Henderson thought about that and then considered how right the butcher was. His son had been one of the "good ones," and his life had been cut short, while Abigail Stillman, bad as she was, had grown into old age. "I couldn't argue that," Henderson said. "Only the good die young."

"Don't take this the wrong way, but I'm not the least bit concerned she's missing. Probably off doing something and never told anybody out of spite. She'll live another hundred years and continue to make people miserable."

"Why you so harsh against lady Stillman?" Henderson asked, wondering whether the butcher had known about her sleeping with his father and how it all ended. And did the butcher know that he'd been there when his father died?

"As if you don't know, Carter," Mike finally said, and narrowed his gaze.

Henderson returned the stare. "What the heck are you talking about, Mike? You got something you wanna say, boy?"

"No, I'm just a little upset about my car. All lady Stillman ever did was cheat me on some meat. I know she was your stepmother at one time, and I am sorry if I came off disrespectful."

"Well, that's fine," Henderson said. "Stillman's a snake and willing to do the distasteful things in life to get what she wants."

Henderson glanced around. The waitress and the busboy were on the other side of the diner. "I am not surprised she cheated you on the meat. She was always a cheater," he added. "Old bitch probably ran off with some poor slob."

"Wouldn't surprise me," the butcher said, recalling the day he had learned his father'd been found dead in an alley. A man walking a dog had come across him lying there like a bag of garbage, with a gunshot wound to the belly that he hoped had killed him quickly.

Henderson wiped his mouth with a napkin. "You hear about my son?"

"Yes, of course... I just didn't know how to bring it up. My condolences."

Henderson glanced down at his coffee. He picked it up and sipped it. "Thank you," he murmured. "You hear anything, you let me know."

"Certainly," the butcher said. "If you need anything, just ask."

"Well," Henderson whispered, "can you drop off some giggle water at my house later?"

"You finished it all already?"

"It's been a tough week."

"I can understand," the butcher said. "I'll leave you enough to last a while."

Henderson nodded, "I appreciate that. Whatever it costs, let me know, and I'll stop by your shop and pay you."

"Don't worry about that, Chief. This one's on me."

Henderson fished a pack of Chesterfields out of his heavily starched breast pocket with brass buttons. "You think it'll be all right if I lit this up?"

"I am done anyway," Michael said, and threw money down on the counter. "Let me get out the door before you strike that," he concluded, exchanged pleasantries with Henderson and the waitress, and left.

18

It was twenty past seven in the evening when Chief Henderson sat down at his desk in the police station. He jotted down some notes and began to think of Freddy. He wanted to convince himself there was a higher rationale, a greater purpose for his premature death, that only his Maker knew, a reason he'd never understand. "We're dust," he muttered, clenching his fist. "And to dust we shall return." He felt a rush of anger spike through him, felt the hairs on the back of his neck prickle, followed by flashes of heat. He crumpled the sheet of paper in his hand and threw it across the room. It hit the brick wall and dropped onto the wooden floor. He stood up, picturing in hazy shades of black and gray the man who had killed his son. He couldn't see color; luminosity was limited. The man's face was washed over, ghostlike, murky and obscure, hidden in shadows, like a duck swimming through steam rising from a lake covered bleakly by the light of a cold moon. He rolled his shoulders, thinking, took his seat again... if he didn't stop the recent crime wave, he'd be unemployed and worthless too, his name destroyed. He needed a body, soon.

The wind rattled the old windows. During periods of heavy rain, it would leak, and he was careful not to leave anything of value on the sill.

The police station, inside the small brick municipal building next to a park, had been opened in 1908, and been built to last, since a fire had destroyed the original one in 1906. It was fireproof, all block, metal, and brick. The police portion consisted of three small rooms—the larger one contained a steel prisoner's cage that was fitted for two and sometimes held five or more, two desks piled high with dockets and old notebooks, and three single bulbs shining dimly. The second room was solely for storage, and the third, used for interrogations, had a refrigerator for meals.

Henderson rose from his stool and stumbled over to the phone. He lifted it, thought briefly, then hung it up. He looked around his office. A few years before, when the economy was better, a former mayor, Lester Brisol—a man bred from the soil—had had plans to refit the building with plaster walls, but Henderson hadn't seen the need to waste money on things like that. He was content with the wooden floor and the brick walls.

He liked that mayor a lot. Brisol supported the police department one hundred percent. A truly great man—that he was. Talking about improvements to the cell, Henderson had once told him to save the funds and not to worry. "The cage is steel, and steel lasts forever. Nobody's escaping." There was a point one couldn't argue. Criminals never escaped; some of their blood still stained the wooden bench and paint-chipped steel bars. But Lester Brisol was nothing like the current mayor, Wilson Alexander Fitzgerald, who went by his first name. Henderson and the mayor didn't see eye to eye. They constantly argued, and truth was, Henderson was figuring a way to arrest the mayor and remove him from office. There had been times he had considered framing the fellow; but he'd known that, sooner or later, Wilson would slip up, and Henderson would be the one to see he was punished.

Henderson was anticipating retirement soon; closing in on fifty-four, he'd always known it was a young man's job. But what could he do now? Looked like it was only going to be him for a while. Dankert had cleaned out his locker the day before, and Wilson had refused Henderson's request for additional officers, had blamed the economy and said he'd do his best to appropriate funding. But Henderson had known he wasn't sincere.

To compound matters, Henderson was seeking comfort in the bottle. The butcher had dropped off enough to keep him drunk for a week. Henderson squinted and recalled the terror in his son's eye as he lay there dying in the dirt. How could I've let it happen? he thought. If only I had stayed with him when he went into that house. Then there would've been two of us. I could've shot the bastard. I could've saved him.

Henderson began outlining what he knew in a Big Chief

notebook on his desk. He knew Charlie Burgess had been murdered. He knew Abigail Stillman was missing. He knew his son had been murdered. What he didn't know was who had done it, and how he'd tell his wife the truth.

Then Henderson thought about the bullet that had entered Frederick's belly and wished he himself had taken it instead.

He rubbed his bloodshot eyes and noticed his fingertips shaking. The wooden desk drawer creaked as Henderson opened it and fished out a long glass bottle of whiskey. He yanked the cork and put the bottle to his lips.

Then he lifted his son's gun belt off his desk and folded it across his lap; he was brushing the new leather with his fingertips when his wife Molly called out, "Carter, you there!" she shouted. "Dinner's cold, and the priest is coming by. You know this." She entered the office in a black blouse and black pants. She had a sad look in her eye, and the stress lines on her face were ominous. She narrowed her gaze, standing over the desk of her drunk husband.

"Just a minute, Molly. I'm finishing up some paperwork," he slurred.

"Nonsense," she shouted, hands on her hips. "Your drinking is only making this harder for us. Give me that bottle."

Henderson grudgingly handed it over.

She looked deeply into his bloodshot eyes. "You stink like booze and you're staring at me like you've never seen me before. Helllooo. You there... Carter." She waved her hand in front of him.

"Cut it out, Molly. I know I am drunk. No need to point out the obvious. Hell, I don't care if I stay drunk till my liver falls out of my belly."

In a flash, she slapped him across the cheek, "Snap out of it!" she shouted. "Now, let's go home for dinner."

He rubbed his cheek and rose out of his chair, steadying himself on the desk. "I'll be fine, honey. Trust me."

"Well, you better, because Damien needs a father. And right now I need a sober husband. Let's go home and pray," she said, stifling a sob. "God ain't gonna give us nothing we can't get through… It says so in the scriptures."

"Sometimes I wonder where God is at times like this."

"Don't say that, Carter. You have to have faith. It's what we need."

He threw his arm around his wife, and they hobbled out the door, the big man towering over her. He closed the door behind him, muttering, "Charlie didn't kill him, Molly."

She looked up at Henderson, her eyes filling with tears, the crows' feet deep and dark. "Who done it, then?" she asked.

"I don't know."

"He was murdered?"

"Yes," Henderson sighed.

"So who done it?"

"I told you, I don't know."

"What do you know?"

"I know the killer's dust," Henderson said. "And to dust he shall return."

19

Tucker awoke to bright morning sun pouring around the edges of the window shade, dust motes dancing merrily as if signaling a beautiful day. He stretched and raised the shade to a sweeping view of the town and its people going about their business. He looked closely and observed a man in a suit carrying a brief case head for the trolley, which was at capacity with business people and school kids holding onto the side railings. In the distance, though, a second trolley was heading in from Leonia to accommodate others. The sky had a few clouds low on the horizon, making it seem longer and clearer.

Tucker saw the wind was blowing leaves and debris across the roadway. The browned tips of the leaves on the trees were turned up, waiting for rain after a long hot summer.

But as beautiful as the day promised to be, there seemed a solid chance another wind storm would soon develop, rain only a distant hope.

He turned to his still-sleeping wife. "Wake up, Emma. It's past eight already."

She murmured, and her eyes held his. She kissed him. "Morning," she whispered.

"Looks like you could sleep all day," he said.

"I slept well last night. You?"

"The whole night through."

There was a pile of clothes on the chest with a note from Lillie that he guessed she'd placed there sometime during the night. It read: Good morning. See what fits.

When he showed the note to Emma, her eyes beamed. "Those are for us?"

"You bet," he said, slipping into a pair of blue jeans. "How do these look on me? And this work shirt? I'm guessing they're Dominic's."

"They fit well. I love you," she said.

"You, too."

She swung her long legs out of bed and padded to the clothes pile. She let her nightgown fall to the floor and began sifting through the pile. She was as comfortable naked as dressed. Tucker loved that naturalness in her. Another thing that he loved was that she had never pretended or tried to act like anybody else. She was herself, and others he'd known including him looked up to her. It was rare in a world full of pretense—and even rarer for a woman who'd been beaten and tortured by the hand of another man to be that open and comfortable.

She chose a soft white dress with a red velvet belt that she tied into a bow in the back. It was too big, looked a bit funny, but she wore it proudly.

They stood before an oval dressing mirror and modeled the new outfits. "Swanky," Emma said.

"You look damn sexy in that dress."

"Sexy enough to take me here, right now?" she said, her smile so enticing that it was tough to resist.

He didn't even have to think about it. He curled a finger under her chin, kissed her, wet tongues swimming back and forth, thrilling them before they fell backwards onto the bed with Emma on top of him, those smooth legs straddling his powerful hips. "You've got great gams, honey," he whispered.

"Take me," she murmured breathlessly.

After another minute of kissing and watching for the door, Tucker slid Emma next to him, their eyes locked deeply. "One second," he said, and rose from the bed, making certain the door was locked. He slid back into bed and parted the tent of Emma's hair that had fallen over her face. Staring deep into her speckled brown eyes, he kissed her again and unzipped himself.

When he entered her she began breathing heavily. "Be quiet," he reminded her. "These walls have ears."

20

Tucker and Dominic wheeled the truck into the gravel parking lot of Palisades Park Lumber and Supply, going over the tracks that ran along the side of the large building to different docking points. It was early in the morning, and two men in the yard were sitting on a pile of lumber, smoking cigarettes and watching the clock. In five more minutes the whistle would blast, and they'd head back to work—whatever work they could find, since business had mellowed a lot over the past few months.

"Baker's down to two men," Dominic said. "Five years ago he had over a dozen in the yard. A lot of my friends worked here."

"If things don't get better fast, you think he'll close?"

"Six more months of this, and he'll have no choice."

"Something has to break. We can't be in this depression forever."

"Hopefully, the country will turn around sooner than later."

Dominic parked in an open parking space in front of a towering barn that had been converted into a lumber-storage facility, with tall racks of neatly organized wood stacked with plates indicating their length, width, and type of wood. There was lots of balsam, pine, even some harder mahogany. In the middle of the barn sat pallets of plywood, shingles and five-gallon pails of tar.

Making their way through the barn, Dominic said, "We'll get everything for today, but if we run out of something and I need you to make a run, this is where I need you to come."

"Seems fairly direct from the job site," Tucker said. "Just a few blocks."

They came across a large sawing table with an electric saw used for cutting bigger lengths of wood. Dominic commented, "When I was in high school, I worked here, and that's where I was stationed. I'd cut wood all day by hand. Went home with sawdust all over me, my ears, eyelids, my mouth... everywhere."

Tucker chuckled. "Ah, that smell of fresh cut wood reminds me a lot of when I was younger too, working with my old man."

They continued through the barn and, on the other side, crossed a gravel parking lot to a large house with two small steps into the back door. Inside, they strolled around the store. A customer sitting at the counter was discussing the latest Goodell-Pratt hand drill. The man held it and tested its precision drilling through a piece of pine nailed to the counter for demonstrations. "Makes life a lot easier," the proprietor said. They'd known they'd have to wait.

Dominic explained that the proprietor, Baker, enjoyed his job. He was handy and had built the store himself, thirty-three years earlier, after he'd gotten married and had his first daughter. Dominic had gone to school with his daughter. Baker assembled at the railroad tracks so shipments of lumber could be received directly at the barn.

Tucker looked around the store. "These tall shelves," Dominic went on, "were once filled with supplies, tools, doorknobs, solvents—just about everything one would need to build, fix, or clean anything. But nowadays, look—the higher the shelf, the barer it gets. This place was fully stocked a year ago."

"He's got potential to survive," Tucker whispered.

"I hope so. He's got little competition," Dominic said in a low voice, leaning into Tucker. "He just needs people to start building more, like they did a few years ago."

"I see."

"Lately Baker only replaces what he's certain he'll sell. I guess it doesn't make sense to let his money sit on the shelves. So for now, he keeps the basics. Everything else is on back order. Or at least that's what he'll say when he runs out of something."

Tucker and Dominic moved closer to the counter and heard the customer say, "I'll hold off on the drill right now. Let me get a good stainless saw instead."

Baker turned around picked a stainless saw with a wooden handle off a hook. "It's the same one you always get."

"It'll do," the customer said.

"I'll be with you in a second, fellers," Baker said as he packaged the saw for the customer, who turned to Tucker and Dominic and nodded. "How's it going, Dominic?"

"As they say, Mike, the road to success is always under construction."

The butcher smirked. "That it is."

"Still working on that roof, Mike?" Dominic asked.

"I fixed that already."

Tucker interrupted, "You're the butcher who drove us here?"

"Well, I rode in today by myself, unless I missed something." The butcher smirked again, then smiled like a politician would.

"Well, I meant—"

"I know what you meant," the butcher said, winking. "How's the lady?"

"She's fine. We found some new friends," Tucker said, patting Dominic on the shoulder. "He's great... Hey, thanks for the ride."

"Well, it's nice to see things are shaping up for you. I'll see you around."

The butcher stuffed his receipt into his breast pocket, tucked the saw under his arm, and left.

"Can you call on the boys?" Dominic asked Baker. "We're going to need their help loading the truck."

Twenty minutes later, the truck was loaded, and Dominic and Tucker rode off to the job site.

"That butcher," Tucker said. "You were saying something about him?"

"He's a drugstore cowboy. Everybody's cautious with their wives around him."

21

It was dark on the side of Dominic's home when the butcher crept up to the washroom window in the cool night. He was wearing a dark blue shirt, a gray fedora that sat low hiding most of his face, and a pair of black pants. He wanted to see Emma again, even if only for a moment.

It wasn't unusual for the butcher to be peeping into that window. He had been staring at Dominic's wife for years, had propositioned her on many occasions, and believed, sooner or later, he'd catch her at a weak moment. He liked Lillie's full figure. One day, she'd forget she was married, and he'd have his way with her. But for now, it was Emma who occupied his mind daily—and his thoughts of loving her, and of marriage, were growing stronger.

He hadn't expected to find her the way he did. She was naked in the bath, humming, when he peeped into the open window. He was tall enough to see in without having to stand on his toes. He felt his heart thump; it made him feel alive. She was running her fingers through her soapy hair, squinting as to not to burn her eyes as the butcher watched closely, his breath stronger. He became aroused and wanted to climb in there and take her. But kidnapping a soapy naked woman wasn't going to work.

He watched her wash her neck and breasts. She was what he needed to fix all the horrors of his past—somebody to love him, who'd care about him, somebody innocent and sweet who knew nothing about him or the small town gossip.

She rose, and the butcher studied the soapy water run off her smooth body, contouring her full breasts, slender waist, and full hips. Her slim ribs seemed to accentuate the size of her bust. His eyes fixed on her nipples, and it got him even more aroused. It wasn't just the sight of a naked woman that had him so excited, but of one he believed he'd marry. He had it all figured out. The wedding ceremony was going to be performed by the justice of the peace, with the justice's wife as the witness, the justice saying after he pronounced them man and wife, "Good to see you two are desperately in love with each other," Emma kissing him on the cheek. He could smell her powder and perfume.

He unzipped himself as he stood there at the window, thinking about the honeymoon they'd have in a small seaside motor court. He'd give her a baby there, no doubt.

Just then he heard a loud noise and some rumbling, and was startled to see Chief Henderson approaching him. What does this damn fool want now? he thought.

"What you doing in the alley, boy?" the chief demanded. "Who is that?"

The butcher backed away as Henderson staggered toward him. He could smell the alcohol. "It's me, Mike."

"What are you doing?" Henderson again demanded.

"Take it easy, Chief. I'm just tying up the garbage. Everything okay?"

Henderson leaned into him, his eyes a deep bloodshot red and watery. "Have you seen Abigail Stillman?"

"You already asked me that. I told you no."

"Well?"

The butcher's brow's furrowed. "Well what, Chief?"

"Nobody's seen her in two weeks. You hear anything, Mike?"

The butcher wondered why the man had asked him again. Did he have suspicions? But then, when Henderson nearly fell over, the butcher realized he was only drunk, and decided to play along. "No, sir. I'll ask around tomorrow. If I hear anything, you'll be the first to know."

"You do that," Henderson slurred. "Let me know. Yeah, you let me know."

The butcher relished the moment. "Don't take this the wrong way, Chief. But shouldn't you know where your stepmother is?"

"You know I ain't talked to her in years, Mike. You trying to be funny?" Henderson spat. "Cause if you are," he said, clenching a fist.

"No, no, I forget. It's been a long day... Maybe she went to Atlantic City for a holiday."

Henderson sighed, unclenched his fist. "She has been known to disappear every now and then. That's what she did the last time."

"She always said she loves the beach and boardwalk down there. Maybe she packed up and moved." The butcher thought what a fool the Chief was to be having this conversation again. And he loved every second of it.

"That would be nice," Henderson hiccupped. "But listen— if you see or hear something, let me know."

Henderson stumbled off.

"Hey, Chief," the butcher called out, "how's the stock look? You need another drop-off?"

Henderson put his index finger to his temple. "It never hurts to have a little more comfort."

"Okay. Tomorrow, I'll drop some off."

Henderson reached for Dominic's house to steady himself. "Thanks for the steaks you sent the other day. We appreciate it."

"You're welcome... Say, Chief. Have you asked that new guy and his wife?"

"What?"

"I think the name's Tucker. But I ain't good with faces, names, or places."

"Who is he?"

The butcher wrapped his arm around the Chief's shoulders, both big men walking out toward street. "He's a vagabond... a wanderer... seedy-looking guy."

"Where would I find this man?"

The butcher could feel the man's weight. He was practically holding him up. He pointed to Dominic's front door. "I saw him go in there a few hours ago. He was working with Dominic earlier down on West Ruby. Tall guy? Looks maybe thirty-something?"

"You sure he's in here?"

"Yes, sir."

"Thank you." Henderson staggered for the sidewalk and

spread his legs wide for balance. "I'll come looking for you if I need any further information."

A little later, the butcher opened his car door and climbed in behind the wheel. He rolled down the window as he approached the swaying chief walking down the sidewalk as if he had just disembarked from an ocean liner. "He seems like the kind of man who could cause a lot of trouble," he ventured to say.

"He's got more trouble coming his way then he'll ever cause. Wait until I get my hands on him."

"If you need anything from me, you know where to find me." The butcher nodded. "Anything I can do to help."

"Hold on a second, Mike." Henderson swallowed and again took a wide stance to stop the swaying and regain his balance. He rested his elbows on the butcher's car door and said, "Can you do me a favor?" The strong smell of booze quickly permeated the interior of the butcher's car.

"Sure."

"Keep an extra eye on this guy."

With a confused look, the butcher said, "You want me to keep watch on him?"

"Yes," the chief said.

"My pleasure," The butcher smiled, accelerating lightly, and the V8 grumbled down the unimproved roadway. Shaking his head, he thought how alcohol could make a fool out of some.

22

Sitting before the piano in his parlor, the butcher was playing a somber tune. He wasn't in the mood for anything else. The rush he had felt from seeing Emma naked in that window had subsided. There was no trace either of the joy he'd felt from toying with the intoxicated chief. No matter what he did, he couldn't shake the blues. It was late in the evening, and he was preparing himself for bed. Sometimes the piano allowed him to free things bottled up inside.

In his youth, he had been much to marvel over, a prodigy. People had come from all over to hear him play. But they hadn't been the ones he wanted to hear him—men with motives who gathered at his home, where his mother worked and he sat playing all the songs they enjoyed, especially Scott Joplin's ragtime hit "The Entertainer" (how they loved that one) while, over the noise of the piano, he heard his mother slyly panting in a bedroom not far away. She wanted every customer to think she was enjoying it. And when her panting stopped, a man emerged from her bedroom, a smile on his face from ear to ear, and usually tossed a coin on the piano—a tip for Michael. The money was what kept him on that bench. He'd nod and play some more. It went on every Saturday night after the underground fight club, the men sitting in the formal parlor, listening to him play and waiting for their turn to have their futures read, as she claimed.

He finished the song, stretching the notes and ending on a low D, holding it down and letting it vibrate through the house. His mother was listening, in the same bedroom she had worked in all that time. He rose from his stool; I wonder what she's doing, he was thinking.

He entered her bedroom; she lay there sleeping, her chest moving softly up and down. The memories started coming on stronger, and before long all he could picture was men, and more men, on top of her, and he could hear her panting in ecstasy as she pleased her customer and he played the piano in the formal parlor. He recalled her most regular customer, Charlie Burgess, before he began going steady with his mother—when they weren't exclusive to each other. Burgess would always leave her room, zip himself up, and, with a grin, sit next to Michael at the piano and part the boy's hair. Michael hadn't known then how desperately Burgess wanted him. The thought of a man being intimate with a young boy sickened him.

But worse now, the image of Burgess brought on a stronger and more painful memory that Michael couldn't shake, from during a period when Burgess and his mother had been exclusive, when they appeared to be loving and caring to each other. It was the night of the World Series. He recalled Burgess saying, "Ah, that's my boy," and wiping the corner of his mouth before patting his bare, shaking inner thigh. *Ah, That's a my boy*, raged inside his head.

Through a haze of spiraling grays and black, the butcher again remembered the day he had caught his father humping Henderson's stepmother Abigail Stillman on the butcher block, the day that had changed his life forever. No matter how hard he tried, he couldn't erase it. At least old lady Stillman, and old man Burgess, had paid for what they'd done, he thought. His mother and Henderson were the last two yet to pay.

The butcher walked around his mother's bed and lifted a silver-framed picture of his father from the nightstand. It was tarnished, the photo gritty and dirty. He could smell the dust. In the photo, his dad was smiling in his uniform outside the store. Michael had never understood why a woman who'd done so much since his death would sleep every night with a picture of a man she'd betrayed, a man who had in turn betrayed all of them.

A single tear dripped down the butcher's cheek as he recalled a bright morning so long before when he and his father were tossing a baseball on the green grass in the backyard. His father would bend down, and Michael'd wind up and toss him a strike nearly every time. He was that good even at a young age. "Now, let's work on that fastball," his dad would say, showing him where to wrap his fingers around the laces, big smiles on both of them.

He held the photo against his chest, tilted his head back, and drifted back to that afternoon. In his mind's eye, his mother was behind him on the back porch. She was walking toward him with a tray with two large glasses of iced tea. "Come and have a cold drink," she'd called out in her apple-embroidered apron. But when he walked over toward her, arms out reaching for a glass, he'd looked around and couldn't find his father. He lost his place in his dream and wondered where he had gone. Standing behind his mother was Charlie Burgess, naked, his member hard. He was smiling and playfully shouting, "You ready for another inning? I'll pitch," he said with a deep laugh that sounded like it was coming from a barrel.

The butcher shook his head, trying to erase the dream.

He threw the picture across the room. It shattered and fell to the floor. He made a fist and slammed it into his other hand.

That's when he reached for a pillow, the other hand seizing his mother's throat, and pressed the pillow against her mouth. "Just go to sleep," he said.

She squirmed and fought and, with muffled shouts, cried, "What in the heck are you doing?"

"I'm clearing out space. I guess you can call it junk removal."

She struggled with him as he pinned her down and tried again to suffocate her. "Let me go," she cried. "I'm your mother."

"You're in the damn way," he seethed. "You're always in the damn way."

She rolled onto her belly and, with a solid effort, rose on her knees and elbows and attempted to shake him off her. "I'm your damn mother," she repeated. "Stop this now!"

"Too bad you're going to miss the wedding, Nancy," the butcher raged and struck her with a sharp elbow to the back of the head. "You just couldn't make this easy, Nancy, huh?" he spat.

He rolled her over. She had a woozy look in her eyes. She was reaching for the bed post to steady herself, but her hand kept missing on the attempts. "Please," she said, her voice almost a whisper.

"If it's anything to you, don't feel that special. You're not the only one who needs clearing."

With both his hands he pressed the pillow against her face, applying tremendous pressure around her mouth and nose. He heard something crack, and then blood began saturating the pillow. He watched the life drain from her like water running from a gutter and seeping into the ground. Shortly thereafter he pulled the sheet over her head. "You let me down," he said. "Emma would never approve of you."

He left her bedroom and found himself back at the piano, playing a song for his mother.It was "Ave Maria."

23

"Promise me you'll quit the drinking today, honey," said Molly, handing her husband his police man's hat at their front door. She ran her hand along his chest. "Hand it over, Carter. It's for the best."

Henderson frowned, reached into his breast pocket, and pulled out the flask of whiskey. "Here," he said, handing it over. "Sooner or later I'd have to quit anyway."

"Yes, and when you see Michael, tell him no more deliveries."

Henderson said nothing.

"I mean it, Carter. Cold turkey. Not a drop. You were so drunk last night, you kicked in the back door. You scared the hell out of Damien and me."

"Sorry about that, honey. But I misplaced my keys."

"Don't make excuses, Carter. If you don't quit drinking, Damien and I are leaving you."

Henderson swallowed. He had known his drinking was getting out of hand, and that, sooner or later, he'd push his family away. He wasn't willing to risk that. And the thought of it allowed a wave of guilt to consume him. Surely last night they must've thought it was the killer coming for them. "Okay." He bowed his head. "It's for the best. No more drinking."

"Do it for me and Damien, honey."

Henderson nodded. "Okay."

"I'll have dinner ready for five."

Henderson bent down and kissed his wife, saying, "I'll call if I'm running late."

"Why would you run late today?"

He let out a long breath, "Yes," he said. "I may be late. Today may be the day I get him."

"What makes you think this guy killed Freddy?"

Henderson stayed in the doorway. "He must've needed a

place to stay, so he killed Charlie Burgess, and he was staying in his house when we arrived. Maybe he thought we somehow knew. It's the only thing that makes sense. He's a vagabond. A nomad of some kind."

Molly's eyes were rimmed with tears. "Sounds terrifying. I don't want to think about it anymore. But it's the only thing on my mind."

"We need justice."

"Yes." Molly sniffed back a tear.

"It's the only grace that will help."

"I pray every day."

"I don't need the prayer," Henderson muttered.

"What?"

"He needs it."

"Well, don't go killing anyone unless you're certain."

"God help him."

"Calm down, Carter. You're getting all worked up."

"...I'm real angry, Moll."

"I know," she said and rubbed his shoulders. "Please, though, calm down."

"I am."

"Seriously, honey. You'll need all your senses to get him."

"I will, don't worry."

He pulled the doorknob and swung the door open. The morning air was crisp, the sun still hidden behind the hill. He heard the train whistle in the distance. In a little while, the depot platform would be filled with commuters. The passengers debarking from overnight destinations would soon be dragging their luggage through the dirt streets and concrete sidewalks that had replaced many of the wooden ones. "Whoever thought it would be like this," he grumbled.

"I know."

Henderson nodded. "It'll change."

"I hope so."

"Maybe today."

She rubbed the small of his back. "Damien and I are going to take the trolley out to Hackensack Cemetery later," she said. "We'll sit a while with Freddy. I'll let him know what's going on."

"If you wait till tomorrow, I'll go with you."

"I'll go both days."

"Okay."

"Be careful."

"I'm always careful."

"...You know what I mean."

"I know."

Molly took a deep breath of the morning air. "Is Dankert going to help you?" she asked.

"I had to let him go."

"I thought you said—"

"They came served him the papers."

"Who came?"

"The County."

"...Senseless," Molly said.

"You're telling me."

With wide eyes, Molly said, "You shouldn't go after this thing alone."

"I'll be fine."

"Maybe put a call into the county and see if they'll send men to help."

"No."

"Why not?"

"They've already took two of my men. I wouldn't ask them for nuttin'."

"Call one of the neighboring towns."

"No."

"Extra hands couldn't hurt."

"No."

"But—"

"I'll take care of it, Moll."

She said nothing. There was a brief moment of silence before Henderson called into Damien's room, "Come here and say goodbye before I head off to work."

From the room emerged a five-year-old boy with big blue eyes and curly blonde hair. He ran to his father and wrapped his arms around the big man's legs. "I love you, Daddy," he said.

"I love you too, son."

The boy looked up to his father with pleading eyes. "Later, can we play catch, Daddy?"

Henderson bent over, and the boy draped his arms around his neck like a chimp holding onto his parent. Henderson straightened up and held the boy in his arms. He gazed into his eyes, smiled, and said, "After dinner, son."

Fifty-four years old and still playing catch. It's what happened when you marry a much younger woman.

The boy kissed him on the cheek, slid down his long frame, and ran back into his room, obviously pleased.

Henderson adjusted his police man's hat and set off for work. In the driveway he turned back to Molly and said, "Stop at the druggist on your way, and pick up a small American flag for Freddy. And get one for that boy Carlson. I still can't believe he killed himself the way he did."

"It's all so tragic. How's Veronica doing? Poor thing. First she loses Freddy, and then her ex-boyfriend, too."

"From what I hear, she's a mess."

Molly said nothing.

"Do me another favor, Molly."

Molly softly nodded. "What is it, Carter?"

"Let Freddy know I'll be there tomorrow." He winked.

24

The police cruiser coughed a bit before it fired up. Henderson held his foot on the accelerator to allow the engine to warm faster. He was impatient with vehicles, especially one he hadn't paid for. Since he was the only cop left on the force, he took the cruiser home with him last night. For years, he walked the same path to and from work every day like clockwork. He'd seen the same people along the way. Days when he was late coming home, they'd known something had happened. They'd be certain to check the newspapers the following day because anything that was worth reporting would be there. That is of course, if Henderson cared to report it. He was careful about what he told the newspapers. Too much and his small town wouldn't feel safe. Too little and the townspeople would become too naïve. It was a careful balance he struck. And perhaps, the hardest thing he had reported to the press was the murder of his son. He'd sat there in his office across the desk from the journalist and fought with all his might to speak calmly and sternly without hinting that he was crushed inside. In times of tragedy and great despair, Henderson had known that being the town's police chief required leadership. What would they think if they'd seen a police chief sobbing like a boy?

As he rode through town, dawn broke and the katydids began buzzing, birds singing their morning songs. A gray squirrel scampered across the roadway. He swerved to miss it.

He thought of Freddy, of when, ten years before, he had brought home a three-month-old black lab puppy with very big paws. Young Freddy, a big smile on his face, had run around the yard and house all day until he'd finally fallen asleep with the pup on the formal parlor floor. Henderson had bent down and kissed the boy, then lifted him and pup and tucked them into bed. In the morning, Freddy would come crying into his room with puppy urine on his t-shirt.

Henderson smiled briefly, tears in his eyes, and slammed his massive fist against the dashboard; a puff of dust rose from it, which he wiped from his very red eyes. "I'm going to kill the bastard!" he muttered through clenched teeth.

A short time later he pulled up in front of Dominic's house. Both Dominic and Tucker were motoring out, tires crunching on the gravel of the driveway.

"Stop!" Henderson shouted, motioning with his big hand out the window. He pulled his vehicle in front of theirs and got out.

"I need to speak with you," he said.

Dominic rolled down the window. Henderson approached and asked, "Where you fellers off to?"

"Finishing up on West Ruby," Dominic told him.

"Who's your friend?" Henderson went on, gesturing with his chin. "Yeah, you," he added, pointing.

"Tucker Hammond, sir," he answered in a polite voice.

"Kill the engine, Dominic," Henderson muttered, came around the front of the car, and opened the passenger's side door, his weapon out and trained on Tucker. "I need you to step out. Make one fast move, and you're a dead man."

"What's this all about?" Dominic gasped.

"Just need to ask him a few questions. It won't take long."

Tucker, wide-eyed, raised his hands above his head, cautiously stepped out of the vehicle, and felt Henderson's big hands running along his belt, then down both legs as the lawman frisked him. "Any weapons, boy?" Henderson demanded.

"No... This is a misunderstanding, I assure you."

"Why is that?"

"Why is what?" Tucker spat, slightly flustered. "This is a misunderstanding."

"Says you," Henderson told him.

"...Why are you doing this?"

Henderson wrenched Tucker's hands behind his back. "We're going to my office."

"Why? I ain't done nothing."

"You're pushy, huh, boy." Henderson slapped on the cuffs.

"Nonsense," Tucker thundered. "I've done nothing."

"God help ya if you did."

25

Henderson opened the cell door and said, "Step out of there."

Tucker rose from the cot, wondering what was next. Having been a cop himself, he knew the psychological games cops played with their arrestees, told himself he was prepared for whatever Henderson threw his way, because for one thing—the most important thing—he was innocent of any charges the chief might level at him.

Henderson pointed him toward a small windowless room with a table and two chairs. An ashtray full of half-smoked butts sat on the table, and the room stank of smoked cigarettes and cold sweat.

"Have a seat," Henderson ordered, and when Tucker took one of the chairs, Henderson sat across from him, spread a clasped brown folder on the table, and tapped it with a thick forefinger. "Your story checks out," he said in a Northeastern twang that was like taut fence wire. "What surprises me more is you had a clean record as a cop—more than clean. Exemplary. But I am not sure why you left." Henderson's gaze narrowed as it locked onto him.

"Does it really matter?"

"I like to know who I'm dealing with," Henderson said. "Why'd you leave a good job and come to Palisades Park?"

Tucker shrugged. "Needed a change of scenery."

"It's a lot prettier scenery in California than it is anywhere around here," Henderson countered. "My way of saying I don't believe you."

"Am I free to go, or are you charging me with something else?"

"I can charge you with about anything I care to, son. We might not be as sophisticated as you big-city boys when it comes to the law, but in this small town, I'm all that passes for law and my word pretty much goes. So unless you're willing to camp out in my cell for awhile longer, you'll tell me what you're doing here."

"I still say that's my business."

"No, that's where you're wrong. Whatever happens around here is my business."

Tucker met Henderson's stare with his own cold hard gaze.

Henderson knew he wasn't going to break the boy down. There was something in those eyes that told him Tucker had faced a lot worse than a typical small-town cop ever would.

"I'm not your enemy," Henderson said, changing tactics.

"No, I never believed you were. I'd like to call my wife, if I could use your phone, tell her I'm going to be a little late getting home."

Sarcastic but in a subtle way, Henderson thought. "Not to worry—she called earlier, and I told her you were down here talking with me."

Tucker said nothing.

Henderson glanced at the square ivory-colored face, the spider black hands and Roman numerals, of his Bulova wristwatch. He liked that watch a lot. It'd read five thirty-three.

"Well, do you?" Tucker said.

"Do I what?"

"Do you have any charges on me, or am I free to go?"

Henderson glanced from his watch. "What if I said yes? You got anything to say about that?"

"No, I get it. Either way, I can't win... But I didn't do a damn thing."

"So you got anything else to tell me?"

"Yeah, I'd like to speak with a lawyer."

"You got money for that?"

"You know I don't."

Henderson smirked. "There's one across the street on the second floor."

"Am I being charged with anything?"

Henderson shook his head. "Nothing," he said.

"Then I'd just like to go home."

The chief rose, closing the file with the casual air of some-

one closing a Bible he'd just read a passage from. Then he shifted the weight of his gun and holster to a more comfortable and
accommodating position around his waist—and maybe to let
the young man know too who was still in charge.

Tucker followed him out of the room into an anteroom
where Henderson grabbed his policeman's hat from a peg by
the front door, settled it on his head, and fished around in his
front pocket for a small ring of keys.

The two men crossed to where Henderson's vehicle sat
parked black and lonely as a waiting widow.

"I got my eye on you, boy," Henderson said. "You can't
breathe around here without me knowing about it."

"I can do whatever I damn well please," Tucker said. "I'm
innocent."

"Real independent son of a gun, ain't you?"

"It comes from my raising," Tucker said.

"I got my eye on you, boy," Henderson said again.

"I know. You already said that a thousand times today,"
Tucker said, rubbing the pain knotted in his shoulder.

Henderson watched Tucker walk across the street and
start for the hill.

I got to get the hell out of this damn town, Tucker was
thinking.

26

A day had passed in the butcher's house, the heat at times climbing over a hundred—hardly ideal for a decomposing body. Even in the middle of the cool night, his mother's remains stank as badly as they had earlier in the sweltering heat. He knew he'd have to do something. The smell was worse than that of a piece of beef that had gone bad. Gases from deep within would eventually burst through the swollen greenish and blue-veined skin and soak into fabrics, even walls. Once a smell like that spreads, you can't ever get rid of it.

He turned on the Philco. Nothing but white noise. It filled the house. He liked sitting there and listening to the static. The very thought that invisible radio waves were flying through the air fascinated him. He sniffed at his shirt and realized the time had come. He couldn't wait any longer to bury her.

The moon was casting a somber luminosity over the terrain at fifteen past three in the morning when he carried his frail mother's corpse into the backyard. He bore her over his shoulder like a bag of rice. She was no burden for his strong back and powerful legs. Along the way he stopped to stare into the darkness. The world was asleep. It was surprisingly cool, breezy, and quiet until the cry of a crow shattered the silence. He looked out into the distance and felt the stillness. Soon the moon would begin to welcome the day, and the land would awaken from its rest. It sent a calming feeling through him.

After a brief consideration, he selected a spot thirty feet from the back porch, beside a shallow grave he'd made five years before for Patches, an old cat that, when her right leg broke jumping off the dining room table, he'd put down. That should do. It'd be far enough from the house, and she'd be next to her cat—an animal Mike never liked. It was fitting and, quite frankly, he didn't care enough about her to consider it any further. It would do.

He dug the rounded edge of the shovel into the soil and leaned one foot on the back of it before heaving a shovelful over his back. The dirt was softer than usual, making the job go faster than he'd anticipated. He kept digging and soon felt the tip of the shovel strike the cat's small wooden casket. He removed it and lifted the lid. For a fat cat, it had small bones, its canine teeth protruding from the thin jaw bone. He set it aside.

Far off in the east, a pinkish glow was breaking the horizon. He continued to dig, stopping a few times to wipe the sweat from his brow and catch his breath. Two feet down, he came across a large rock, clawed his fingers around it, and hefted it out of the hole, his back straining as he sat it on the edge.

The eastern glow had stretched wider and higher by the time he was waist-deep in the earth. He peered out of the grave as large oak trees began welcoming the morning sun. Should be deep enough, he muttered, and tossed his shovel out. He hoisted up his arms and dragged the body in, adjusting her to lie flat on her back. He stuffed the tiny cat's coffin under her arm, as if she's carrying it to where she was going. Seconds later he climbed out.

"We all make decisions," he said aloud, tossing a shovelful of soil into the grave without any emotion, as if planting a tree. "And for each there's a consequence."

After covering the body with a foot of dirt, he rolled the hefty rock into the grave. It landed flatly with a loud thud. "Give my regards to Father."

He continued backfilling the grave. His forearms were beaded with sweat and dirt; his blue jeans had large stains at the knees and on the thighs where he continually wiped his hands. He was filthy and needed desperately to wash, his hair grainy with dirt and sweat.

Looks like another hot day, he was thinking as he tossed in the last shovelful, tamped the soil, and headed for the house. He closed the screen door behind him, made certain each window was fully opened, and let the morning breeze pour through. It'd be at least another day before the smell dulled a bit.

He filled a large glass with water and sat on the settee,

chugging most of it down in one long gulp. He turned on the Philco and picked up the signal. It was NBC broadcasting their morning radio program. There was satisfaction on his face, and that calmness he'd felt outside flushed over him.

27

"I suppose you're right, Dominic," Tucker said. "I guess I'd question me too if I was the chief."

Dominic nodded. "He's really not that bad of a guy. Just a little pissed off right about now. Could you blame him?"

"No, you're right."

At half past nine on Saturday morning, they parked out front of the local pistol range. It was situated next to the railroad tracks and behind a large junkyard, where an old man sat rocking on a porch with a long shotgun resting against the side of his faded blue jeans. He wore a threadbare shirt and a frown. People were being extra cautious lately. Truth was, they were scared to death. It was warm and bright, the sun promising another hot day. On an exterior ranch house wall hung a large banner for the upcoming annual turkey shoot, held every Thanksgiving. It was nearly three months away.

Inside, they found a man sitting behind a counter with lots of wooden cabinets affixed to the wall behind him. The place was set up like a makeshift bar, with three stools and a pine counter. Dominic and Tucker slid on the stools. There was a sign over the door that led outside to the firing lines. It read: *Obey the range master or be gone.*

"Good morning," the man said.

"Hey, Gregg." Dominic dropped his elbows on the counter. "Mind if we fire a few rounds? With all that's going on around here lately, it couldn't hurt to brush up."

"You ain't kidding," the range master said. "But you'll have to wait a bit. The line's busy."

The popping of repeated gun fire spilled through the white cinderblock walls. "Can we get a box of .45s and .38s?" Dominic asked, handing the man a folded bill. "Two boxes should be enough for today."

The other cupped the bill in his hand and reached behind

the counter, opened a cabinet, retrieved the bullets, and slid them across the counter. Tucker had noticed the bottles of hooch tucked in behind the boxes of bullets. There were also numerous trophies on a shelf next to the cabinets.

"Can I get you some pop?" the range master asked.

Dominic shook his head. "No, thanks," he said, turning to Tucker. "You want something?"

"You mean pop like that giggle water in that cabinet?"

"There ain't none in here boy," the range master sneered. "You got a lot of gall."

Dominic reassured Tucker, "Pop meaning 'soda.' You want a soda?"

Tucker shook his head. "No," he muttered. "Pop's for kids."

With curious eyes, the range master asked, "This guy okay?"

"He wouldn't be sitting next to me if he wasn't," Dominic declared.

"Where you from?" the man asked. "I've never seen you around here."

"Colorado. What's it to you?"

The range master narrowed his gaze. "If you got a problem, you can see your way to the door."

Tucker let out a sigh. "Look, I don't mean any disrespect. Just got a lot on my mind, that's all... I could use some hair of the dog."

"He's solid," Dominic pledged. "As solid as they come."

"I know what you want... But if you mention one word outside of here—" Gregg adjusted the substantial revolver on his belt— "you and I will have problems."

Tucker raised an eyebrow. "I wouldn't care enough to say something."

Dominic paused, and it appeared the gears of his mind were spinning. "I guess it never hurts to loosen up a bit... Good for the aim. We'll take two." He was digging into his pocket for more money when Tucker grabbed his arm.

"This one's on me." Tucker fished the five-dollar bill out of his pocket. "It'd be my pleasure. Straight up good for you?"

"Yes."

The range master dawdled briefly before he said, "Friend of Dom is a friend of mine."

28

Twenty minutes passed; Tucker and Dominic continued sipping their illegal booze. The whiskey seemed to go down smoothly and without complication. They had another, then another. It was the first time Tucker and Dominic had had a moment's ease; it was as if they were waiting to watch a baseball game. No wives. No worries of work.

Sipping his drink, Dominic said, "Tell me a story. Tell me the first thing that comes to mind."

Tucker said nothing.

"Just one," Dominic pressed. "It'll pass the time. Looks like it will be a while before the spots open for us."

"Well...."

"Interest me," Dominic said.

"First thing that comes to mind, right?"

Tucker watched the range master go through a door out into the firing lines. When he opened it, the sun poured in briefly. It seemed to allow Tucker to think clearer. "Well, the first thing that comes to mind was on a chilly night in October of 1918."

"The war, huh."

Tucker nodded gravely. "It's seems, first or last, it's always on my mind."

"I can understand," Dominic chewed on an ice cube. "So."

"Well, my company was advancing through the Argonne, heading for the railroad hub at Sedan. If we captured that hub, we'd break the rail net supporting the German army."

"You had a lot of soldiers in your company?"

"Enough to force the enemy's withdrawal."

The popping of gunfire continued. Somebody must've been a good shot, because they could hear the men celebrating.

Tucker sipped his drink. "So there I was, working my way through the thick, hilly forest terrain that the Germans had spent the past four years fortifying. France ain't like what you think. You probably think Paris and all that stuff, right?"

"I've never been there. Actually, I've never been anywhere, really. So what happened?" Dominic fished a Chesterfield from his breast pocket, lit it, and offered Tucker one.

"Thanks, Dom." Tucker pinched the cigarette between his lips. It hung loosely as he lit it and then took a long drag. The alcohol had gone a long way to easing his anxiety. "We known the terrain didn't favor us, but we were there to fight. We were like machines."

"Brothers."

"Yes." Tucker felt a numbing and buzzy feeling on his lips. It rolled over his head and into the back of his neck. He finished his drink in one long swallow.

"I'd've been there, Tucker, but I am flatfooted," Dominic explained self-consciously.

"Lucky for you," Tucker said, then, in a more serious tone, leaned in closer. "Sure you wanna hear this?"

Dominic nodded.

"Well, listen good, cause you ain't gonna hear me say it again."

"If you don't want to, I can understand," Dominic said. "No big deal."

Tucker waived a dismissive hand. The alcohol had loosened him. "No, I think I need to tell you."

"Okay... Go on."

"We came to a high ridge from which we could study the terrain in the distance. We saw nothing but the tops of tall trees, and heavy brush. Not even the cherry of a cigarette." He glanced at the Chesterfield between his fingers. "The only thing audible was the squawk of a bird gliding through the cloudy sky. It seemed grayer and darker than usual. I turned to Tommy, my most loyal friend in all of the ADF. He watched my back, and I watched his. I asked him what he thought it was going to feel like when we were back home. He chuckled and whispered to me that the first thing he was going to do was take a long hot bath."

"You felt that grimy, I bet."

"Oh, yeah," Tucker snickered. "And I told Tommy, 'As soon as I get home, I'm gonna marry Emma.' I showed him the photo of her that I kept in my pocket, and he bit his lip and told me she was beautiful."

Dominic raised the glass to his lips, finished the drink, and coughed. "He was right about that. Did you marry her right away when you got home?"

"No, that wasn't possible."

Dominic gave a curious look. "Why?"

"That's another story," Tucker said. "You want me to finish the one I'm telling you now or what?"

"Go ahead," Dominic said cautiously.

"Where was I?" Tucker asked.

"The long bath. Your friend Tommy craved it."

"Yeah," Tucker adjusted himself on the stool. "At that point, my socks were stiff with weeks of sweat, and lots of overuse had torn holes into the fabric. I had blisters the size of quarters, and I knew that being home would give me the time to heal and forget... And throughout every battle, it was the promise of returning home to Emma that kept me alive."

"I can understand. I feel that same love for Lillie."

"Speaking of Lillie," Tucker said. "She wasn't there earlier. Where'd she go?"

"She went by her sister's in Washington Heights."

"Manhattan, huh?"

"Yeah, she goes at least once a month."

"It's all right that Emma's in the house alone?"

"Of course it is," Dominic said. "Go on with the story."

"Okay. So after another hour of observation, an order came down to advance. We came down the ridge and, within minutes, we were met by heavy fire from massive numbers of German troops. There were bullets everywhere—and the only thing we knew was that the Germans were dug in somewhere ahead of us. Tommy and I circled out to the east with the company, and before too long we had them in our sights. We traded fire, and then we got up close and personal. I stuck my bayonet deep into an enemy stomach. His eyes flared open, and he screamed and fell to the ground. I made certain to stick another two holes in him to make sure."

"Was it easy to kill somebody?"

"I wouldn't call it easy. I'd call it the best option at that moment."

Dominic nodded.

Tucker exhaled a lungful of smoke. "I turned to my right and saw another Hun fire at point blank range, striking Tommy in the gut. Worse, he hit him with another round in the thigh before I fired my .45 and dropped the bastard."

"Damn, you say."

"By then the gunfire had fallen off, and most of the Germans had retreated. We'd held them off."

"What happened to Tommy?"

"Well, you said first thing that came to mind, so this is— and always will be—it. I'll never forget standing above Tommy as blood spilled from his mouth in a thin stream that pooled on the ground below him." Tucker felt a chill run through him. "He was gasping and shaking like the earth was quaking. In his bloodied right hand was a photo of his two younger sisters. He struggled to raise it in front of his face. He cried to me that the pain was too much. Said it was a burning pain."

Tucker finished his drink. "I told him to hang in there, that the medics were on their way... you sure you wanna hear this, Dominic?"

"Yeah, sure I do."

"Most of the bleeding was coming from his thigh, so I knelt before him and cut open his BDUs and pressed my fingers into the hole. His uniform was soaked. With each heartbeat a spray of blood spurted like a fountain. That happens when the femoral artery is severed."

Dominic nodded.

"I looked down at my blood-soaked fingers and gathered his hands and folded them across his chest. But he clenched his fists and began to bite at them. He was in tremendous pain. Tears were streaming his cheeks, and he gagged even more. I couldn't wait any longer for the medics so I hefted him over my shoulder and charged him toward the medic's tent."

"That was... very noble of you," Dominic said simply.

"No," Tucker said. "Noble would've been preventing him from dying."

Just then the range master called into the range house, "Line's ready for you two."

29

Tucker and Dominic were soon standing outside. The range master pointed down the line. "There's two open down there. The last two. Nobody goes down range unless I say so. Got it?"

They nodded and shuffled toward their lanes in a constant popping of gunfire. Dominic was carrying a black duffle bag; Tucker had the boxes of ammo. The range was six lanes wide and twenty-five yards deep with a sand pit and a tall cement wall behind the targets, which were silhouettes of a bank robber pointing a gun directly back at the shooter. There was lots of brass on the ground, and Tucker felt the empty cartridges crunch underneath his feet. When they got to their lanes, Tucker chose the one against the long block wall and Dominic the inward one. With their boots, they broomed the brass on the ground around them and set up against a thin wooden ledge that stood before them and the target.

Tucker felt an uneasy sensation when he gazed off to his left at the back of a big man firing down range in rapid succession. He knew who he was. And when Chief Henderson turned to him and caught him glancing, they meet with a hard stare. Just great, Tucker thought. Just great. He watched slyly out of the corner of his eye as Henderson reloaded.

Dominic opened his duffel bag, took out two handguns, and handed a Colt 1911 .45 ACP to Tucker. "I thought you'd like this," he said.

"Where'd you get this from? I thought you said you weren't in the war."

"I wasn't. It's my brother's. He brought it home."

Tucker accepted the weapon and ran his palm over the cool steel of the barrel. He felt the weight of it and rubbed the long smooth wooden grip. "Brings back a lot of memories," he said.

"I'll bet it does."

Tucker plucked eight rounds from the box and loaded the gun—seven in the magazine, one in the chamber. "Now you can really feel its weight," he said, and set the gun down on the ledge.

Dominic handed him a Smith & Wesson .38 Special six-shot revolver with rubber grips. He liked the blue steel of the barrel, brushing it and saying, "This here's a beauty. It's police issued."

Dominic nodded, "Uh-huh."

"Where'd you get it?"

"I bought it from a state cop a few years back."

"It's the duty weapon back home." Tucker smacked open the cylinder and loaded the rounds, pressing each one into place with his thumb. "It certainly is a beauty."

"Your pick, Tucker." Dominic gestured with his eyebrows. "What'll it be?"

"Holding the Smith & Wesson, Tucker said, "This'll do." He looked down at the sights, adjusting the dots on an empty brass cartridge that lay aimless on the ground. Spot on.

Dominic handed him a brown leather holster. "Take this. Give me the .45. I'll have some fun with that."

Tucker handed it to him, lopped the holster through his belt, and stuffed the .38 into it. For a moment he thought of the days in Colorado, shooting with his fellow officers at their police range. They were all part of a pistol team that was very competitive in the local circuit, taking home a few sizable trophies they proudly displayed in the police station. If only he could go back to those days, Tucker thought.

Dominic drew and fired all eight shots down range; the slide slid back, and he turned to Tucker. "How about that, huh?"

Tucker tasted the sweet, filmy gunpowder residue in the air and glanced down range. "Not bad, Dom. Not terrific. But not bad either."

Dominic sat his goggles on top of his head. "What do you mean, not terrific? I got all eight in, didn't I?"

Tucker squinted and looked down range at the target. "Yeah, but they're all over the place. None of them's a kill shot either."

"They're all in, right?"

"Yeah, but there should be a grouping." Tucker put his thumb and index fingers together making a circle. "The tighter the grouping the better the shooter."

Just then Henderson approached. "You any better?" he asked, curling his lip. "Let me see what you got, boy."

Tucker turned to him and noticed a metallic glint from the gun holstered on his hip. The man had his hands tucked into the front of his belt, which made his shoulders seem to flare wider. "What's it to you?"

"You're a tough son of a bitch, huh?" Henderson took a step closer. Tucker thought he'd smell booze, but from what he could tell, Henderson was sober.

"Not at all. Just taking it easy on a Saturday."

"Well then, show me what you got."

Tucker didn't like the tone in his voice. But he went ahead and fired, striking the target with perfect heart shots and one between the bank robber's eyes. He holstered his weapon and took a step back. "That's all I got," he said, with the trace of an edge to his voice.

"...You're one heck of a shot, boy. Very impressive." Henderson moved in towards Tucker's lane, quick-drew his weapon, and fired, striking both eyes on the target, even put a round in the barrel of the robber's gun.

"You're not so bad yourself," said Tucker.

"And that ain't nothing," Henderson said.

Tucker studied him. "You didn't empty your weapon."

Henderson stuffed his revolver in his holster. "Neither did you, boy."

30

Saturday night the butcher made the journey to Harlem in a black tuxedo and white pleated shirt with a black bow tie, his hair brushed back with Brylcreem. He looked like many of the slick ones who had somehow managed to prosper when many were scrambling to survive.

The moonlight was falling on his crooner jaw, pronounced cheeks, and the soft hazel eyes that made women dream of long lives of love and promise. Staring at his reflection, he knew what was looking back at him. He knew of his quirks. Knew the townspeople saw him as a drugstore cowboy. Most men would go to great lengths not to be labeled a womanizer. But what did that matter? He did what he wanted, and nothing kept him from his desires. He wasn't the restrictive type. He'd gotten that from his parents.

It was after ten when he reached an underground speakeasy. There were no signs on the building. Nothing indicated what lay behind its doors—a large ballroom in a four-storey red brick residential that appeared to be an extemporized bodega. But none of that mattered. Everybody knew about its existence. The proprietors were part of the underworld that controlled most of the illegal alcohol flow in and out of the city. The butcher had a contact that allowed him to make small drop-offs every other week. The underworld knew that using men like the butcher, who was less likely to be followed by the feds, would allow them to operate deeper under cover. The feds knew who all the key players were, and the butcher and others they used were considered small time—nobody worthy of the feds' time.

He killed the engine and studied the area. Lots of fashionably dressed men and women crowded the sidewalk, going to and from the many hidden venues.

When he climbed out, he smelled the sweet aroma of caramelized onions coming from a nearby hamburger joint. At least the patrons sitting on stools in the plate glass window, framed by bright round electric bulbs, seemed happy with the food. Ten at night, there was a lot of vehicle congestion; wide billboards sat above most of the lower buildings. There was no indication that Harlem had originally been a Dutch village.

Harlem lies between the East River and the Hudson, where, uptown, it meets Washington Heights; to the south, it stretches down to Central Park. But since the Great Migration, the movement of two million African Americans out of the South, many blacks had found Harlem as their new home. Most clubs played jazz.

He could hear the rhythm booming from beyond the club doors, and it beckoned him. A police officer with a long baton hanging from his belt walked past the doors, whistling, and continued down the street. Was he that blind to what was going on inside? Mike knew the cop was on the arm. At a time when money had been hoarded, any dished out could silence the world. Even the feds knew they couldn't control its power. But this part of the city was different. Maybe it was the illegal booze that had many people trudging by; the promise of taking an edge off was just what they needed. But one would not have expected that vicinity to be an adequate portrait of a county in financial ruin.

More people were out than on a typical Saturday night because the sky was endless and clear, the summer sun cooled a bit. It was going to be a long night of dancing, booze, and late-night romance. The very thought of it put a bounce in his step.

He knocked on a solid wooden door next to a bodega. From a sliding window in the door, a set of dark eyes appeared. They studied him up and down. "Mike?"

"Yeah, Slim. Let me in."

The door opened, and a large, burly door attendant with hard features, a barrel chest, and large muscles that weren't defined appeared to the right in a narrow hallway. A heavy smell of cigarette and cigar smoke permeated the tiny space. "There was a reflection of something coming from behind you, Mike—I couldn't make you out."

"Cut the shit, Slim. Not every white guy is a cop."

The black man snickered. "Well, not many of you folks come here, that's all."

The butcher handed his car keys to the man. "Make sure Trevor brings my car back when he's done unloading. I want it parked right out front, not down the block."

"Right out front is where it'll be," the attendant said. "It's tight in there already—try looking for a table along the sides."

"Thanks, but Trudy's handling my reservations."

The butcher worked his way through the heavily congested lobby. Silver ashtrays sat on the tables, and groups of black men huddled around them, smoking cigarettes, laughing, and glad-handing. The ceilings were lower in the corridor until moments later, when he entered the double doors into a wide and expansive ballroom. There, a black woman in a red-fringed slip dress, complete with red sash, white gloves, and a red feather boa, approached him. "Michael, your reservation is up front." She smiled, a long cigarette holder pinched between her fingers.

"Thank you, Trudy." He slipped her a folded bill. "How's the family?" He loved this big-shot gesture, the way people reacted, the way they kissed up.

"We're doing fine. And you?"

"I couldn't be better," he said.

"Should I hold a reservation for you in two weeks?"

"Nah, I got something to do."

"You're still making a drop-off, right?"

"Always...."

The woman winked. "Your date is a cutie."

"Where is she?"

"Up front. Toward the center of the stage."

He turned and, saying nothing further, ambled off.

"Enjoy, Michael," she called after him.

He nodded and weaved around the crowded tables filled with booze, cards, and poker chips. The place was brimming with plumes of cigarette and cigar smoke. Most men acknowledged his presence; some women gave him a guarded glance. It wasn't common to see a white male and a white female in the club. But when you did, you knew those folks were people of importance.

The butcher found his reservation. "Hello, Lillie."

31

"Hello, Mike," Lillie grinned.

She was wearing a blue dress cut high above the knee, and when she crossed her legs, the butcher caught a glimpse of her stocking, where it was clipped to the garter belt, that aroused him. She had a striking appearance that reminded him of Mata Hari. "Is this where you meet all your dates?" she asked, a smile playing on her face.

"Only the special ones."

"Cut it out," Lillie said. "I know why you chose this place."

"Why's that?"

"Come on, Mike. Look around. The chance of running into somebody who'd know me in here is nearly impossible."

"It's not just that," the butcher countered. "It's the music and the ambiance. How do you like the band?"

Lillie leaned in, her full breasts pressing tightly against the bodice of her dress, a blue shawl draped around her shoulders. She had a long mane of wavy brown hair pulled away from the ears with Bobby pins at the back of her head. She briefly thought of Dominic and knew she shouldn't be there with the butcher. Her eyes caught his wandering glance, and she smiled. "Whadja say?"

"I said how do you like the band?"

"I've always loved jazz."

"Well, I'm glad you finally looked me up."

Lillie was folding a napkin in her hand. "I'm really nervous, Mike. If Dominic ever found out, he'd kill me."

"Well, who's going to say anything? Like you said, none of these colored folk know you."

"It's just... You know I should be faithful."

He chuckled and shook his head. "I wouldn't know what that's all about."

"Well, it's just..." Her voice trailed off. "I mean, it's not like—"

"Relax, Lillie."

"I know, but…"

"But what?"

"…Forget I mentioned it."

"I know you'd like to," he said. "See what it's all about. I know you think about it. You want to know what it's like to live without limitations."

Warming up to him, she said, "You are hard to resist."

He wrapped an arm around her shoulders. "So are you."

But then a wave of guilt swept over Lillie. "No," she said, pushing his arm off her. "I'm very nervous. Let me have a few drinks first."

He glanced around for the waiter and threw two fingers up to get his attention. "So," he went on with a trace of sarcasm in his voice, "where were you before you got here?"

"By my sister's."

His face twisted. "Your sister's?"

"Yeah. You knew that."

"And you went by her place for the weekend for what reason?" "To spend some time with her and…"

"And what?" He lit a cigarette and blew the smoke overhead.

"…And to see you."

"So then why all of a sudden the worry? You obviously planned this."

Lillie rubbed her arms. "Don't pay no mind to me. It's my nerves talking."

The band finished the number, and the crowd applauded. People were whistling and calling out for more. "Let's hear it for them," the butcher exclaimed. "Now, that's some of the best jazz I've heard in a long time."

The waiter arrived and sat the drinks down on the table. Lillie had a glass of red wine and Michael a jigger of his product. He liked sipping it openly in an establishment. It made him feel proud and allowed him to sample for quality control. He sniffed at it and then took a long swallow. He liked the burn of the whiskey and how it warmed his insides. In many ways

Mike saw his product as much more than just illegal booze. When somebody had a headache, a cold glass could erase it. Whiskey also cured the blues, anxiety, toothaches, insomnia, and stage fright. Mike had known that for some it could be fatal. He learned that from his uncle. But in moderation, he saw nothing wrong with it, even if it was illegal.

Lillie finished off her wine quickly.

"Can I get you another drink?" he asked, playing the suave gentleman to the hilt.

"Yes," she said.

"Waiter." He snapped his fingers. "We'll have another round," he called out with a grand gesture.

The waiter pointed at the table, making a mental note of their drinks, and nodded.

Just then, a young, attractive colored woman in a red-fringed dress approached and paused before the butcher. She wore deep red lipstick, and black eyeliner dramatizing her big green eyes. Her raven hair neatly framed her face, with a big blue bow on top. Her little black dress accentuated her curves, and when she leaned in she smelled of booze and cigarettes. She had that after-sex glow, a kind of mellow ambience. She was, in fact, a floozie the butcher bought and paid for on occasion for sex, but he'd gotten tired of her and was always on the make for new meat.

"Uh, yeah, who the hell is this?" she scoffed, pointing to Lillie. "What the hell do you think you're doing?"

Lillie looked her up and down for a long moment before she turned to him and whispered, "This is beyond me. I should get going."

"Hang on," he told her, and pointed a stern finger at the woman. "Get out of here, Tamara," he seethed.

The colored girl rested a fist on her hip. "Why should I?"

"You will if you know what's good for you."

"So this is how it's going to be, huh," Tamara sneered. "This is what I get?"

"Goodbye," the butcher said, pointing behind her. "Just you walk away," he said.

Tamara rolled her eyes and slithered out of the bar and

into the hallway. Michael watched her every move. He noticed her slip into the ladies' room.

"What was that all about?" Lillie asked. "You dated a colored woman?"

"No."

"Then what was that all about?"

"She's a delusional loon," he said.

The waiter approached, served the drinks, shook the butcher's hand, and asked her, "First time here?"

She nodded.

"Well, it's like no other in the city, ma'am. Enjoy," he said, and left.

Michael told her, "I need to use the wash room. Be right back."

The wine was overcoming her by then. She forced herself to sit up straight and continued sipping it.

32

Michael navigated out to the hallway and positioned himself along the wall outside the ladies' room, waited for Tamara to come out, and when she did he grabbed her by the arm. "We need to talk. Now."

Her eyes were wide with inquiry. She smelled of face powder, and a residue of it clung to the shawl around her shoulders. "Take it easy. You're hurting me."

The butcher's grip on her bicep grew stronger, and he dragged her through the crowded hallway into a deserted alley behind the club. "What is it, Mike?" she hissed. "Is this some sick joke of yours?"

"I wouldn't call it a joke. That'd be a stretch."

"Who the hell are you with in there?"

"That's not your concern."

Her lip quivered. "I thought it was just me you were interested in, baby."

"You're a colored hooker. You screw guys for a living. What makes you think a guy like me would have a thing for you?"

"You didn't used to mind what I did for a living, boyo."

"Yeah, well that was then and this is now."

"But nothing's changed, baby—you're still you and I'm still me."

"Wrong. You ain't nothing to me no more."

"Why would you say that if you didn't mean it?"

"I wanted to get me some for free."

"You bastard." She swung her purse at him. "I should've known better."

The purse struck him in the shoulder.

"You know what they say, right?"

"What?" She asked in a huff.

"Men pay hookers to leave. That's what makes you so desirable."

"No," she snapped, and swung the purse at him again. "I was falling for you, you big galoot. What a sap I was."

He clamped his hand around her mouth and dragged her down the alley, knocking over garbage cans. She kicked and squirmed, but she was no challenge for a man his size. When he got to a spot behind a restaurant where garbage bags and refuge were piled high, he knocked her to the ground. She screamed. He jumped on her and tied his handkerchief tightly around her mouth. "Now, shut up." He thought about raping her. But then he thought about Lillie. The prospect of having his way with her was more alluring, and he didn't want to spoil it.

She looked up at him with eyes full of fright. She kicked as hard as she could, but he held her with one hand and ripped away a cord tied around one of the garbage bags. He used it to tie her wrists and ankles to a drain pipe on the side of the building. She tried pulling free but couldn't, her legs bound at the ankles and hands above her head. She bit at the handkerchief but couldn't get it out from her mouth.

He pulled out a snub-nosed revolver. "Should I kill you? Or are you going to be a good girl and shut up?"

She glanced at the revolver and then back at him, and he wanted to laugh because she looked exactly like a colored version of one of those dames on the cover of a True Detective magazine, with tears streaming down her cheeks.

"You go to the cops, and I'll kill you. You can trust me on that."

She continued to chew at the handkerchief but, gagging, couldn't respond. Her screams were muted.

"You need to understand your role," he spat. "Be thankful you're not dead."

The butcher covered her with the pile of garbage bags and was soon back at the table with Lillie.

"So how you feeling?" he asked, smiling and wiping beads of sweat from his brow.

She grabbed his arm and hugged him. "A lot younger," she cooed.

33

After a few more drinks, Lillie, overcome by the effects of the wine, collapsed into the butcher, and he folded his arm around her back. "This is so wrong of me, it feels right," she mumbled into his chest. A trumpeter was standing at the edge of the stage, weaving back and forth, blasting away while the band kept the beat. As he went into a wild improvisation, what some called "jungle beat," everybody's eyes were riveted on him—except for the butcher's and Lillie's, whose eyes could barely focus on her drink.

"Forget about Dominic. Tonight is about you."

"Okay," she said, her speech buzzy.

"He'll be there when you get home. Nothing will change."

She sat upright. "There's something very mysterious and exciting about you," she said, wrapping an arm around his shoulders.

"Tonight it's about you, baby. About you letting your hair down."

The maroon curtain fell, and an announcer in a red-and-white vertical-striped shirt and a white skimmer hat appeared at the microphone. He tilted the brim of his hat low to visor the blinding spotlight. "The band's taking a short break," he announced. "We'll be right back with all your favorite tunes."

The crowd applauded, and the man bowed and disappeared into the darkness.

When the waiter set down more drinks, a spray of booze rolled over the rim. He wiped it up with a towel that hung from his apron and handed Michael the bill. "Is there anything else I can get you?"

"No, this will do," said the butcher, who glanced at it, took a ten-dollar bill from his pocket, and cupped it into the waiter's hand. "Thanks, Johnny."

He so much loved making such grand gestures, it was almost an addiction.

"You need change?"

"Nah, pal, all yours."

The waiter flashed a mouthful of choppers.

At an adjacent table, an older colored man with a gray fedora and long cigar grumbled through the side of his mouth, "Johnny, get me another right away."

An attractive colored woman at an opposing table called out, "Johnny, a pack of Camels and another gin."

The waiter held up a finger. "Be right with you folks."

The butcher raised his glass and sipped. "How 'bout we hit another club or find something else to do?"

Lillie thought about it and, in two long swallows, finished her wine. Her face had gone numb.

"You must really like that," he said with a smirk.

She set down the glass and examined the polish on her fingernails. "Should we have another?"

"Nah, let's head out."

The butcher rose from his stool and steadied himself. Lillie did too but without poise. She fell onto the open chair next to her. "I guess I got up too fast," she mumbled through the tent of hair that'd fallen over her face when a bobby pin went flying onto the rug.

He reached around the table and helped her to her feet. "Be careful, Lillie. It's tight in here, and you can easily trip."

They locked arms and squeezed through the crowd. Once outside he helped her into his vehicle, got behind the wheel, and started the engine. As he pulled away from the curb, she turned to him, kissed his neck, and cradled her head in the crook of his shoulder. "I think I'm falling for you, Mike," she whispered. "I know I shouldn't, but I think I am."

There it was. The go ahead. He rubbed his right hand up her thigh and around her full hips. "There's something about you I love, too. And it's not just your beauty."

She looked petulant but grinned anyway.

A short distance down the road, he parked in front of the Monroe Hotel, a five-story building with a large overhang covering the double glass entry doors and white crown. Trees were planted in wooden tubs on the sidewalk beside the main entrance.

He got out, walked around the vehicle, and opened the passenger door. "Only the nicest place will do for my lady."

She gazed into his eyes, still an enigma to her, and wrapped her arms around him. "I should get back to my sister's," she said only half honestly.

Looking up into the stark velvet-black sky at the bright stars shimmering, he motioned and said, "It's a beautiful night. We'll rest off the booze, and then I'll drop you off."

She looked at him, too intoxicated to understand. She hugged him, murmuring, "Sobering is good."

He lifted her from the car and stood her upright, wrapped an arm around her waist, and they swept into the lobby.

Before too long, they found their room, tore away the sheets, and fell into each other's arms. He rolled her onto his side and pressed his lips against her neck. She squirmed with a tingly feeling that ran from her toes all the way to the base of her head. He continued, smelling the booze from his breath on her neck.

"Your skin is so soft," he said as he parted strands of hair that had fallen across her face, looking now deeper into her eyes.

"Feels so good," she purred.

He cupped his hands around her full hips. She raised her arms above her head, her breasts rising with the gesture. There it was—the final signal. She pulled him on top of her and their hearts began to beat wildly. When he entered her, she gasped, and her eyes rolled back in her head.

"Sex is always better," he whispered into her ear, "when it's just sex."

34

Chief Henderson wasn't sure what time it was. He knew it was early Monday morning. He knew he'd had a horrible night's sleep. Sitting up in his bed, he thought about how he'd spent most of the previous afternoon sitting at the grave of his dead son, the dirt still loose and grainy. He knew it wouldn't be until next spring that the thick grass would regrow. He had adjusted the American flag that Molly had left there. Before he left the cemetery, he had also stopped by the grave of Carlson, the boy who'd killed himself, and offered a somber prayer.

He tried to close his eyes, but the images of the boys dying before him shook him to the bone.

No matter what or how much Henderson was doing everyday to keep himself busy, he couldn't shake the consuming thought of it, and at that moment he realized he would not be able to fall back asleep. He rose from his bed and said to his sleeping wife, "This is the hardest thing I've ever done in my entire life."

She rolled over, squinted, and sighed, "I hardly slept. What time is it?"

"A little after five."

"Go back to bed for another hour," she said, and pulled the sheets up to her neck.

"I can't sleep," he whispered. "I tried, but I can't."

"After the killer's caught, that will help."

"That's if he ever is," Henderson muttered, feeling self-conscious. "Other than that Tucker I told you about, I have no real leads."

"I thought you said he was the guy."

"I don't know about that anymore. He was a cop. From what I could find out, a damn good one, too."

"So what's he doing here?" She sat up, placed a pillow in her lap, and dug her elbows into it. "Seems strange."

"Not really, honey. His car broke down. I checked his story out. It's all legit."

"But why here?"

"I don't know." Henderson wiped the sleep from his eyes. "But he's telling the truth. I can tell when a man's lying."

She fell silent. Then she said, "I got up a little while ago and put the coffee on. It's fresh."

"Thanks, honey," he said, shaking his head.

"What's on your mind, Carter?"

"I was thinking about that poor girl Veronica. She tried killing herself on Saturday."

"Our son's girlfriend?"

"Yeah, she's severely depressed, and I hope she doesn't try something foolish again. She's lucky she's alive. I raced her to the hospital Saturday, and they stitched her up. She cut across both wrists. Doctors said a little longer, she'd have bled out."

"Oh, my," Molly gasped. "That poor girl."

"I guess she's too young to know the value of life. Does that make sense?"

Molly nodded. "I'll pray she heals and doesn't try anything like that again."

Henderson sighed, kissed her on the forehead, and strode out of the bedroom and into the kitchen. The smell of fresh coffee filled the home. He sat in silence at the kitchen table, deep in thought, his mind still racing. He feared the only way of identifying the killer would be through another murder. He had to admit the case had gone cold.

A short time later, he went outside to check the milk box. Like clockwork, a quart sat in the metal insulated box. There was also a bottle of booze. Henderson reached in and retrieved the milk. He left the booze in the box. A promise was a promise, and he'd keep his word with Molly. No more booze. It was tempting and he considered having a glass, but no. He turned back inside.

If the milk was delivered, that meant it was after six. The milk delivery man was about as reliable as one got. He had that delivery there every morning at six sharp. You could set your watch to him. Had Henderson been paying attention, he would have heard him put the milk in the box. But he was mentally so far away from that kitchen table, a tornado could have taken the house down and he wouldn't have noticed.

He sat back down at the kitchen table and considered angles and motives he never had figured before. He had to admit, as he stirred milk into his coffee, some of these notions were, well, extreme. Beyond reality. But he reckoned it was his mind playing tricks on him, and that, at periods of intense stress, the mind could do that. It had when he was fighting down in Cuba. It'll do it again, he thought. He sipped his coffee and thought about what his life had become. Never in a million years would he have been able to predict it.

Shaking his head, he reclaimed his police man's hat from the hook where it hung behind the front door, and soon thereafter he was driving down to Broad Avenue, where he opened the door to his office and sat behind his desk with lots of papers piled high.

Mid-morning, the phone rang. He picked it up. "Henderson here," he said.

"Yes, I've asked around... Nothing yet." Henderson pressed his fingers into the bridge of his nose, slid the hat back on top of his head, took it off, and laid it on his desk. The voice on the other end of the line sounded squeaky and piercing like fingernails on a chalkboard.

"Yes, Mayor Wilson. I've already told you I went to old lady Stillman's house. Nothing was disturbed. I'm still working the Burgess case. Heck, I'm working on all the cases."

The voice grew louder from the receiver.

He let out a long sigh. "If I knew who was responsible, Mr. Mayor, don't you sorta think I'd have him already in prison?" The mayor said nothing. "Who do you think killed em?"

The mayor's squeaky voice spilling from the receiver was aggravating. "...As soon as I know, you'll be the first to know."

Henderson sat back in his chair and put his big boots up on his desk. Some of the papers inadvertently got knocked to the floor. He'd pick them up later. "If you got a tip for me, then give a call. But for now I'm doing the best I can with nothing," Henderson said. "Say, how we making out with the hiring of more cops? That's a conversation I'd like to have with you. First you said it was the lack of money. Then you said my selections weren't tall enough. One was too fat. So what's your excuse now? "

When the mayor ignored his request, Henderson tossed the receiver onto the desk, put his legs down and repositioned himself in his chair. As he retrieved the papers that had fallen, he could still hear the mayor's voice coming through the receiver: "Hello, you there? Hellooooo?" Henderson's eyes fell on his son's gun belt, still sitting undisturbed on a filing cabinet, the leather still new and bright, the silver buttons on the holster brightly reflecting the overhead light and the sun spilling through the window.

Sonofabitch, he thought as the mayor continued to talk. He retrieved the receiver, slammed it down, and began mumbling to himself. Amazing how far handsome looks and a good line of bullshit could get some people.

35

Early Monday morning, Lillie found Emma sitting fresh out of the bath in the formal parlor, her hair damp and frizzled, smelling of lavender and pear. She'd known she'd find her there. It was part of her routine. Every morning Emma would wait in the formal parlor for Tucker to finish his bath, and then they'd chat for a while before he headed off to work.

That day she was going to ask Tucker about what had transpired at the pistol range. She'd listen to him and then find a way to talk him into leaving town earlier, maybe even as soon as tomorrow. But she'd known a job was tough to come by in those days, and that he was interested in making some money while he could. It might be weeks or months until he found another person willing to pay him a day's wage.

Lillie was holding a tray with two steaming hot cups of tea. "I figured you'd like one," she said, setting the cup and saucer on a side table next to the chair Emma was sitting on. The rising sun in a cloudless sky was beaming bright and luminous through the bay windows. Emma's chair was positioned so she could look out over the town. "Thank you," she said. "I still can't get over this view, Lillie. From this high on the hill it seems like you're queen of the land... I watched the sunrise earlier. It was beautiful."

"I ain't watched a sunrise in a while," Lillie droned. There was a softness in her voice that Emma hadn't heard before. Lillie dragged a chair next to the side table, and the two of them glanced out the window.

"No sunsets either?" Emma asked. "Tucker and I both agree that's better than a sunrise."

"What's the difference really, honey," Lillie remarked, her eyes heavy, the left one bloodshot. "Does it matter at all?"

Emma's brows furrowed. "It's beautiful. It... in a way, it makes me feel alive."

"It's all the same."

Emma shook her head. "No sunset is the same," she said. "Every sunrise is special, too. This morning there was lots of orange and pink, and I thought I saw some violet wash across the horizon."

Lillie thought about that for a moment, and how she hadn't noticed the sunrise the day before when she left the hotel with the butcher. All she had thought about then was how it was getting light out and that she'd need to race back to her sister's in Washington Heights before her brother-in-law awoke. "Is everything so perfect in your life?" she sighed.

"How can you say that?" Emma asked hastily setting her tea cup down. It clanged loudly in the saucer. "Are you blind?"

Lillie paused for a moment and then, in a careful tone, said, "I didn't mean it that way. I know how difficult things are for you. Look, I'm not picking a fight with you. What I meant was, is everything always so perfect between you and your husband?"

"Yes, it is."

"Well, then, my mistake," Lillie said. "Everything must be a fairy tale to you."

Emma leaned over and made certain to look her coldly in the eye. "Everything is not always a fairy tale."

"Seems that way."

"You don't even know me. What I've been through."

"Just saying," Lillie said, and brushed her hair over her shoulder. "No need to get all upset. What was so bad in your life other than being stranded?"

Emma paused for a moment before she uncrossed her legs and said, "I was married before I met Tucker."

Lillie said nothing.

"My ex-husband laid his hands on me more times than I care to remember. I'm lucky to have Tucker."

"...He hit you?"

Emma rolled up her left sleeve and revealed the letter "R" scarred into her skin. "It was more than that." The brand looked like a cord of yarn. "My ex-husband came home drunk one night, snuck into the bedroom with a hot branding iron, and this is what woke me up." She rubbed the scar. "He said it was so nobody'd be able to take me from him."

"You poor thing." Lillie swallowed. "How'd you get away from him?"

"He died."

Lillie said nothing.

"He was drunk and fell asleep in his car with the windows rolled up. They found him dead the next morning. The fumes killed him."

Lillie reached out to rub Emma's shoulder, but Emma pushed her hand away. "This isn't about me. What's gotten into you, Lillie?"

"...I don't know," the other at last replied. "After hearing your story, it's no longer important."

36

Lillie and Emma continued to stare out the bay window. Tucker and Dominic had already left for work. Lillie thought of Emma and of how fortunate she had been to escape her ex-husband. And then of how Emma had come to truly love a man.

Did she truly love Dominic? She told herself she did, but it didn't settle right inside her. She thought of how stale her relationship with him had become. The previous Saturday night had been the first time in years she'd felt alive, exhilarated, important to somebody—somebody not her husband. And she had done what she'd sworn married women should never do.

But she didn't feel guilty. And that concerned her. She should at least have felt that. Wasn't it what all women who cheated on their husbands felt? Lillie wondered if something was wrong with her. She considered the likelihood that the butcher wanted her solely for sex... and that was all she wanted from him. Her promiscuity excited her, and the way the butcher was arrogant and callous and strong and how, when he entered her, she had felt salubrious.

Then she fought the urge to continue reliving her misdeed. Everything was going to be fine, she told herself. She'd go back to being an attentive wife, and what had happened was water under the bridge.

Lillie turned the knob on a homemade crystal set on a coffee table that was picking up Louis Armstrong blasting away on his trumpet at a radio station in New York City. Many people loved listening to him. With the advent of the clear channel, they had a signal. Emma loved jazz, that all-American form of music with its roots in the old Negro gospel sounds of the South, and from the jazz houses of New Orleans and Harlem. It was because of the close proximity to Harlem that they were able to pick up the signal free of static.

Lillie wanted to blurt out how she had seen a colored trumpeter Saturday night play the best trumpet she'd ever heard. But she thought it best to keep the thought to herself.

After their brief argument, neither had said anything to each other. Emma decided to break the silence. "Look, I'm sorry I exploded on you. You've done a lot for me, and if there's anything I can do to help you, just ask."

"Don't apologize, Emma. This was entirely my fault."

"What's wrong?"

"Nothing."

"...Don't take this the wrong way, Lillie. But if it was nothing, it wouldn't be written all over your face."

"You can tell, huh?"

Emma nodded. "What's wrong?"

Lillie glanced back toward the door and into the hallway. There was nobody around. She studied the young woman before her and considered her no threat. Emma had said she would be leaving town in a few days. What would it matter if she confided in her? She was about to change the topic of discussion when she said, "Have you ever considered cheating on your husband?"

"Of course I've thought of it, but...."

"Exactly. Everybody thinks of it. That's what I meant about not everything being a fairy tale."

"But I didn't say I'd ever do it. Tucker's been nothing but a blessing."

"All I'm saying is that—" Lillie turned the dial up on the radio—"this is strictly between us girls, right?"

"Wouldn't matter anyway, Lillie. Who am I going to tell?"

"This past weekend, I did it... I finally had the courage."

"Did what?"

"You know," said Lillie. "But what's bothering me is that I don't feel guilty or badly about it. I know I should, but I don't."

Emma chewed on that for a minute. "Maybe there's something wrong with your marriage?"

From the rim of her tea cup, Lillie said, "It's gone stale, but don't all relationships get to that point?"

"Maybe the affair meant less to you, though, than what Dominic means to you?"

"Maybe... maybe that's it," Lillie said. "But in a way, I guess it's not like anybody got hurt. I'm still going to be a good wife and take care of the house and my husband."

"What's done is done," Emma offered. "But I would suggest not doing that again."

"Are you always so moral?" Lillie asked with a wry smile. "Does that make you feel better than me?"

"I am not judging you."

Lillie set her tea cup on the side table and began to whistle listlessly to the music that was filling the room. "It's just, he's so gorgeous. And he's tough. Not just physically strong. Mentally, too."

"You probably shouldn't be thinking that way if you want to save your marriage," Emma whispered.

"But have you seen him?" Lillie asked somewhat proudly.

"Seen who?"

"Mike the butcher."

"You slept with Mike the butcher?"

Lillie grinned. "He's dreamy."

"From the way you're talking, this is more than just a fling. You best be careful, Lillie."

Lillie waved her hand dismissively. "Don't worry about that," she said. "I've already promised myself it won't happen again."

37

Tucker and Dominic entered a small luncheonette across the street from the police station. Everybody called the place "Alphonse's." Alphonse was an Italian immigrant who'd moved into Palisades Park twelve years before. He had a sizable family that lived at the top of the hill, where many other Italians had bought property and raised a family. Standing by the front door, next to a sign that read *Wait To Be Seated*, Dominic told Tucker, "The food here is great. You'll like it."

"Smells delicious," Tucker said, observing a short, portly man, with a white cook's uniform and a white towel draped over his shoulder, stirring a large sauce pot on a stove behind the counter. His back was to them; he was balding a bit and had combed his long hair over the spot in an attempt to hide it.

"That's Al," Dominic said. "Good man. Got a real heavy accent, and loves to talk about his homeland. Especially if you're new around here."

"That's fine," Tucker said. "Where's he from?"

"He's going to tell you... more than once," Dominic chuckled. "He's from the Calabrian countryside, which he says produces some of the best red wine in the world."

"Never had any of that."

"It's actually pretty good. Better than good. It's made from the Gaglioppo grape. Grows mostly in southern Italy, particularly in Calabria. Al claims it's the best in the whole world—and he's probably right."

"Stuff is that good."

"Oh, yeah."

"Sounds like something Emma and I'd like."

"He makes his own. Orders the grapes and stomps them in his garage. Recently he gave me a bottle, and Lillie and I loved it," Dominic went on. "It was damn strong stuff, too. Lillie got tipsy on one glass."

"Even better," Tucker smiled, and, feeling a groan in his stomach, said, "You think he's going to seat us soon?"

"Of course. Give him a second to finish what he's doing."

Shortly thereafter, Alphonse turned around and said, "Table or the counter? Itza up to you."

"Counter's fine," Dominic said, and they slid onto stools before a long lacquered mahogany counter that separated the consumer from the cook and all his pots and pans behind him. It was small luncheonette that seemed to be efficiently using the space. There was a stove and lots of stainless steel. From the sauce pot where steam was rising, the handle of a wooden spoon protruded. Off to the left, a cold-cut slicer and a freshly baked roast beef sat on a big wooden cutting board. There was a bread box next to it. Tucker smelled fresh parsley, meatballs, and sauce.

Al came over and dropped his elbows onto the counter. He wore a big smile and had a pencil pinched behind his ear. He wiped the counter, then fixed two place settings and plucked a pad from his breast pocket. "What'll it ah be, boys?"

Tucker turned to Dominic. "Some of those meatballs on a hard roll would be nice."

"Make it two," Dominic said. "Extra sauce on mine."

Al began scribbling in his pad. "How about da drink?"

"Coca-Cola will do," Dominic said. Tucker nodded.

Tucker heard the door swing and heavy steps approaching. He turned and spotted Henderson in his uniform. Everywhere I go, he seems to show up, Tucker thought, stealing another glance at the big man, whose expression made it clear something was bothering him. His eyes had dark bags under them and looked heavy. The crow's feet and stressed lines seemed more pronounced. He looked like an insomniac; even his shoulders seemed to be hanging like weights.

Henderson took a stool to Dominic's left. "Morning, Dom," he drawled.

Dominic turned to him, sliding a bit closer to Tucker to allow for more room for the big man. "Morning, Chief," he said.

Glaring straight ahead, Henderson muttered, "You're still around, Tucker, huh?"

"I stay where the money is."

Al slid a Coca-Cola in front of Dominic, who poured it over the ice in his glass.

"Make what you can, Tucker," Dominic offered. "Because, after this house, I don't know of anybody with any money to build for a while."

"That's what I told Emma," Tucker said. "When the job's done we're out of this town." Tucker glanced at him. "Nothing personal, Chief."

"This current situation isn't an adequate portrait of what Palisades Park is all about," Henderson said without looking at the young man. "But make what money you can while you can."

"Who isn't a slave to the dollar nowadays?" Tucker said.

Henderson called out to Al, "The usual. And make it quick—I ain't got all day."

Al nodded and continued stirring the sauce pot on the stove.

"That wife of yours seems nice," Henderson said, turning now to Tucker. "She was worried sick about you. Called my desk a lot that day you visited the station."

"Visited?" Tucker smirked. "Is that what you call it?"

"Yeah."

The sounds of gunfire interrupted them.

38

It was brief but effective: Somebody had fired a single shot through the plate glass window. Surprisingly, the window hadn't shattered, but a Coca-Cola bottle behind the counter had, and its contents had been sprayed all over.

Everybody at the luncheonette had ducked—everybody but Henderson and Tucker, the cop and ex-cop. They looked at each other, swung off their stools, and raced to the door, Henderson with his gun drawn and Tucker wishing he had one.

But whoever had taken the shot was gone in a squeal of hard rubber tires and into the immensity of bright sunlight pouring down on the storefront.

At that moment, Henderson realized that something dreadful had changed in his small town—something more dreadful than he could have ever imagined and that he wasn't going to be able to fix, not alone anyhow.

He glanced at Tucker, who was standing cool as a cucumber beside him without so much as a twitch in his hand or nervous eye, as if he was waiting his turn to buy a sandwich.

"I suppose you got lots of this kind of stuff back in the city, huh?" Henderson said, slipping the weapon back into his holster.

"...We got our share."

"The war too, eh? I suppose you got used to getting shot at in the war?"

Tucker leveled his gaze at him. What he saw was a brave soul in a world not of his own making, caught up in real violence that threatened to rip his small town apart, change it forever, and, behind that, a boy with his finger stuck in a dyke, trying to hold back an ocean.

"You never get used to getting shot at, Chief," he said.

The others at the luncheonette were just then peeping out of the imaginary holes they'd jumped into.

Alphonse saw Coca-Cola running down his back counter. In a nervous attempt to do something, he reached for a rag to wipe it up.

Dominic examined the hole in the window, small and neatly round and just big enough to slip the tip of his pinky through. He turned, tried to study the path the bullet had taken, and realized that it had to have missed Tucker's head by mere inches. "You know how close that bullet came to killing you?" he asked.

Tucker nodded. "I heard the snap. That's what you hear, the snap."

Dominic whistled between his teeth.

Henderson, who knew exactly what Tucker was talking about, said, "You don't hear the snap, it means you're dead."

He and Tucker eyed one another with renewed respect.

"You been shot at before?" Tucker asked, somewhat confused.

"I fought in Cuba," Henderson said. "I... I could use your help on this problem, son."

Tucker shook his head. "Not interested in anything but eventually getting to Buffalo, Chief."

"Not even in finding the man who nearly killed you?"

Tucker patted his pockets for a smoke, remembered then he'd promised Emma he'd quit, but just then he could have used a Chesterfield. His pockets were empty.

"Maybe it wasn't me he was trying to kill, Chief."

"It came closest to you."

"Maybe the guy's just a bad shot. He can't know too much about it."

"Why not?"

"He fired from a moving automobile. Without luck, you're not going to hit much doing that."

"Maybe he just wanted to warn you."

Tucker weighed whether he wanted to go buy a pack of smokes and hide them from Emma. It was damn hard quitting cold turkey. With little money lately, he had gone from periods of smoking to spells of withdrawal. Now that he was making money, he had been able to avoid the withdrawal feelings. A cigarette sometimes saved your sanity in the trenches when you were pinned down and couldn't even take so much as a piss.

"Maybe he wanted to warn you, Chief."

Henderson straightened his police man's hat, as was his habit, and said, "If you decide to change your mind and do some real work that doesn't include swinging a hammer, come see me. Just don't wait too long. I intend to catch those responsible for this... for all this," he added in a rough voice. "It just might take me a little longer without another exerienced man to help me."

They watched him walk out.

"He's a good man," Dominic said. He had come up next to Tucker. "The pay would be more than what I can afford—and you'd get your police job back. You said that being a cop was in your blood."

Tucker looked at him but didn't answer.

"And you'll be able to have some money in your pocket," Dominic went on, "when you head out to Buffalo. You'll have a better start on things."

"Unless somebody puts a bullet in me first."

"Yeah, unless that."

39

A local man who had followed all the gossip entered Henderson's office. He was wearing a white collared shirt with a very obvious sweat ring, a blue tie, and a pair of brown slacks. His salt-and-pepper hair was messy, and sweat had beaded on his forehead.

"What is it, Skips?"

"I've got some information for you that you'll find interesting," the man said with a buzz from the fan. He combed his fingers through his hair.

"About the shooting a couple hours ago? " Henderson said impatiently. "Cause that's all that really matters at this moment."

"I wish it was," Skips said. "I debated whether or not to come in here and tell you about this, considering all that's going on."

"I'm very busy," Henderson said and reached for the telephone. He picked up the receiver and looked at the door.

"It'll only take a minute, and I'll be on my way," the man assured.

Henderson knew the man was consistently truthful. "Spit it out, Skips. Say what you gotta say."

"Can I sit?"

Henderson nodded to an open chair in front of his desk. The humming electric fan forced a warm breeze into the office. Skips felt it flush across his forehead when he sat down in the chair. He opened his mouth as if to drink in the breeze.

"Same deal as always?" asked the man. "I tell you what's going on, and you leave me out of it?"

Henderson hung up the phone and readjusted himself in his chair. "I've told you a hundred times already. I don't repeat what you tell me. If nobody can trust me, I may as well close my office door, because ain't nobody gonna walk in and give me any information."

"...It's Doctor Anderson," Skips finally said. "He's doing them scrapings again."

"Are you certain?"

"Earlier I had my lunch on the bench outside his office. I saw two young girls go in there, and they both came out crying."

"Is that all you got?"

"You know he's the only doctor in the area who'll do those scrapings."

"But Dr. Anderson practices all kinds of medicine. Why you so certain they was there for a scraping?"

"I overheard one of them crying on her friend's shoulder. The friend said it was the right thing to do, since she wasn't married."

Henderson rose from his chair and stretched his arms. "Thank you," he said. "I think it's about time I pay Dr. Anderson a visit."

The man rose from his chair and met Henderson at the doorway. "...And I think you should know, I saw your son Freddy's girlfriend Veronica walk in there about an hour or so ago."

40

When Henderson arrived inside Dr. Anderson's office, Veronica was walking out. He noticed the bandages on her wrists, her face pale white, ghostlike.

"Everything, uh, okay?" he asked.

She nodded and continued toward the frosted glass front door with the doctor's name etched into it.

"...Veronica?"

She didn't turn her head, simply walked out of the doctor's office.

"Can I help you with something?" Dr. Anderson had appeared in the doorway.

"Yes," Henderson snapped. "What's going on here today?"

"...It's a doctor's office," Dr. Anderson's brows furrowed. "I practice medicine."

Henderson stepped in from the doorway and glanced around the waiting room. Dr. Anderson had a small office, with a drab colored shag carpet that complimented an olive and white floral print wallpaper that although bleak was brightened by an undersized front window that was pouring sunshine onto the rug and coffee table. On a wall next to a receptionist window was Dr. Anderson's Columbia University School of Medicine diploma, framed in oak and conferred twenty-one years prior; and a red poster with a physician smiling and holding a pack of Lucky Strike cigarettes. The poster claimed 20,679 physicians say, "Luckies are less irritating" and offers, "throat protection against irritation and cough." Dr. Anderson had openly told Henderson on a prior occasion that smoking cigarettes was safe and beneficial. Henderson didn't care either way. He liked to smoke. Henderson fixed his eyes on a girl in a bright orange shirt and frowned, tapping her foot on the floor. Her eyes were wide as she watched the policeman and the doctor stare at each other.

Henderson hit him with it. "You doing scrapings, Doc?"

"What do you mean?"

"Don't play stupid with me doc."

"Are you asking about abortions?"

"You know what I'm asking."

"But I've already answered you months ago," the doctor said. "Why you asking again?"

"I've got good reason."

"But."

"Don't bullshit me," Henderson said. "Answer the question."

Dr. Anderson tilted his thick spectacles down the bridge of his nose and looked up at Henderson. He had cold dark eyes, the kind that'd cause a man to worry. "If you make another attempt to defame my character," he finally said, "I'm going to call my attorney."

"You didn't answer my question," Henderson sneered.

"I'm not answering it again," the doctor countered.

Henderson took a step closer and grabbed the doctor by the collar on his white coat. His pens fell from the yellow pocket protector he kept in his right breast pocket. "I said it before," he whispered hotly, "and I'll say it again. I will catch you, and when I do, I'm gonna haul you in, and you're gonna fall a few times on the way."

"Okay, I'm calling my attorney—and you're gonna be the one falling when I drag you into court."

Henderson reached up, plucked the doctor's medical school diploma from the wall, and split it over his knee, shattering the glass and oak. "It's people like you who are sending this country to hell in a hand basket," he said. "Have you no soul?"

The doctor rolled his eyes. "Stacy," he called to his receptionist. "Come here, and bring the dustpan and broom. This buffoon needs to clean up the mess he made."

"Like hell I will," Henderson said, and punched the doctor in the face. The doctor fell to the floor. "You bastard," he exclaimed, clutching his nose and cheek. "You'll pay for this."

"Send me the bill," Henderson said, and laughed. "And you

can kiss my ass for not scraping you."

The doctor hurried out of the room and locked himself in his office. He glanced at the receptionist, who, in a nervous attempt to do something, began to rummage through papers on her desk.

Henderson turned around, opened the door, slammed it, and left. The frosted glass broke, and the jamb splintered and cracked halfway up the frame.

Now, where did Veronica go? Henderson wondered as he climbed into his vehicle. He could see north on Broad Avenue there were people walking on the sidewalk. He pulled away from the curb and, shortly thereafter, spotted her. He trailed her for a block then pulled ahead of her, parked his vehicle, got out, and waited for her to stroll by.

As she approached, he noticed tears streaming down her cheeks. Her eyes were heavy, bloodshot, with deep caverns. Her hair was mangy and mussed. She looked like she was fixing to hop aboard the trolley.

"Veronica," he called softly. "Don't run. You're not in any trouble."

The trolley chugged closer and Veronica again glanced at it.

"Come here," Henderson said sternly. "It's okay."

He stretched out his arms, and Veronica came into him and wrapped her arms tightly around him. He cradled her in the crook of his shoulder. She began to sob.

"What were you doing at Dr. Anderson's?" he asked in a low voice.

She pressed her head deep into his chest. He felt her trembling. She cried, "It was just a follow-up."

"Follow-up for what?" he asked. "Your wrists?"

"No," she said, and rubbed her very red eyes. There were lots of tears in them, and she had a faraway look. "You don't know what you got until it's gone," she sobbed.

Henderson held her tighter. "What do you mean by that?"

She looked up at him. The big man seemed even bigger against her small frame. She was speechless.

What Henderson saw before him was a young woman who

had encountered more than she was capable of dealing with. She couldn't make a rational decision, couldn't even compose a sentence. She had been no different when she cut her wrists or watched Carlson burn himself to death.

"Was it Carlson's baby?" he finally asked.

"No," she said, her voice barely audible. "I'm terribly sorry."

"Huh?" His brow furrowed.

"It was your son's," she gasped, and fainted.

He carried her to his car and dropped her off at the Oak House. They in turn drove her out to Graystone, a psychiatric hospital. Henderson knew that a girl without family would have slim chances of ever getting out of the place, but she needed care.

He stormed back to headquarters and, within hours, had Dr. Anderson screaming in his cell. He had never beaten a man as hard as he had beaten that doctor.

PART TWO

Demon Chaser

41

Henderson tossed a silver badge across his desk. "Take this one, Tucker," he said somewhat grandly. "Glad to see you and I will be working together."

"I appreciate the opportunity—but how'd you dig up so much of my background?"

"Does a Captain Louis Greenfield ring a bell?"

"Of course, he ran my sector."

"Well, he and I've spoke a lot lately. I called him again last night. He seems to think the world of you," Henderson added, and leaned back in his chair. It creaked as he did. He put his big boots on the desk and combed his salt-and-pepper hair with his fingers. "Not that hard to make a phone call nowadays."

"He and you were in the war, eh?"

"I didn't know him down there in Cuba. But our talks brought back a lot of memories." Henderson exhaled. "But we also spoke a lot about you."

"Did he tell you about the time—"

"Everything," Henderson assured him. "He told me everything."

"I reckoned that." Tucker pinched the pin on the back of the silver badge between his fingers. He held it up to the light, like a jeweler appraising a diamond. "Why the number two?" Tucker asked.

"You got something against the number two?"
"No, just trying to figure out why."

Henderson leaned forward. "That's Walker's badge, and I'm pretty certain he won't be needing it."

"Because he's incarcerated?"

Henderson's brows narrowed. "How'd you know that?"

"Small-town gossip."

"Another place and time for that... You're getting the number two becauseDankert is three and my son was four. And you ain't getting his."

"I can understand that... Why not Dankert's, then?"

"You ask a lot of questions, eh?"

"Well, when you're new around a place, sometimes asking a lot of questions is what helps paint the bigger picture."

"I'm keeping badge three because I'm still trying to find an angle to get big Dankert back on the force," Henderson said. "I got some ideas about that."

Tucker felt the cool metal on the badge. He knew what it mean to be a cop. He knew why he always wanted to be one. What he didn't know why was Henderson would call on him. "And me?" Tucker said. "Why you hiring me when there's a lot of men around here who could use the job?"

"Cause I ain't got to train you, that's why." Henderson replied. "And you're tall and can shoot. Not as good as me, but, good enough."

Tucker let Henderson's braggadocio roll. He'd known the truth and simply nodded as he glanced around Henderson's tiny office. A metal fan was humming on a small table behind him. There was a white mug overflowing with pens and pencils, even a large pair of orange-handled scissors. There was lots of paper piled high on his desk, held down with paperweights to prevent the fan from blowing them all over the place. A black typewriter was dusty. There were files stacked high on a cabinet. About a dozen photos of criminals holding a mini chalkboard that bore the criminal's name and date of arrest lay haphazardly among the mess. Tucker studied the photos. Each had a front and side profile with a ruler on the right side to illustrate the criminal's height. One criminal caught his eye. He'd seen him before and he stood out from the others. He didn't look like the typical criminal. Didn't have that atavistic look, the narrow jaws and close eyes, or the pock marks on the cheeks. He was sharply dressed with a shirt and tie that had been wrinkled, his hair messy, lip swollen with a trail of blood from the right corner of his mouth. It looked like both his eyes were blacked as if somebody had struck him in the face with a brick. He looked closer and saw that it was Dr. Anderson, the cold eyes telling. He was about to ask why Dr. Anderson was beaten so badly, but then thought better of it. Instead, Tucker asked, "Why so cluttered?"

Henderson leaned forward. "Because the mayor has been piling stuff in the other rooms, making it tighter and tighter as the days go by." Henderson looked at his wooden office door with a frosted glass etching with the legend Chief of Police. "I'm the only one with a key to that door behind you. Anything confidential needs to be locked up in here. If I tell you to leave the blotter or something else in my office, that's because I don't want any other eyes on it."

"I know all about police confidentiality and classified information, Chief. No need to worry about that. If you need me to sign something, I will."

Henderson waved his hand dismissively, opened a drawer under his desk, and handed a Smith & Wesson Model 10 .38 special police revolver with wooden grips to Tucker, who liked that center-fire revolver a lot, took it, and thumbed open the cylinder. It was empty. "Beautiful gun," he said.

Henderson tossed a box of ammunition across the desk. "Load it and stuff whatever you can in your pockets. Make sure you keep those extra rounds on you."

"How about a holster and a uniform?"

"Here," Henderson said. "And behind you in that bag is one of Dankert's old uniforms. Have your wife resize it for you."

Tucker retrieved the holster and slid the revolver into it. He unbuckled his belt and adjusted the holster to his hip. When he felt the leather press against him and the cool metal end of the barrel touching his thigh, he felt pleased to be doing the job he loved so much that he had lost and now had again. "How about getting paid, considering those restraints? The wife ain't keen on this. At least I can tell her I'm making decent money."

"You help me get this killer, and I'll make sure you have enough money," Henderson said, lifted the black leather mat on his desk and fished out a check. He handed it to Tucker. "Take this for starters."

Tucker beamed when he read it. "One hundred dollars. That's a lot of money," he said.

"It's a month's pay. And you better cash that today, before the mayor finds out. He's going to throw a fit."

"Why not simply pay me every week?"

"You ask a lot of questions, huh? Let me worry about that."

"Okay... but I got one last question, Chief."

Henderson's gaze told Tucker he was growing impatient.

"Say we get him tomorrow and I set out for Buffalo—you going need some of this money back?"

"No," Henderson said with a chuckle.

"Thank you." Tucker rose from his chair. "I'll be right back. I'm going to cash this across the street and drop it off with my wife. I'll have her start resizing the uniform right away." Tucker picked up the brown paper bag with Dankert's old uniform in it.

Henderson nodded. "Hurry up. We got work to do."

At the door Tucker said, "I'll be back in about an hour. And by the way, the mayor sounds like a real buffoon."

"That's only the half of it," Henderson replied. "He's constantly asking questions about who I'm suspecting. I'm starting to believe he may know something he's not telling me."

42

Mid-afternoon at the butcher shop, the bell jangled above the door. The sun was rainbowing through ammonia residue as the butcher wiped the storefront windows. The place was clean, had that antiseptic smell in the air. Fresh links of sausage hung from stainless steel hooks behind the counter. He'd finished making them earlier and was allowing them to hang there briefly before he'd refrigerate them. His customers loved their snap. That they did. There was a rounded glass case display with fresh cuts of beef and pork. Inside, on the bottom, Cornish hens were sitting in a bath of ice. On a small table behind the counter stood a hefty scale with big round black numbers and a long red arrow to indicate the poundage. The place was sparsely stocked, considering how badly business had spiraled downward from what it had once been. Fortunately, Michael was very frugal and mostly only prepared what he knew he'd sell. He wasn't the type who liked to throw stock away.

He set down his cleaning solvent on the counter and turned to a man who had come in and stood there watching him. "What'll it be, Mayor Wilson?"

"How about Uncle Wilson? Is it possible for you to ever acknowledge me as that?"

"Are you not the mayor around here?"

"Cut this shit, Michael." The mayor's face told the butcher he was impetuous and angry. "What are you wasting your time cleaning for?"

The butcher came around the counter and stood before him. "Butcher shops are supposed to be clean. What's it to you, boyo?"

The mayor shook his head. "You never had respect. That's your first problem."

"Why should I respect a man who doesn't acknowledge my mother as his sister-in-law?"

"You know why I had to stay away."

"If you'd taken care of her when dad died, she wouldn't have had to do what she did."

"I'm not here to talk family."

"Say what you got to say, then, and leave." The butcher nodded toward the door. "Door's behind you. Don't let it hit you on the way out."

"You didn't answer my question, Mike."

"I ain't got to answer nothing." The butcher took a step closer to his uncle. "Cut the bullshit, Wilson, and turn around and leave. I'm not in the mood for your intellectual jargon."

"That's Uncle Wilson to you."

"Whatever Wilson," the butcher said. "I'm not in the mood for your shit right now."

Wilson ignored the butcher and continued, "Well, do you know why?" He gestured with his hands on his hips. "There's a reason and I think you should know."

"You ain't leaving unless you say what you got to say, huh?"

The mayor pointed to the dwindling stock of bread on a wire rack against a long wall. "Five years ago, you had the largest shop in the county, and now you got three loaves of bread. Does that seem right to you?"

"I sell meat. You want bread, go to the bakery."

"Your business is failing because of you, not the economy."

"What about you?" The butcher gestured. "You're the mayor around this town. Shouldn't you take some responsibility?"

"It's you, Mike. You're the reason." The mayor glanced around. He was in his middle sixties and wore a pinstriped navy blue suit with a white collared shirt and solid red bow tie. He had a matching navy blue fedora and, pinched between his lips, a corncob pipe, the kind that Mark Twain was known to smoke. He liked the idea of playing an intellectual. He took a long drag and then let it out, filling the area with smoke. An overhead belt-driven fan cut most of it. "Is there anybody here? Anybody in the back?"

The butcher shuffled back behind the counter. "When have you known me to hire anybody? What do you want?"

"Business is down, right?"

"Yeah, so what's your point?"

"Ever wonder why?" Wilson approached the cash-register where boxes of Hershey chocolate bars were on display. He reached for one and began tearing away the foil. He took a bite and tossed the rest of the chocolate bar into the garbage.

"You going to pay for that?" the butcher said. "Twenty cents."

"Answer the question, Mike."

"It's the economy, the depression," the butcher answered knowingly. "Obviously things are tough. Nobody is working and this damn economy has the country in shambles. Hoover hadn't done a damn thing to fix this. FDR is in way over his head. "

Wilson removed the pipe from his lips and continued chewing on the chocolate bar. "So you're going to blame it on the Government, huh?"

"And you." The butcher smirked. "It's your fault too."

"You're a buffoon," the mayor said and held his hand out to silence the butcher.

"Who you talking to like that?" the butcher seethed. "Don't raise your hand to me... Leave, now."

The mayor half turned, then met the butcher's grueling stare. "You make all that extra money running the booze, and you're still an idiot."

The butcher grabbed a large vintage meat cleaver that hung from a hook behind him. It had a worn wooden handle and had belonged to his father. He'd turn it on its side to slap and tenderize meat, mostly when his customers ordered chicken breast. "I could easily kill you right here," he growled. "I don't think Dad would mind. Mom either."

"Cut the tough-guy jazz, Mike. You ain't killing me, and you know it."

"Don't be so certain," the butcher said.

"I ain't worried about that," Wilson said with arrogance so potent the butcher found it hard to swallow. He tried to refocus the conversation. "So what did happen to the bread rack?" he said. "You had those shelves full a year or two ago. Ever seriously wonder why it's the way it is now?"

"I already told you my thoughts."

"Well, then maybe you're not as bright as I once thought you were."

The butcher narrowed his gaze at his uncle. "Twenty cents for that chocolate bar, and our business is done here."

Wilson came around the counter and stood toe-to-toe with his nephew. "If you're going to kill me, then do it."

43

The butcher's chest grew hard and he moved in closer to his Uncle Wilson. He couldn't believe the stark resemblance to his father in the man. They were both tall, and they both had the same square jaw and icy eyes. The butcher felt his hand choke the wooden handle on his cleaver. Their noses were nearly touching, eyes staring into each other's. "You're treading uncharted waters," Michael said hotly.

Wilson, sensing the cleaver in his hand, took a few steps back. "What am I going to do with you?" he said. "You're scaring the heck out of everybody. That's why your business is suffering."

Mike chewed on that for minute. The he said, "Suppose you tell me how I'm scaring everybody."

"Because he molested you, huh," the mayor said coldly. "Is that why this all started? Or was it old lady Stillman having your father killed?"

"Nobody molested me," the butcher retorted.

"Come on, Mike. Cut the shit."

The butcher took a step back and the wheels of his mind began to spin. The thought of reliving that day brought anger, and lots of it. Coupled with the embarrassment of his hidden past, he became dizzy. Shaky. "Who else knows about this?"

"Nobody."

"How can you be so certain?"

"It's family business," Wilson said. "I don't repeat family business. Especially things embarrassing like that."

"Mom told you, huh?"

Wilson nodded. "Yes, she said you've been acting strange lately. I've bit my tongue on this. And speaking of your mother, I haven't been able to get in touch with her."

"So what?"

"Did you kill your mother too? You sick sonofabitch."

The butcher didn't answer him. His mind, still heavy in thought, trudged back to the day old man Burgess first molested him and the subsequent times it had continued over the years. He thought of how cold Burgess had been on those encounters and forcibly gotten what he wanted. In his mind's eye he saw Charlie Burgess the first time in the desolate cornfields and how he'd slid his hand caressingly on his thigh then surprised him with a kiss. He felt a slimy feeling of saliva on his lips. He recalled the way Burgess had smelled horribly in the merciless heat. Then he pictured the knife and heard his deafening cries for help. He shook his reverie. The butcher reached for the counter with his free hand to steady himself. He held the meat cleaver tighter. A chill ran through him. "What the heck are you talking about, Wilson?"

"Look, if I have to turn you into the authorities, I will. You're leaving me no choice. This has gotten way out of hand, and I can't continue to ignore it."

The butcher felt a rush of white-hot fury, felt his heart kick out more beats. "And how are you so certain it was me? I've done nothing."

"Who you kidding, Mike? Part of me thinks you're now doing this to sleep with that new guy's wife."

"What new guy?" The butcher asked unconvincingly.

"Don't go there."

The butcher shrugged. "Anyway, it ain't true."

"No?" Wilson challenged. "Then why do you unzip yourself and stare at her every night in the bathroom window?"

"How would you know that?"

"Let's see," Wilson said. "Where do I live?"

Mike took a deep breath and exhaled slowly. He was regaining focus. "I get it. You live across the street. And I never unzipped myself."

Wilson raised an eyebrow.

"Has anybody else seen me?" Mike asked.

"Not that I know of."

"...Well, I'll stop that."

Wilson let out a long exhale. He shook his head, then in a serious tone, said, "And I keep calling Chief Henderson. At first he was clueless, but now I sense he's starting to suspect something. So ride out of town tonight and never come back. That's the best I can do for you, son. When you're far enough away, get some help."

The butcher plucked the sharpening stone from a drawer under the counter and began sharpening the cleaver. The sun was brightening the plate glass store front. It shown onto the floor and dust motes floated in his rays. "Why should I leave?" he asked without looking up. "Who's gonna run this place?"

"What difference would that make if you're in jail or, even worse... dead?"

"I've already told you, I'm innocent."

"Bullshit!" Wilson shouted and reached for a loaf of bread. He held it in the air and said: "If your father was alive, he'd lay a beatin' on you right now."

"Put the bread back on the shelf," the butcher said. "Dad wasn't a good man."

Wilson threw the bread on the shelf. It hit the shelf with such force that it fell onto the floor. His voice rose. "Have respect for your father. He loved you, and look what you've become. Leave tonight, and never come back. You're leaving me no other options."

The tone brought on another memory. Wilson's voice and Michael's father's were so similar, he thought he was hearing the old man, and he again pictured the night he'd come home after hoisting Abigail Stillman onto the butcher block and burying his legs between her bear hams.

And he pictured him kissing his mother with the same lips that'd just caressed lady Stillman's in the room behind him. Then Charlie Burgess entered his mind once more, and how he had forced himself on Mike, and how he had hated the feeling and cried as Charlie entered him.

He threw the clever at his uncle. "Oh, my," he gasped as it tumbled over itself and struck Wilson between his shoulder blades. Wilson screamed and dropped to the tile as the butcher stepped over him and watched him gag and choke on his own blood. The cleaver had punctured a lung. No doubt.

"Shit," the butcher said. "If it's anything to you, I didn't mean it. It slipped."

Wilson was strangling on the blood pooling rapidly in his mouth with a gargle.

It was broad daylight, and anybody passing by could have been a witness. The butcher quickly locked the front door and then, with a Herculean effort, dragged his uncle into the back and hefted him onto the butcher block. Wilson's eyes by then were glassing over, consumed with fear.

"I'm sorry, Wilson. But there's no way you'll survive this? It's too deep."

Wilson was too weak to reply.

"But your concern for me came years too late. You should've stuck by us when dad died."

The butcher clenched his fingers around his uncle's bloody neck. It was the last time anybody ever saw or heard from the mayor. Within minutes, Michael had mopped up the store and reopened for business.

44

A week had passed since the shooting at Al's Luncheonette. Tucker figured he'd maybe be able to develop a lead by returning to the crime scene on the same day and time it had taken place. It was a long shot, but what else did he have?

First he'd questioned those who'd been walking in the vicinity or maybe waiting for the trolley. People did have routines and regimens. But after countless hours of prior investigation—mostly questioning the locals—he'd heard only a few stories about Abigail Stillman, and nothing about the shooting. He was certain folks didn't trust him, or that they weren't willing to stick their necks out and possibly become the next victim, or both. In this, they were far from foolish. He had learned they were scared to death. The suspicious look they wore while speaking to him in his police uniform was ominous.

He went back to headquarters, gulped down a cup of warm coffee that had been sitting in the pot since morning, and headed back out on the street. It grumbled a bit in his stomach but gave him the boost he needed. On his way out, he paused briefly in the main hallway and read the municipal bulletin board. There was a resolution that concrete sidewalks were going to be added to some of the streets on the eastern portion of the town. It claimed it was being done without having to raise taxes. Next, was a photo of the new Lindbergh Elementary School with a flyer for a political debate that will be held in its auditorium next month. And finally, Tucker allowed the overpowering 8 x 10 photo of Mayor Wilson to soak in. It was a typical political photo with the mayor holding his trademark corncob pipe an inch from his lips with a look of trust and sincerity on his expression. His smile gleamed. Tucker noticed the Bulova watch with the black hands and gold face that hung loosely from his wrist. In gold leaf on the bottom right corner was singed Arthur Camp from Arthur Camp Studios located on Broad Avenue. Chief Henderson had told Tucker that if he needed a photographer at a crime scene, he was to summon Arthur Camp immediately.

The sun was still high and shining brightly when he left through the municipal building's double doors. He had a pad in his hand and a pencil stuffed in his breast pocket along with a pack of Chesterfields. He liked those cigarettes a lot. It was the taste of a smoke after a meal that he'd loved the most.

He rolled his shirtsleeves up and adjusted his tie to fit loosely around his neck. It was hot, in the high eighties, with few clouds and lots of humidity. He fished a comb from his rear pocket and combed his wavy brown hair to the side. He watched a worker from a restaurant empty a mop bucket into the street. When the worker went inside, two brown birds splashed in the soapy water. It was quiet, save for a milk delivery truck that chugged past, water spilling from its bumper leaving a trail on the cobblestones that evaporated quickly. Surely there had to be something to learn, Tucker considered.

A half hour later of canvassing the area and questioning a dozen or so people, he'd again come up empty. He entered Al's Luncheonette and spoke with the proprietor. Alphonse was in his usual spot behind the counter, stirring a smaller sauce pot. There was a heavy smell of chopped meat and onions coming from a sizzling frying pan next to it. Alphonse grabbed the frying pan, emptied the meat into the sauce pot, and stirred it into the sauce. On a counter was a dome-shaped Crosley Harco radio that was covering the NY Yankees game across the river. Tucker heard the announcer tell how Red Ruffing was pitching a hell of a game against his former Red Soxes while Babe Ruth, another former Red Sox, had already hit a home run in the 2nd and caught a critical fly ball in the 5th.

"Don't suppose you've heard anything have you, Al?" Tucker asked.

Alphonse looked up from the pot. "I don't hear a thing. You know. I just work and do my job, and sometimes the people they tell me things, and sometimes they no tell me nothing."

Tucker noticed the empty chairs, the garbage can. By that time on a normal day, the latter would have been filled with discarded items. There would've been food-stained plates and silverware stacked in the sink behind the counter. Tucker commented on it: "Slow today."

Alphonse put a silver lid halfway over the pot and let the sauce simmer. He turned the heat down low and left the wooden spoon in the pot. "Everybody's scared, Tucker. They all afraid to come in here. They think they gonna get shot."

"I can understand that," Tucker said and looked at the store front window that was flush with sunshine, the bullet hole covered with a piece of cloth tape.

"Was it you?" Alphonse asked. "Chief says that bullet was for you."

"If it was, who would want to kill me?" Tucker asked. "I hardly know anybody."

"Everybody going crazy," Alphonse shrugged. "It's not like this back home." He went into a long story about how nice it was in Italy and how the Italians wouldn't let such a thing happen. "Is a matter of respect," he concluded.

Tucker stood there listening, but his mind was busy. He moved slightly to his right, to where he had been sitting when that bullet came through the window. The shooter'd been one hell of a shot if it was me he was trying to kill, he said to himself, and felt chills recalling how close he had come to death. With a nervous twitch, he reached for his comb and ran it through his hair again.

Alphonse turned the black knob up on the radio. He leaned into the radio and then distracted Tucker, "That Ruffing got a hell of an arm. He is pitching a no-hitter."

"So is the guy who fired this shot through your window."

Alphonse fell silent and went back to his sauce pan. He slowly stirred the wooden spoon, and sprinkled in fresh basil.

The sun continued to pour on the wooden floor, dust motes dancing. He peeled off the patch of tape Alphonse had stuck over the bullet hole and reconsidered the angle, and where exactly the vehicle would have been at the time the shot was fired. He put his index finger in the hole and felt for a slight angle, if any. The roof, Tucker thought. He would have to get to the roof of the Bank of Palisades Park for a clear, unobstructed view of the crime scene. That'd show him exactly how it had happened.

"Don't worry, Al." He headed for the door. "He'll be caught, and your business will return to normal."

"Be careful," Alphonse paused from stirring the sauce. "It's not worth dying for."

45

Outside on the street, Tucker studied the remains of the rubber the squealing tires had left on the pavement. Most had worn off, but he was still able to imagine the kind of vehicle that was capable of laying down that rubber. It'd have to be fast, with a big engine. It wasn't any Model A. Those tracks had been made by something powerful, like a V8. That much he was convinced of. Another telling sign was the width of the tire marks.

A man in a blue fedora, dressed in a fashionable blue suit with a white shirt and blue bow tie, was staring at Tucker in his police uniform as he bent down and swabbed some of the rubber.

Tucker noticed the attaché case in his hand, rose from his crouch, and approached him. "Sir, were you here around the same time and on this day last week?"

The man nodded. "I'm here every day at this time. I teach late afternoons at Columbia University, and I take the trolley to 125th Street Ferry."

"...So you wait here every day?"

"Monday to Friday," the man said.

"Did you witness the shooting?"

"Witness?" the man muttered. "I am not a witness."

"Right," Tucker said evenly. "What I meant was, did you see anything that could help me locate the shooter without me ever mentioning we spoke? I promise you I will keep you out of it."

The man studied him briefly, pulled at his collar, took a step closer, and said, "I don't know... I have a wife and kids, and what if you don't keep your word?"

"My word is all I got," Tucker said. "I don't even need to know your name."

"...Okay." The man. "It was a black Ford. That's all I know."

"Did you see the shooter?"

"Heck, no," the man said. "I saw the car after I heard the shot, and then I hit the sidewalk and covered my head with this." He waved his case slightly.

"So you didn't see anything other than the car being a black Ford?"

"You usually don't see much, Officer, when you're flat on your belly covering your head."

"Thank you, sir."

"Does that help at all?"

"Yes. Yes, it does, as a matter of fact."

Tucker had begun to walk off when the man called out, "Officer?"

Tucker turned back.

"Not a peep. You promised," the man said.

"You got my word, sir. Thanks again."

Five minutes later, Tucker was on the roof of the bank and laid his pad on the cement edge. He studied the area, saw the municipal building, the overhanging electrical wires above the sidewalk, the firehouse, the trolley tracks with a trolley approaching from Ridgefield, and the creek in the distance with it looked like seven boats anchored, probably fishing. He saw where the sun shone, the shadows it was making behind him, and how it poured onto Al's. Seconds later, he saw the man he had recently spoken with board the trolley. Something told him the professor, if that was what he was, knew more. He'd press him again another day.

He leaned against the ledge, adjusted his gun so it wouldn't scrape on the concrete, and began to consider where the shooter's vehicle would've been on Broad Avenue. He had already concluded it was facing south because of the rubber marks. But he reconsidered the position of the vehicle, and how the shooter had managed to fire that single round. From his bird's eye perspective, Tucker saw how the shooter could get off a precise shot. He swallowed. It was possible it had been for him. But why? It didn't make any sense.

He paused for a second, then pulled the pack of smokes from his pocket and lit up a cigarette.

"Tucker," shouted a voice from below. "Get your ass down

here and in my office."

Tucker exhaled the smoke. "On the way, Chief."

16

"Have a seat there, Tucker." Henderson gestured to the open chair across his desk. "The mayor is missing."

"What?"

"His wife just left. She said he didn't return home last night."

"Really?"

"Yes. And what'd you hear out on the street there? I saw you talking with Mr. Parker."

"Who's that?"

"The Columbia professor you were talking to in the blue suit."

"Oh, him." Tucker scratched his temple. "He didn't know anything. But somebody else who didn't give his name said the shooter was driving a black Ford."

"A black Ford, huh," Henderson thought aloud. "You hear anything else?"

"I did hear a few stories about Abigail Stillman."

"Forget her," Henderson snapped. "...Things around here are going to get worse with the mayor missing."

"You think he's dead?"

Henderson shrugged. "Wouldn't be much of a loss, but if so, folks'll become even more terrified than they already are. Things are spinning out of control pretty fast."

Tucker considered how cold Henderson was and realized that, over the years, the man had become so hardened to the life of a cop, his emotions were buried so deeply, not even a sledgehammer could bust them open. At times, Henderson was callous, and his disregard for another human, especially one he didn't care for, got Tucker thinking. "Why aren't we re-examining the Burgess homicide and the Stillman disappearance, Chief? Maybe those cases can offer us something." He was careful not to mention Henderson's son.

"One case at a time," Henderson told him. "It's only us

here."

"We need to look again at those two cases is all I'm saying," Tucker went on. "We have to be missing something."

"Forget that old bag and that dirty old man."

"But there seems to be a connection."

"They're both old bags?" Henderson suggested skeptically. "That's the only connection I got."

"No, Chief," Tucker said. "The connection is you."

Henderson looked up from his desk. "What? What are you saying?" he snarled.

"Abigail Stillman was your stepmother, right?"

"...So?"

"And Burgess and she dated after your father died, right?"

"How'd you find that out?"

"You sent me out to talk with the residents of this here town, Chief."

"And how is it connected to me, Sherlock?"

"That I'm not sure about."

Henderson toyed with a pen in his fingers, looked out the window at people making their way up and down the street in front of the building, and pointed to them. "It's called small-town gossip, Tucker. Don't believe everything you hear from them."

Tucker hadn't wanted to provoke him. "Okay," he said calmly, "but we need to reconsider the Burgess murder. Did anybody know you and Freddy were going there to serve that warrant?"

Henderson rubbed his chin and sat back in his chair. He thought about it for a moment before he said, "Mayor Wilson knew about that."

"Are you sure?"

"Yes, of course. The neighbor whose horse Burgess killed called the mayor, and then they both came in here."

"'Allegedly killed,' you mean?"

"No. The neighbor saw Burgess kill his horse."

"You sure?"

"Yes," Henderson said. "What does this have to do with anything?"

"Wait," Tucker continued. "Tell me about the day the mayor came in here with the neighbor to report that crime."

Henderson's brows furrowed. "Mayor sat right where you're seated. He picked up that phone, and called the judge, and had me take the warrant to the judge's house and sign it right there on the spot...."

Tucker said nothing.

"He was adamant about charging Burgess," Henderson went on, "and having the warrant served the following afternoon. They never liked each other."

"So he was certain you'd be going over to serve that warrant the following afternoon."

"Yes," Henderson said. "He and the neighbor knew about that. We showed up early."

"Why?"

"Because Freddy was bugging me to make an arrest." Then it came to Henderson in a blinding light. "You said the vehicle was a black Ford, right?"

Tucker nodded. "Yes."

"And the butcher has a black Ford."

"That's right. He drove me and the wife here in it, but there's a lot of black Fords."

"Not around here," Henderson said.

"But why would he want to kill *Burgess*?"

"That I don't know. But it looks, I'd say, like we have ourselves a suspect."

47

After stopping by the butcher's shop and his home, Tucker and Henderson were unable to locate him. He seemed to have vanished into thin air. It was getting late and even the streets had fewer people on them. They were all huddled up in their homes with their doors locked—a weird feeling for the residents, Henderson knew. Up to the recent spate of violence, nobody had ever locked their doors. Mothers and children would typically be out walking to and from school and the stores along Broad Avenue on such a beautiful sunny day. After dinner families were known to stroll along Broad Avenue and frequent the Paris Confectionery Company for ice-cream floats and sprinkled cones. The proprietor, a generous and humble man, had cut the prices to allow families to continue to enjoy his homemade ice cream during the difficult economic times. Even the Park Lane movie theatre had slashed ticket prices, but right about now, even free wasn't enticing enough to get the families out of their homes. Henderson had known the peacefulness his small town enjoyed was compromised.

Back in the chief's office, Henderson commented on it: "Like everybody's left town."

"Butcher, too," Tucker replied from the file cabinet he was standing in front of, flipping through papers. He saw the picture of Dr. Anderson beat up and he smirked. "I was going to ask you last time I saw this. What happened to Dr. Anderson." Tucker held the photo in his hand.

Henderson didn't answer the question, but said, "Have a good look at doc, cause when I catch the butcher, he's going to look a hundred times worse."

Tucker continued flipping through the papers. "Reminds me of that day you dragged me in here. I sensed you thought a bunch of times about beating me."

"So," Henderson said. "What's your point?"

"Is that the standard operating procedure around here?"

"Did I hit you?" Henderson countered. "Check yourself for bruising... Go Ahead."

Tucker fell silent.

After a long pause, Henderson smirked: "Dr. Anderson deserved every bit of it."

"I bet."

Henderson had meanwhile sat in his chair and pulled himself into his desk. He plucked a pencil from the mug on his desk and had begun to write something down when he stopped and said, "It's not like Mike to close his store during the week."

"I've seen 'be right back' and 'out to lunch' notes posted on his window before. Do you find it strange that he didn't leave one this time?"

"That's a good point, yes—but then again, he's a rum runner, and it is possible that he's out doing that," Henderson countered. "But that doesn't seem right either. He usually does that at night."

Not looking up from the document he was reviewing, Tucker said, "Not always. It was daylight when he drove us in... I heard a lot of clanging, and he said it was milk jugs he was hauling."

"What'd you expect him to say?" Henderson said. "Running booze is still illegal."

"That's it!" Tucker exclaimed, and turned to Henderson. "We can drop a warrant on him for that, and bring him in here for questioning, and then we'll have some leverage on him."

Henderson shook his head. "That's impossible."

"Why?"

"He ain't going to buy that."

"Why not?"

"He just ain't," Henderson grunted. "Forget it. That won't work."

Tucker wanted to ask if it had to do with Henderson being a customer of the butcher, but he thought better of it. Tucker thought back to the day he'd driven him and Emma into town. At that time, he considered him a petty criminal and perhaps a womanizer, but not a killer. He swallowed thinking how foolish he was to put his wife in the car of stranger like that. It could've turned out badly. But it wasn't the first time they'd hitch a ride with a stranger. Actually, there were few vehicles on the road and many people who didn't own a car. Everybody at one time or another hitched a ride with a stranger.

Henderson put down the pencil and drew a comb from his top drawer. He brushed his hair back over his ears. "We'll wait until later, and go back to his house and shop, and keep looking for him. We'll find him."

"Are we still going to keep the same shift hours until we get more cops?"

"Yes," Henderson said. "Same two twelve-hour shifts. Ten in the morning till ten at night. Second shift is the overnight."

"Okay, tonight I'll handle the overnight," Tucker said. "I'm going home for chow. I'll see you later."

Henderson grinned. "Thanks. And don't forget... When you're working the overnight, make sure you keep a full tank of gas. The gas station doesn't open till six in the morning."

48

"Have a nice night, Patrolman," Chief Henderson said with a smile.

Tucker smiled back, drained his coffee mug, cinched up his belt laden with weapon, holster, ammunition, and nightstick, and prepared to begin his shift patrolling the town. He looked down and was pleased with how neatly Emma had ironed his uniform. He noticed the overhead bulb reflecting from the glossy polish on his boots.

It was ten at night, and the police station was almost silent except for the constant humming of the metal fan behind the chief's desk and the little noises every building makes when nobody is around. Somewhere, something is creaking or thumping.

As Tucker finished his routine preparations, checking the Eveready flashlight, making sure he had enough battery power, patting his breast pocket for his pad and pens, he said, "Still no sign of the butcher?"

Henderson didn't turn his head from his desk but said, "Nope."

Tucker shook his head and headed for the door. At the door he stopped and threw out another question: "How about any word on when the new cops are being hired?"

"Three weeks... three weeks, and we get two new cops."

"That's comforting," Tucker said.

Henderson forced a slight grin and called out, "See you, Tucker. Anything comes up, you give a holler."

"Sure, Chief."

Tucker double-checked the equipment in the police cruiser. It wasn't much—an extra flashlight, some bandages, and a flotation device in case a swimmer in the creek became distressed. He pulled away from the curb and into the night.

It was dark and balmy, but not quiet. The chirping of insects was loud enough to cover a gun shot. Later it would quiet down. Tucker's lunch and newspaper sat on the passenger seat, available for his break around the time a glow in the east began erasing the stars.

A creature of habit, Tucker started his patrol on the usual streets. He noted the names as he traveled down them. There were some dead-ends that required him to make a three-point turn to reverse direction.

Unless something interrupted Tucker, he'd be able to make a complete patrol circuit at least four times during his shift. But that night he wanted to try something different. He parked in the shadow of the big billboard on Bergen Boulevard. He was going to see who was coming and going from town.

Tucker had just had a roast beef sandwich, which he washed down with hot coffee from his thermos, and read the little note that Emma usually put in his lunch bag, just as she had all those times when they were back home. It was usually a poem she had written or a little hint about her birthday gift or, sometimes, an I love you note. That night's had to do with some much-needed intimate time.

He pulled up at the billboard and was cleaning up the napkins from his lunch when a car passed. It didn't look like it was speeding. If times were different, a vehicle traveling at a safe speed wouldn't have aroused any suspicion at all, but that night Tucker wondered. He hadn't gotten a good look at the car other than to see it was black. What seemed odd was that the motorist was coming into town so early, that is, if he was coming into town so early and not just passing through. None of the town's businesses were open, not even the coffee shop.

Which made Tucker even more curious.

He eased his vehicle out of its hiding space and began following the car. He didn't want to be obvious—the car had done nothing illegal—so he followed at a distance and kept the red tail lights in sight.

Tucker had passed through town and was about to break off when the car turned down one of the side streets near the Overpeck Creek.

He pondered that for a few seconds. His curiosity was aroused, so he followed. He lost the car briefly and couldn't tell whether it had turned down Columbus Avenue or Commercial, the two streets were that close together. Tucker turned onto Columbus, and drove to the end of the street. There was no sign of the vehicle. He made a U-turn, returned to the main road, and was soon on Commercial, the only street where the car could have gone.

There it was, parked in front of a house just before the end of the street. Tucker could barely make out the glimmer of the creek and the weeping willows in the distance, the only light coming from a house across the water. He took a closer glance and noticed the vehicle was parked in front of Henderson's house. It looked like the butcher's, but Tucker was uncertain at that moment.

He looked around and saw no movement. He parked the police vehicle on a grassy incline across from the house, grabbed his flashlight, and turned toward the place. He crept around back—he didn't want to alarm anybody that late at night, so he relied on his night vision, which had become pretty good after years of night duty back home and this being the middle of the shift.

The backyard was messy with children's things everywhere—sit-on toys, a tricycle, and some other things Tucker couldn't make out. What didn't seem right was the short ladder propped under a first-floor window. He advanced cautiously and climbed the first two steps of the ladder. He was high enough to see inside. He flashed his light into the room to see a man dash from the room and heard the squeal of a child. As he hastened to get after the man, he caught his foot on something and got hung up halfway in the window. With a solid effort he propelled himself into the room and landed with a thud on the floor.

Just then the lights in the hallway went on, Chief Henderson's voice cried out, and footsteps thundered down the stairs. Tucker met Henderson in the front vestibule. Henderson's face dropped as he spotted Tucker running through his house with a flashlight in hand. "What the heck?" he screamed.

Tucker blurted, "Chief, is there a child in that back room?"

Henderson's eye's bulged. "Oh, my gosh—Damien! My son sleeps in there. Is he all right?"

"He's okay, sir. There was an intruder. I didn't get a look at him. But I'm almost certain it was Mike the butcher. I think that's his car parked out front."

Tucker dashed out the door with no further explanation. Henderson followed barefoot in his shorts and t-shirt. The V8 was still parked out front.

Tucker drew his service revolver and advanced on the car. A quick inspection proved there was no one in it, but it was without a doubt the butcher's; his white uniform, and a half bottle of booze, were lying across the passenger seat.

"He either went down or up that way," Tucker said, pointing in opposing directions. His senses told him toward the creek. "I'll check down that way."

Henderson shouted, "Go ahead. Go. I'll grab my gun and boots, and check the other way."

Tucker jogged down and was soon searching along the Overpeck Creek, keeping his eyes focused. He looked both ways along the reedy bank—but saw nothing but moonlight on the rippling water. He kept checking back to see if the vehicle was still there. It was.

For ten more minutes he searched every likely hiding place on the creek bank except an area of high reeds and bulrushes bordering the creek further downstream.

He was knee deep in the rushes and weeds, startling a few resting ducks, when somebody hit him from behind and shoved him into the river. He was shocked by the suddenness of it: A strong pair of hands were gripping his throat from behind, forcing his face into the mud. Trying to breathe, he gulped down some water and was choking even as the man squeezed his throat harder and harder. But he called on all his reserves and, with the adrenaline running, hurled his attacker off him, splashing around in the waist-deep water, fighting for his life against an assailant struggling back with the strength of desperation. He had a madman's power and he was squeezing the life out of him. Tucker had only a thin thread of breath left when he felt the other go off balance, and, taking advantage, again threw his attacker off, rolled him to his back, coughed up some water, got a small breath before the other turned and grabbed him again.

Whenever he tried to get a look at his assailant, he was forced to fight him off. But when the man once more rolled him onto his back, Tucker saw he was the butcher. "You're under arrest, Mike," Tucker spat, coughing. "Stop resisting."

The butcher momentarily got the best of him and again dunked him. Tucker brought his knee up hard into the butcher's groin, heard him groan and push away into the reeds. Tucker was disoriented enough to lose him.

As he staggered out of the water, panting and gasping, he saw the dark figure of the butcher dashing up the bank toward his car. He lost a few precious minutes searching for his .38 by running his hands along the muddy creek bottom. He didn't want to go after such a madman armed only with his fists. If the butcher had a gun, he was a dead man.

Bent over, hands on knees, was still gasping and trying to catch his breath. He started back to the Henderson house, which by now was lit up, and other lights were coming on in the neighborhood. He felt a tightness in the pit in his stomach when he saw the tail lights of the butcher's vehicle come on, heard the engine roar, and watched it take off into the night.

He raced to his car as quickly as his soggy clothes would allow, jumped in, and started after him. When he got to the top of the street, he had to make a choice. If it was the wrong one, he would lose him, because the butcher would already be a long way down the road in the opposite direction.

He cut the wheel to the left, back in the direction the car had come from. There was no police work involved in that, only an educated instinct. He thundered north on Grand Avenue.

When he saw no sign of the butcher's vehicle a few minutes later, he knew he had lost him. He drove straight for the butcher's shop and checked for his vehicle. He checked the man's house. Again nothing.

Dawn was casting a pinkish glow over the horizon when Tucker eased his vehicle into the grassy area across the street from Henderson's house.

His soggy clothes were extremely uncomfortable. He crossed the front porch into the parlor. "Is everybody safe?"

Henderson was sitting on his settee with his pistol in his lap. "I didn't want to leave them alone in case he came back." He got up and said, "Come on, we'll leave Molly and Damien with the Sinagra boys down the block. They own enough guns to protect them while you and I pay Mike a visit."

"I already checked his shop and store. He's on the run."

Molly's eyes darted from Tucker to her husband to her son. She was terrified. The boy seemed calm, probably didn't know how close he had come to being kidnapped.

Henderson placed his hand on Tucker's shoulder. "Good work, son," he said proudly.

49

Tucker and Henderson rushed toward the butcher's house. The sun was casting subtle shades of blue and yellow everywhere, silhouetting the stately maple against the skyline as they rounded the corner up East Homestead Avenue to the top of the hill, where a few homes were secluded in a heavily wooded area. The motor raced as it came to the steepest part. They drove into the glimmering sun rising from behind the hill.

Within a minute or so, Tucker slid the police vehicle onto a patch of gravel on the side of the road about a half a block from the butcher's home. Lots of trees and sun-scorched brush and overgrown weeds provided cover for their cruiser.

"He's got to come home sooner or later," Henderson said.

"You think he can see us?" Tucker asked, drawing his weapon. He let it hang loosely by his side. "If so, we should take cover."

Henderson, not turning his head, said, "Not from this angle. But if he sees us, he sees us. That's why we shoot first."

Tucker nodded gravely. He felt the weight of his .38 and double-checked his uniform pockets. He had another twenty rounds. He glanced down at the revolver cylinder. He could see the shell ends pressed into it.

When they reached the front of the butcher's home, they noticed three steps that led to a deep red-colored porch. One side of the middle step held two flower pots that had water leaking from the base. Two plants hung from hooks on the right side of the porch and they too had water dripping. Henderson said, "It's possible we just missed him."

"Why would a man on the run, stop home to water his plants?" Tucker considered. "That doesn't make sense."

"Forget that," Henderson said. "Flank right, and head to the back of the house. Cover the rear door."

Tucker observed the path he'd take into the backyard. "Are you going through the front door?"

"Yes. Cover the back door."

Tucker glanced around. "I don't see the V8."

"The back door," Henderson whispered. "Go quietly."

Tucker crept into the backyard while Henderson moved stealthily up the front porch and tried the doorknob. "Damn it," he whispered to himself. It was locked. He glanced into the front window. Nothing was moving. He thought of kicking in the front door but thought better of it. He wanted to be in enough of a tactical position to get the drop on the man. Henderson concealed himself at the front window with his gun up and ready to fire. He watched carefully, and noticed a lamp on in the front parlor. A newspaper was laid out across a settee and papers from a desk that sat in a corner were messy and littered on the floor. It appeared that somebody was in a hurry.

Moments later he found Tucker, who had his gun drawn on the rear door, in the backyard.

"Pssssst," Henderson whispered to him.

Tucker nodded.

"What's that behind you?"

In a far corner of the yard was patch of loose, grainy dirt. There was a rounded shovel hanging from a hook on the exterior of the garage, next to a ten-foot wooden ladder. "Stillman?" Henderson asked inquisitively. "You think old lady Stillman is buried there?"

"Maybe the mayor?" said Tucker with his gun still trained on the rear door. "We'll check it later."

"Front door's locked," Henderson said.

"Check this door," Tucker said softly. "I got you covered."

Henderson approached the rear door, slithering under an open double-hung window where lacy curtains were blowing in the wind. He lifted his weapon into the frame and his eyes followed. Nothing. If the butcher was inside, he was either completely unaware of their presence or lying in wait to ambush. Henderson figured the latter.

From a neighboring yard, a set of eyes appeared over a tall wooden fence. Tucker saw the movement and turned when a man shouted, "Don't shoot."

"Show yourself now," Tucker spat. "Hands up."

The man stood on his toes and his face appeared above the fence. In his right hand he held a watering can.

"Did he ask you to look after his plants?"

"No," the man said. "I just do it."

"Get back in your house, Warren," Henderson said.

The man disappeared behind the fence; seconds later, they heard the man's rear screen door slam. Henderson turned to Tucker. "No more shouting—as if it'd make any damn difference now." He tried the back door. It was unlocked. He waved Tucker on. "Let's go."

Henderson went in first and cleared the kitchen, which was the first room inside from that direction. The place smelled of frying grease and rotten milk. There were ants on the counter where a sandwich was left half eaten. Above the sink was a clock that looked like a chicken coop with a rooster on its peak. It had stopped at half past one. It was already a week into the new month and the calendar next to the stove read August, 1933. Tucker followed, and they moved methodically through the house, checking closets and every likely hiding spot, expecting the butcher to surprise them.

"What's that smell?" Tucker asked. "It's putrid."

Henderson sniffed the air. "Smells like a dead body."

Tucker didn't answer. He inched up the stairs to the second floor and into the larger bedroom. A large pair of black boots on the steps caused Tucker to slightly roll his left ankle as he crept closer to the top. At the top, Tucker stopped and held his index finger to his lips. An open hallway window allowed a breeze to cut some of the smell. They listened briefly. It was quiet. Tucker continued on while Henderson waited in the hallway: Should the man try to ambush both of them, one could provide cover while the other searched the room, checking the closets and under the bed.

When Tucker was leaving the main bedroom, he tripped over a cane that lay haphazardly on the floor. "Old lady Stillman's?" Tucker asked.

"No," Henderson replied. "His mother's handicapped. And I didn't hear about her dying or anything."

"That smell is real bad. You think it could be...?"

"Let's finish searching the rooms then have another look at that dirt in the backyard." Henderson started for the bedroom on the other side of the hallway. "Maybe it's just that old-folks smell."

Henderson checked the second bedroom and a small anteroom that held an armchair with clothing piled on it. The butcher's belongings were all over the place. There were two photos on the bed and one on the floor. The two on the bed were of his parents and the photo on floor was of the butcher with a man Henderson didn't recognize. He picked up the photo and on the back read: 'Roger and me, April, 1928.' The contents of a dresser drawer lay messy on the bed. On the dresser was a blue and gold trophy with a man in gold shooting a basketball on top along with athletic ribbons and other sports memorabilia. A glass jug on the floor was filled with coins and had a pair of men's underwear hooked around its rim. Somebody was in a hurry to find something, Henderson thought. And the butcher was too old to be living like the way he was.

They went downstairs, closed the rear door when they left the house, and sauntered over to the disturbed dirt. Henderson knelt and ran his fingers through it. It reminded him of Freddy's grave. Somebody had recently sprinkled grass seeds on the soil. In the distance a dog was barking. Henderson considered that maybe somebody was approaching. But the barking stopped, and it wasn't all that much. But a dog still had barked, and he didn't want to chance it.

50

The hot sun was pressing through their clothes as Henderson and Tucker stood in the backyard of the butcher's home, the day growing hotter and hotter. Both knew the longer it took to apprehend the butcher, the farther away he could flee.

"To find out whoever, or whatever, is buried here, will have to wait," Tucker said, pointing at the makeshift grave. "No sense digging now. We'd be sitting ducks."

"Another time for that," Henderson agreed.

"Let's check his shop," Tucker suggested. "He either went there or home, and we've already established he's not here."

"I'm not sure where he went, Tucker," Henderson offered. "Nothing is adding up."

Tucker wiped the sweat from his brow. "You said the mayor was related to the butcher. And that's probably how he gets his inside information, right?"

"Yeah, but for as long as I can remember, the two of them ain't been on speaking terms."

"You said that already, but they're still family," Tucker said. "And family is family."

"Not always," Henderson glanced toward the roadway. "The mayor doesn't even acknowledge his own Fitzgerald name. Goes by just Wilson."

"Interesting," Tucker said.

"These people on the hill are more of a family than most blood relatives."

"I don't understand."

"The Italians. Remember I told you about them. In one way or another, they're all related. Some have similar family names spelled differently and they too are somehow relatives. People from the same hometowns in Italy are considered family."

"Ah, like the Irish back home," Tucker said, knowingly.

Henderson tapped Tucker on his shoulder, then gestured

toward the police cruiser. "Let's not waste too much time."

The men began walking. In the front yard Tucker paused. "What doesn't make sense is why he'd try to kidnap Damien," he said.

Henderson let that sink in for moment. "Beats me."

"Sir—" Tucker cleared his throat— "it's obvious he also has a problem with you. Why is that?"

Henderson knew he'd been there the day the butcher's father died years before. But did the butcher know that? How could he? He had been a young boy at that time, and by all accounts there were no witnesses. He'd left the man dead in the alley, and nobody'd mentioned anything. Henderson had been a young constable at the time, and he'd cleared the case, ruled it a homicide by an unknown assailant.

And even if the butcher did know, why wait till now for vengeance?

Henderson rubbed his chin against his shoulder and looked Tucker in the eye. "I don't want to scare you, Tucker. But if you're only considering me here, you're forgetting about yourself. Maybe it's you he's after."

"First off, I've already fought him. He doesn't scare me. And secondly, that makes no sense. He tried to kidnap your son earlier. Aren't you willing to acknowledge that?"

"Like I said, Tucker I don't want to scare you."

A warm breeze swept through the backyard, but it was no match for the baking sunlight. A chime in the neighbor's backyard was ringing. And they could smell the bacon and eggs coming from the neighbor's kitchen. The smell forced Henderson's stomach to roll. He was hungry, but so deep in concentration he didn't realize it.

"If you think I'm scared, why ask me to help you catch this guy?" Tucker said, plucking a smoke from his cigarette case. He put it to his lip and stuck the match on the side of the house.

"Never mind," Henderson said. "We've got a long day ahead of us."

Tucker pulled in a long drag and watched the cherry glow on the tip of the cigarette. He was deep in thought. "Stillman was your former stepmother, right?" Tucker offered Henderson a smoke.

"Forget that," Henderson replied, lighting the cigarette. "I caught him in the alley, side of Dominic's house."

"Huh?"

"At the time, I didn't think anything of it."

"In Dominic's alley?" Tucker asked inquisitively. "What would he be doing there? Dominic lives four or five blocks from here."

Henderson didn't answer.

"Wait." Tucker bit his lip. "The mayor lives across the street from Dominic. And you said they're not on speaking terms, so it wouldn't make sense he was in the neighborhood to see him."

"I wish I'd had all my senses that night," Henderson said and exhaled a short drag from his nostrils. "But I'd had a few too many pops."

"What does that mean?"

"What does what mean?"

"You're losing me," Tucker said.

"What I'm saying is, I was drunk."

"I get that—but what was he doing in the alley?"

"Said he was putting out the garbage."

With a confused look, Tucker said, "I've been putting the garbage out since they took us in. Emma and I were helping with household chores to show our appreciation for their hospitality. So then," Tucker said, rubbing his elbows, "what was he doing in Dominic's alley?"

"He was peeping in the windows."

Tucker swallowed.

"He's been known to do stuff like that. When I questioned him, he told me I should question you. That's how I came about to picking you up that morning."

"...Why did you wait until now to mention this?"

Henderson nodded. "It slipped my mind... I've been thinking a lot about my son and what if Veronica had had my son's baby. If she hadn't gone to Doctor Anderson for that scraping, I'd've been a granddad. In a way, I think I would have gotten some of my son back. That is, of course, if it was going to be a boy."

"You nearly beat Doctor Anderson to death, and I'll bet even that doesn't help, the way you're feeling right now."

Henderson shook off the memory and said, "Maybe it's your wife he's after?"

Tucker thought back to the day the butcher had driven them in and recalled the uneasy feeling he'd had when the butcher stared at his wife, how his eyes seemed to drink in the sight of her. "Oh, God," he said. It had hit him like a ton of bricks. "Here," he added. "Why here?"

"Huh?"

"Why would he drive us to this town," Tucker glanced around the butcher's backyard. "I mean, when there were so many between where he picked us up and the ferry to Manhattan. Why Palisades Park?"

"And what about that bullet?" Henderson asked, now thinking clearly.

"What?"

In a dismal tone, Henderson muttered, "The one that nearly killed you."

"I'll admit it was possible. But you can't be certain." Tucker felt a chill in his belly. "I still say that bullet could've had your name on it."

"Not a chance." Henderson shook his head. "He's a serious shot."

"Still a tough one to pull off from that angle."

Henderson waved a dismissive hand. "What's so hard? He pulled up in front of the luncheonette, fixed you in his sights, and pulled the trigger."

Tucker chewed on that for a moment. "But he just tried to kidnap Damien."

Tucker felt the warmth on the back of his neck. The sun was casting a long shadow on the butcher's house. In the distance the dog again began barking.

Henderson leaned on the revolver on his hip. Tucker could tell he was searching deeply. He tapped his index finger against his lip. "But if he tried to kill you, and he was in that alley watching your wife through that window—"

A gunshot rang out, reverberated over the hill, and echoed

in the distance.

Tucker felt a sharp pain at the base of his neck, like a little knife digging. "Oh my, God, Emma!

51

The door shattered open with a loud bang, wood splitting and cracking as the butcher kicked it into Dominic's house. It fell from the hinges, and a cloud of dust flew up when it belly-flopped on the floor. He stepped over it and crept into the hall-way. It was early still, and the smell of fresh coffee permeated the place. From off to his right Dominic appeared in the parlor wearing his shirtsleeves and blue jeans. "What the heck?" he said. "Who's there?"

The butcher stepped into the parlor, gun in hand, tower-ing before him. Sunshine spilling through an open front win-dow silhouetted the butcher. The wind was blowing through the curtains and over a side chair that was facing the window. Last night, Emma and Lillie were sitting there, marveling at the vast and elevated view of the town. But this early in the morn-ing, they were still tucked into their beds.

"Mike? Is that you?" Dominic asked, rubbing his eyes. "What the heck you doing here?"

The butcher crept closer, saying nothing. Dominic saw the handgun in his hand and suddenly felt queasy. "What—uh, what's this all about?"

"Turn that chair around and sit down." The butcher mo-tioned to the chair. "Make a fast move, and you're dead."

Dominic's eyes darted from the gun, then to his eyes, then back to his gun. He saw something on the butcher's face that he hadn't seen before—anger and determination. "What's this all about, Mike?" Dominic showed his palms. "I've done noth-ing to you."

"That's right," the butcher smirked. "You haven't."

"Then—"

"Then what?" the butcher said. "What brings me here?"

Dominic said nothing.

"Is that what you were going to ask me?"

Dominic turned the chair around and held the back of it. He licked his dry lips. "Why are you here with that gun, ordering me around?"

The butcher fell silent. He was now looking beyond Dominic to see if anybody was in the hallway.

Dominic nearly fell as he sat with shaking legs. His left leg was hammering into the floor. "If it's money, I got some. You can have it all. Honestly, I got some... take it."

The butcher strode over to Dominic, angling the gun at his temple, the sweat now visible on Dominic's florid face, his left eye twitching. "You think this is about money, huh," the butcher asked and placed his free hand on Dominic's hammering leg.

It stopped briefly. But when the butcher removed his hand, it began to pound again against the floor. Dominic looked into the muzzle of the butcher's revolver. It seemed larger and wider at that close range. He saw the cold steel of the barrel and how the man's index finger lay heavy on the trigger. "I got lots of cash in a metal tin in the bedroom. I'll gladly—"

"It ain't about that."

"Then what?"

"I'd like to call it vengeance."

"But I've done nothing to you."

"I already told you that was true."

"So what vengeance you got for me?"

"I said it's not about you."

"Then why you got that gun on me, Mike? Why'd you kick down my door?"

"Sorry about the door, Dom," the butcher said. "I guess I went a little overboard with that." The sarcasm dripped off every word.

"We can work this out."

"Listen, Dom. Hand over my bride, and I'll be on my way."

"You mean my wife?"

"No."

"Emma?" Dominic gazed at the butcher's wet clothes and how his hair was covered with strands of weeping willow and cattail —and him as calm as if he had walked into a church, his breathing even and slow.

The butcher squinted into the sights on his gun as if it would make a difference at that close range. He glanced down at Dominic with distant eyes.

"You're not making sense, Mike. But whatever the problem is, we can work out," Dominic said. "Let me get you a change of clothes."

"And give you a chance to get your gun? No."

"I don't own a gun."

"You own at least two, Dom. You and Tucker were firing them down at the range last week."

"Well, yeah, but I don't keep them in the house. You can come with me into my bedroom. I'll get you fresh clothes and then we'll have coffee." Dominic in fact kept a loaded .38 behind the dresser in his bedroom. But how would he be able to get to it now? he wondered. They'd struggle, and the butcher would get a shot off before he could retrieve it.

It looked as if Dominic had struck a chord with the butcher. There was a brief moment where he appeared forgiving. But just then the gasp of a woman was audible.

"Come on... Come out here, Lillie," the butcher called into the darkened hallway. "Let's go Emma... you too, dear."

Dominic shouted, "You leave them alone, Mike. You got something with me, then keep it between us."

"Shut up," The butcher said, and with the gun trained on Dominic he carefully watched Lillie move into the parlor. She was wearing a white nightgown, eyes wide with concern, and she was trembling.

"Leave my wife alone."

"Emma," the butcher called out. "Emma, come in here."

When Emma didn't appear, the butcher shrugged. "Stand next to your husband," the butcher instructed Lillie. "And if you make even the slightest move, I double tap this trigger, and that'll be it for the both of you."

With Dominic and Lillie before him, he'd have to deal with them before going into Emma's room to whisk his soon-to-be wife off her feet. It wasn't the way he wanted to take her. He had known it'd be hard for her to accept him. But acceptance would come in time. She'd see he was sincere and could be caring, and he believed she would eventually forgive him, that love was blind, and when she eventually fell in love with him, nothing else would matter. It had to be this way, he reassured himself. He had run out of options. He was identified. It was now or never. She'd have to flee town with him today.

He caught a glimpse of Lillie's nipples through her sheer white nightgown. Relishing the moment, he asked Dominic, "Do you know how hard it is to let a woman be when she's kissing up on your neck?"

"What in the hell are you talking about?" Lillie scoffed. "Have you lost your mind?"

"You don't make sense," said Dominic.

"It's not sense I'm here to make," the butcher spat with his gun still trained on him, beaded directly on his forehead

Dominic's eye was twitching. "I've told you we can talk this out. What is it you want?"

The butcher slapped him across the cheek. "Shut up and listen," he sneered. He flashed the back of his hand to Lillie. "If I gotta slap you silly, I will."

She pulled her face away. "Put the gun down, Mike," she pleaded. "Let us be."

Dominic rubbed his red and pinkish cheek that had the print of the butcher's large hand across it. "Yes, Mike. Let us be."

But when the butcher flashed a grin and thumbed the hammer back on his revolver, Lillie leaped at him. "Get out of here right now," she shouted. "Get your crazy ass out of this house." She punched him in the chest.

In a flash he had shoved Lillie to the ground as Dominic was rising from the stool. "Sit back down," he said. "You need to hear this."

Lillie reached out and hugged her husband. "Don't kill us," she cried.

"I slept with your wife," the butcher said.

"What?" Dominic said, rubbing his cheek. "What the hell are you talking about?"

The butcher winked to Lillie. "You're still tight."

"You're a sick son-of-a-bitch," Lillie cried. "You're crazy."

"That's impossible," Dominic said.

The butcher chuckled, "That birthmark on your rump—is that something everybody sees?"

Lillie swallowed and glanced at her husband. "It's not true," she whispered to him. "Honestly."

Dominic had begun to speak when the butcher stopped him. "Shut up." He retrained the gun on Dominic's forehead. "If you had one chance at a deathbed confession, would you come clean?" he asked her, focusing on the man, thinking of his mother's misdeeds and how her promiscuity had cost him greatly. "Would you tell him how bad you were?"

"I've done nothing." Lillie sobbed.

Emma, listening in the other room, was terrified. She considered rushing in and attacking the butcher—there'd be three against one. But she worried that would get them all killed. Maybe he wouldn't kill them after all. She tiptoed toward an open window and climbed out. Help will be on the way shortly, she muttered to herself, and ran down the roadway.

"Go ahead and tell him, Lillie," the butcher scoffed. "Tell him how we necked in that hotel, and how you came home to him and sat at the dinner table across from him without any sign of what you'd done... Tell him how you laid next to him that night."

"I don't know what you're talking about," she muttered. "You're insane."

With a flash Dominic leaped forward and swatted at the butcher's gun. Michael hammered him in the chest, knocking him back. Dominic sprung to his feet and tried again to pounce on the butcher, but his desperate effort came seconds too late.

The gunshot exploded in that tiny space like a bomb had gone off. Decorative plates above the fireplace rattled, followed by a piercing buzzing noise.

Dominic fell bleeding to the parlor floor. Behind him, the view of the town out the bay window looked like a painting, the sky a clear blue with soft powdery clouds. He began to choke and squirm. The bullet had hit him in the throat, and dark red blood was spilling from it. He kicked as he tried to get up, managed to get to his knees and elbow, but when he tried to press himself up, he collapsed and his eyes went wide, his jaw twisting before he went slack.

In the silence that followed, the butcher reached for Lillie. But she struck him in the gut with a closed fist. "You bastard," she seethed. "You go to hell!" She ran to her dying husband. "How could you?" she shrieked. "How could you?"

"It's women like you who destroy families. Destroy society."

"You killed him! You bastard. Go to hell!"

She turned away. He coughed. "If it's hell you want me to go to, that's fine with me. I'll meet you there. It's people like you, Lillie, that have ruined this town," he concluded, thinking of his father, and Abigail and pulled the trigger.

The bullet struck her in the back and she fell to the floor and began convulsing. She let out a piercing scream that reminded the butcher of a pig he had once slaughtered by slitting its throat, only he hadn't cut deep enough and the animal had squealed in horror.

"Collateral," he muttered to Dominic's body before him. "That's what your life has become. Collateral damage."

He slid his gun into the front pocket of his blue jeans. He brushed his hands together and wiped them on his jeans. He glanced down at the bodies. Their blood was pooling on the hardwood floor. It was a thick and dark wine color that began to seep into the crevices and flow toward the butcher's soggy boots. He took a step back.

Lillie managed to drag herself on top of her already expired husband. Was it an attempt to shield him? She was grunting in pain, her arms collapsed across her husband's shoulders. She struggled to push herself up, cantering her head to the side to observe the butcher staring down at her. She was able to speak, though barely, she garbled. "You son-of-a-bitch."

The butcher's face remained unchanged.

Then her body relaxed and went still. Her eyes rolled back in her head before they fixed open.

"Emma," he called out softly into the rear bedroom, as if he was calling her for dinner. "Emma, love," he said again. "I'm not here to hurt you."

When he pushed open the door into the rear bedroom and saw the open window and the curtains blowing, he knew she was gone.

Seconds later he returned to the parlor and swabbed some of the blood that was running toward the fireplace with his index finger. Next to the fireplace on a white wall he wrote in their blood:

MURDER. JULY 28, 1903.
CASE UNSOLVED.
KILLER AMONG US.

52

Tucker and Henderson were at that moment charging north on Tenth Street, the engine on their cruiser panging and screaming as Tucker's foot lay heavy on the accelerator. They were moving as fast as their police cruiser allowed, which wasn't much, but enough to navigate the hilly terrain quicker than by any other means. When they reached the crest of the hill, Dominic's house appeared in the distance. They looked ahead. They could see how the road would dip briefly before the steepness of the terrain continued. There were few clouds and lots of sun. Many trees skirted the roadway where goats grazed beyond a wired fence. The area was sparsely developed with only a few houses on each block.

Henderson was breathing heavily. "Can't this thing go any faster?"

"I've got the pedal slammed to the floor."

"Two gunshots already."

Tucker swallowed. "Oh, God."

Ahead, a large pothole came into view. Tucker swerved to avoid it and the passenger-side tires rose off the roadway. He gripped the steering wheel and Henderson held on to the door handle. The vehicle felt like it was going to roll. But then a split second later, it dropped back and the tires regained contact with the gravel.

"That was close," Tucker muttered.

"Watch!" Henderson snapped. "There's a larger one up ahead. You won't be able to avoid it. Just go straight through it."

They continued down the unimproved road and through the approaching pothole. The wheels creaked, and it sounded like something had snapped. Both their heads hit the roof. Tucker bit his tongue. "Ow," he screamed and held the steering wheel.

"Two more blocks straight, Tucker. Keep moving."

The terrain grew steep again and the engine labored against the heavy drag as Tucker applied enough pressure to crush the pedal. "Let's go, you damn thing! Let's go."

As they crossed the next intersection, Henderson shouted. "Stop the vehicle." He pointed off to the right. "Up East Palisades Boulevard. It's Emma."

Tucker turned onto East Palisades and, moments later, he parked the cruiser on a patch of dirt on the side of the roadway and jumped out. "Emma!" he called to her.

She kept running, approaching a main roadway.

"Emma. Emma!" Tucker continued to shout. But his calls fell on deaf ears. She kept running.

Tucker raced after her and grabbed her from behind. She elbowed and kicked at him. "Leave me alone," she cried. "Leave me alone!"

But then she saw Tucker's pleading brown eyes and she collapsed into his arms. Sobbing uncontrollably she gasped, "He shot them. They're... oh, God."

Tucker's stomach nearly let go with sickness when he asked, "What happened?"

"You didn't hear the shots?" she cried. "The butcher shot them."

By then Henderson had slid behind the wheel. He slid the vehicle up beside them, shielding them should the butcher drive by and start firing. He parked it, leaped out with his gun held tightly in his hand, and positioned himself on the rear bumper, watching the roadway intently. All his training from the war had consumed him. He knew they were under fire—knew all too well what that was like, having watched his brother get struck down in Cuba. Had he provided cover for the boy, either by fire suppression or dragging him to the ground, he would have saved him. No doubt about that. But he hadn't. And he wasn't going to make that same mistake again. "I got it, Tucker," he called out. "Calm the wife down, then saddle her up."

"Yes, sir," Tucker said, then shook Emma. "Honey, breathe. Breath in and out... Now, tell me what happened."

She tried to speak but couldn't.

"It's okay. I'm here now. Is he still in the house?"

Emma shook her head. "I don't... I don't know. "

"Take your time, Emma... Good. Take a deep breath, now... Okay now let it out."

Tucker saw tears in his wife's eyes as she exhaled onto his policeman's uniform. But he also saw something he hadn't seen before—horror, and a lot of it. Her eyes, and the corners of her pretty mouth, were drooping with stress. He continued cradling her in his arms, rubbing her arms; she felt the scar of the branding her former husband had left her. Tucker kissed the top of her head. "It's going to be okay, honey. I'll promise you that."

"Promise," she said. "Promise me we'll get out of here."

"We will," Tucker said. "Promise."

She wiped the tears from her cheeks and said, "He shot Lillie and Dominic. I heard the shots when I was running from the house."

"Did he hurt you?"

Emma shook her head. "No," she said. "He broke into the house, and then I escaped through a window."

"Don't worry. You're safe now. I won't let anything happen to you."

Emma continued to sob.

"Is he still in that house?" Tucker asked softly.

"I don't know. I ran as fast as I could. I never looked back."

Tucker let out a long breath. "We got to find a safe place for you."

Henderson crept backward toward them. "Get in the car. We're easy marks out here."

"Yes, sir," Tucker said.

Emma reached for the rear door handle on the passenger side door. She turned to Tucker. "Lillie was having an affair with the butcher."

"Huh?" Tucker slid into the passenger seat.

"Who was having an affair?" It was Henderson.

"Lillie," Emma said. "She met him on a Saturday night in New York City."

Tucker shook his head. "Surprising," he said. "This whole

town is in bed with each other one way or another."

Henderson glanced at her. "Easy, dear," he said. "Did you notice if he had more than one gun?"

"No."

"What kind of weapon was it?" Henderson asked.

"It was a pistol," Emma said. "But I didn't get a good look at it, other than it was black. I only peeked in the parlor for a second."

"How much firepower you think he's got?" Tucker asked the chief. "Are we outgunned?"

Henderson pulled into the roadway. Two goats were outside the fence on the corner grazing on some dry wild grass. "We have to pick up somebody before we raid Dominic's house... Today, Tucker." Henderson let his breath out slowly. "We kill him today."

"What about Emma? I'm not leaving her."

Henderson raced the vehicle toward Broad Avenue. "I would never jeopardize her safety, Tucker. You can bet your life on that."

53

"What brings you here so early?" asked Chester Dankert, opening his front door.

The expression on Henderson's face was ominous. He pushed his way in, checking back at the street to see if they were being followed. "It's very important." He rushed through the vestibule with Tucker and Emma trailing him. "Tucker, Emma, meet Dankert. He was a cop in Palisades Park."

"I know who you are," Dankert said to Tucker. "You're my replacement."

"That's not true, Dankert," Henderson claimed. "He's nobody's replacement. He's his own man."

Tucker didn't like the remark but let it ride, considering they were there to ask the guy for help. He felt the bruise at the back of his head where the butcher had struck him, a tender knot that had swelled to the size of a half dollar. Emma sat on the settee; he stood beside her. Emma still shaking with a confused look, nervously bit at her fingernails. Tucker calmly put his hand on her shoulder. "It's okay, honey," he said. "Take another deep breath and let it out slowly."

Emma did as he said and was able to relax her shoulders. But the stress mounted heavy on her face. She slowly began shaking her head as she thought about what had transpired. Nobody deserves to die like that. Then she recalled her abusive ex-husband and how he had held her down that day he scarred her with the branding iron. Now she'd known there was a man out there far worse than her ex. A man that her husband was seeking. The thought sent a tremble through her and she held tightly to Tucker's forearm.

"The window, Tucker," Henderson said, pointing. "Keep an eye."

"Yes, sir."

"No," Emma said. "Stay with me."

Tucker bent before her and looked her in the eye. "It's okay, honey."

Emma nodded nervously. "What if he finds us?"

"Let me worry about that," Henderson spat. "The window, Tucker. Watch that damn window."

Tucker strode over. He kept an eye out the window and looked back periodically to check on, Emma. "Think we were being followed?" he asked Henderson.

"We'll soon find out," Henderson said, curling his lip. "He's had this all planned from at least a week ago."

"How do you figure," Tucker asked.

"The calendar in his kitchen. He had every day crossed off up until a week ago. So either he left his house then, or keeping track of the days was no longer important."

Tucker shook his head. "The time had come, huh?"

Emma glanced around. It was a cozy place, the kind in which one could raise a family. Dankert had a fireplace and rocking chairs draped with blue-and-yellow quilted cotton blankets over the back. There were several toys in a wooden crate in the corner of the room. A cuckoo clock was hanging on an exterior wall between two large windows covered with long white curtains. A mirror on the far wall cast a flat, lemony light. The room was otherwise dim, the air humid, the house quiet enough to hear the rattle of ceramic plates in the china cabinet as the chief cleared his throat. "Grab your gun, and let's go. We have to leave now," he said. "I don't have time to explain."

Just then a boy appeared in the room. He was seven years old and wearing red pajamas and a frown. "Daddy?" he said.

Dankert rushed over and picked him up. "Daddy's got company. Time to go back to bed."

When Henderson saw Dankert's son, a chill shot through him. Damien had come inches away from being kidnapped or worse. Henderson shook off the feeling. He'd known Dominic and Lillie had been shot inside their house, and there was a slim possibility that maybe they were still alive, that maybe the butcher had only wounded them and was lying in wait for him and Tucker to come charging through the door. But, he also knew, to save them he'd have to be certain it was safe enough to spare his men. For every battle, there needs to be a plan. Whether when he'd charged up Kettle Hill with colored infantry men, known as the Buffalo Soldiers, or others in the white regiment or Rough Riders, there was always a strategy. And Henderson had seen first-hand how well a plan can come together. Those colored troops fought side by side with him. And were brave as hell. In his mind's eye, he caught a glimpse of a fractured image of the troops, forging up that hill coolly as bullets were searing by them. The confidence he had that day consumed him.

"Get your gun," Henderson said again. "Dominic and Lillie may be bleeding out. We need the three of us to clear that house."

Emma interrupted. "I don't want my husband involved in any of this."

Tucker said over his shoulder, "Emma. Hush, honey."

"But," she said sheepishly, "I don't want anything to happen to you."

"Nothing is going to happen to me," Tucker promised, glaring out the window. "Hurry, big feller," he added to Dankert. "We're running out of time."

Dankert darted into a back room and, seconds later, reappeared with a pistol in his hand. He stuffed his pockets with a handful of bullets into the front pockets on his blue jeans. In his top breast pocket on his flannel red shirt, he slipped in an extra bullet. "Mind telling me who it is we're hunting?"

"Mike the butcher," Henderson spat. "He just shot the two of them."

"That sonofabitch," Dankert sneered. "Let's go."

54

It wasn't possible for either Henderson or Dankert to manage the back seat. Both were too large to bend their legs to fit. Besides, they had to race Emma to the Sinagras, to hide with Molly and Damien, and Tucker wanted to ride next to her. His legs cramped as he twisted them to allow enough room for her. Although he weighed a lot less than the two in front of him, being that he was six foot three and angular, he felt his back strain and the tightness in his hamstrings from his struggle with the butcher in the muddy creek. But he shrugged it off and made certain to keep watch for vehicles approaching from the rear. They had to hurry.

As they charged down the steep hill, Tucker felt the dips of the terrain in his stomach. At the base of the hill, he saw an old man in overalls swinging a sickle at the dry grass that flanked Klaus's pond. The old man had a concerned look on his expression as he watched the packed police cruiser scream down the roadway, dust clouding in its wake.

In the silence that followed, Tucker asked Henderson, "How are you certain these Sinagras can protect my wife?"

"Trust me," Henderson said. "You got to trust me."

They crossed Broad Avenue without stopping and nearly collided with a southbound trolley. The few riders held onto the rails and braced for the impact. "When you're waiting for that damn trolley, it takes forever," Henderson claimed. "And when you're not, it's always there."

"At the Grand Avenue intersection watch for Mr. Jenkins," Dankert called out. "He's usually hauling produce to the market now."

Henderson nodded gravely as he continued to race down the hill. At the Grand Avenue intersection, the road was empty. Henderson made a left, fishtailing it onto Grand, and continued thundering south. He leaned back and applied more pressure on the pedal. Emma's heart was in her throat. She'd had never raced before in a police car.

Moments later they came to a skidding stop outside of the Sinagras, and hurried Emma inside. She protested and grudgingly entered the house, where a man with a long rifle was keeping a watchful eye from a large front bay window. On a side table next to him sat extra boxes of ammunition and a large silver knife. There was another man watching from a window on the north side of the room. He had a long rifle strapped across his back and a pistol holstered to his hip. Molly and Damien were hiding there. An older man appeared from a darkened hallway. "Come, dear," he said to Emma. "I'm Craig. You'll be safe here." When he turned and Emma followed, she noticed he too had a rifle strapped across his back and a pistol holstered on his hip.

"She's going to be fine," Henderson assured Tucker as they reversed out of the driveway. "There's six good men in there who are all handy with those weapons. Two of the boys are decorated snipers. Anybody who gets close to that house will die long before they set foot on the grass."

"Then why ain't they coming with us?"

"We got Dankert now," Henderson said, "We'll manage."

Dankert nodded.

"Why are they not on the force?"

"The sniper boys," Henderson said. "Them boys all messed up in the head from the war."

"But my wife...." Tucker reached over the seat and nudged Henderson, who was driving. "You sure she's safe?"

"She's safe," Henderson said. "Don't worry."

Tucker had an empty feeling in his gut. He had been in the Sinagras' place for mere seconds and rushed back to the car. He'd had only a brief moment to study the men and he prayed they'd be able to protect his wife. It was risky. If something happened to Emma, he'd never forgive himself. And how messed up in the mind were they, Tucker thought.

The engine growled and the cruiser thundered down the roadway. Henderson turned to glance over his shoulder at Tucker. He was still in the clothes he'd left his house in a hurry earlier that morning. "Make sure you got enough rounds, Tucker," he said. "I'm not expecting a long fight, but if he puts up one, we got to have enough ammo."

Tucker patted the pockets of his still-damp uniform. "I got enough."

"Chief, are you sure Emma is safe at that house?" Tucker asked again.

"Yes," Henderson said. "Molly and Damien are there too. You think I would leave them in a place that wasn't safe?"

At that moment it made sense to Tucker. "Okay," he said.

Dankert reached under the passenger seat and retrieved a hidden box of ammo. "It's still here," he said, and stuffed the box into his waistband, tightening his belt on it. "Ready," he said.

55

"All clear," Henderson called out when he reached the master bedroom of Dominic's house. He re-holstered his .38. The last time Henderson had been inside Dominic's house was for the funeral of Dominic's grandfather. He knew the layout well since many homes were built similarly with the typical front parlor off the front porch, formal parlor and dining room beyond that with the kitchen in the back. On hooks outside the rear screen doors were clotheslines strung to the tall trees in the backyard. Many of the builders used the same blueprints to build the neighboring homes. "Let's head back downstairs into the formal parlor and have a good look at the mayhem."

Before leaving the bedroom, Tucker quickly inspected Dominic and Lillie's belongings. From what he could tell, the butcher had not rummaged through his room and nothing had been taken, eliminating robbery as the motive. But Tucker had known that wasn't the case anyhow.

"Downstairs, Tucker," Henderson said. "You too, Dankert."

Thinking briefly about how close he had come to catching the butcher wrestling with him by the creek, Tucker said, "I feel very responsible for this, Chief."

"Why?" Henderson asked skeptically. "That's nonsense."

"I should have caught him."

Astonished, Henderson said, "You saved my son."

Tucker let that sink in. He couldn't help but feel the guilt anyway. It was all part of his whole situation and how being laid off back home in Colorado and breaking down on the side of the roadway and ending up stranded in Palisades Park made him feel about himself, and that would be that, he figured, till it stopped.

They left the bedroom and walked into the hallway where a chandelier hung from a long brass chain. The banister shrank the hallway. "Watch your head, fellers," Henderson said.

"Watch what?" Dankert asked as his left eyebrow struck a sharp corner of the chandelier. "Oh, that." He rubbed it. A small drop of blood fell from the eyebrow into the cavern of his left eye socket then down his cheek. There was a terry cloth towel hanging from the banister. He retrieved it and wiped off the blood.

Tucker followed the two down the stairs, their boots creaking on the old wooden steps that twisted slightly back to the main floor. At the bottom of the stairs, he saw Dominic's work boots. He knew Dominic was off and had wondered if he was sleeping when the butcher burst into his house. Must've been caught by surprise. "Where do you think he fled to?" he asked.

"He could be anywhere." Dankert dabbed his bloody brow with the towel. "I don't think he's the type to hide out at the motor lodge up the road. He has told me he liked the woods."

"Outdoorsman?" Tucker's sucked on a tooth. "'Cause somebody who's that driven for women needs to be at a place where women are. I don't know many women living out there."

"Other than that, I would not have thought he was capable of this," Dankert said.

The sun was slanting through an open window as they examined the crime scene. Out the window was a picturesque elevated view of the small town and the meadows beyond. The glowing sun highlighted the cotton-like clouds across the vast blue openness, evidence that the world would push on regardless of the horror that lay before their toes. Time waited for nobody.

"Gather whatever information you can quickly," Henderson ordered. "Then we're off after this sonofabitch."

Tucker and Dankert did as they were told.

Henderson stood before the bodies and rubbed his chin. Lillie was lying on top of her husband, and the blood had pooled a dark red color underneath them. It ran along the parquet flooring, turning a lighter shade of red as it seeped into the moldings. A chair was knocked over and a lamp was on its side on the floor, suggesting a brief struggle.

"Damn shame," Henderson said. He caught his reflection in a mirror that was hanging in an anteroom. It had a thick walnut frame with flowers carved into the corners. He could see his eyes were heavy and the stress creased onto his expression. He briefly thought back to when he was a younger cop. Horrific events, death, and all the demons police dealt with regularly, hadn't bothered him back then. But especially since Freddy's death, the work was affecting him poorly. There was no shoving things into a dusty corner of his mind, no escape. It had dug its claws into him so fiercely he was becoming an insomniac. And it was showing.

"I've known Mike fairly well over the years," Henderson muttered. "At least I thought I did."

"You didn't think he'd kill somebody, huh?"

"Honest to God, I would never have pegged him for that."

"I see." Tucker examined closely at the scene. "From what I can tell, he shot them and walked out the door into the broad daylight like nothing happened."

"I see that," Dankert said. "The set of boot prints goes through the front door."

"More boot prints over here," Tucker called out and followed the boot prints into the room Emma and he occupied. He swallowed, shook his head, and walked back into the formal parlor. "Should I go and get Arthur Camp? I think that's his name," Tucker said. "To photograph this?"

"No," Henderson said. A light breeze that swept through an open window made a desultory effort to circulate the air in the room. "Let's go," Henderson said. "We're wasting precious time. Somebody cover the bodies with a bed sheet and give me a smoke," he added, tapping Dankert on the shoulder.

Dankert held out his cigarette case. Tucker went and retrieved a bed sheet.

Henderson plucked one out and struck a match. Through the flame, as he pulled on the cigarette, he saw some scribbling on the wall next to the fireplace. "What's that?" he asked.

"What're you looking at, Chief?" Tucker asked.

Henderson stepped over the bodies and squinted. He knew exactly what the message meant, and felt a hollow feeling in his chest. He swallowed as he thought back to the day.

But he wondered how and what the butcher knew. He couldn't have heard it from his father. Dead men don't offer testimony.

"What's it mean?" Dankert asked.

"It means he's escaped us for now. But I'll be dammed if he lives longer than a day."

Tucker covered his dead friends with the sheet and the men left.

56

It was nearly noon when the Dingman's Ferry Bridge came into view, the wrought iron trusses towering from the decking and narrow roadway. The bridge was slimly built and allowed for a single travel lane in each direction. A toll collector with apron and sun hat stood between the lanes on the opposite side.

The butcher wheeled onto the bridge, hearing the Canadian fir decking rattle below him as he crossed the Delaware River into Pennsylvania. Upstream he could see the river washing the rocks and the sun glimmering on the rocky bank. Several people were paddling in their canoes. Others were lying on blankets along the bank, basking in the warmth. It was about as nice and clear a day as one could've desired. A few clouds sat low on the horizon, the sun glowing brightly in the vast open sky where high above, two hawks glided gracefully above the tall pine trees.

A light westerly breeze was filling the compartment of his vehicle. He filled his lungs with the fresh air. He considered turning off, lying down on the shore, and stretching out. He'd nap a while, watch the hawks play, and when the sun became overbearing, plunge into the river like a .45 caliber and let the water cool him off. But he didn't have the proper attire— only had the clothes he had fled in. What would those sun lovers think if they saw a man stretched out before them in blood-stained clothing?

The toll collector signaled him to stop. "Ten cents, sir," the collector said. He wore a bright smile and a pin on his breast that said *Proud Volunteer Fireman*.

The butcher handed him a dime and smiled. "Looks like another hot one."

"Nineties and cloudless" the collector said. "Bad combination for forest fires."

"Try to stay cool," the butcher said.

The engine purred as he charged the V8 up a steep, serpentine hill that lay beyond the bridge. The pavement was loose, with lots of tall green timber skirting the roadway. Too fast, and he'd slide into a tree. Nothing good would ever come from that. He thought about what the toll collector had said. The evergreens were brown from lack of rain and days of intense heat and sunshine. The thick forest felt dry. He passed a wooden sign that read High Risk of Fire Today. Two famished deer stood off to north.

At the summit of the hill he passed three wooden crosses alongside the roadway and, off to the east, a small church, with flaked white paint that was mostly chipped off and a steeple bell, in the center of a cemetery. He thought briefly of the dead people below the surface of the rolling hill, of how their time had come and how some of them might have died.

Fifteen minutes later, he pulled into the gravel parking lot of his country house, a petite two-bedroom ranch with a sizeable fireplace where trophy bucks were mounted. He glanced at the empty passenger's seat. "We're here, Emma," he said to himself, and shook his head in disappointment. She should've been there. It should have been the start of their new life together.

A chipmunk dashed from a rock as it crossed the lawn to the front door. He let out a long sigh, fidgeted with the key in lock, turned the doorknob, and went inside.

The house looked the same as it had the last time he'd spent a weekend there two months before. He saw a thin coat of dust on the china cabinet and wiped it with his finger. He'd dust the furniture later. A strong, musty smell lay heavy in the air. He'd have to open the windows and let in fresh air to remove the dank staleness. He knew the smell was coming from the orange shag throw rug in the living room. It was time to replace it. He entered the tiny kitchen and checked the stock. There was plenty of canned food, enough to hold him for a while. On his way in he'd turn the well water on outside at the water box. He opened the faucet and let the water run for a few minutes before he stuck his head under the stream like a cat and gulped down the fresh water. It was always cool and he loved its crisp taste. He'd gotten into the habit of bottling some of it and taking it home with him to Palisades Park.

He entered one of the bedrooms and rolled the bed to the side. On hands and knees, he felt for the loose flooring. The wood creaked as he opened a compartment from which he angled out a silver box filled with lots of money, mostly hundreds he had saved from running booze over the years. He dug his hand into the box and pulled out a thin bundle. There was in excess of three thousand dollars there. He patted his crusty blue jeans and knew it'd be best to wash and change his clothes, but mostly he wanted to enjoy the silence. Let that overtake him and give him time to plan, to reflect on his shortcomings and how he'd have to raise his game. Bottom of the ninth, bases loaded, full count. He needed to get on base to take it into extra innings. He needed that badly, and he knew exactly what he needed to do... plan, rest, and make certain the next swing he took was the right one. And that he had the right pitch.

He sat at the edge of the bed and leaned over, opening the top drawer on an antique nightstand. Inside lay a single silver framed photo. He laid the picture on his lap and examined it. It was a grainy photo of his father in his butcher's uniform, holding two year old Michael. He wore a frown and Mike held a swirly lollypop the size of a softball. He closed his eyes and tried to remember the day the photo was taken. It had to be springtime and was probably on his birthday since lollipops that size signified a special occasion. As hard as he tried to recall, he couldn't. So he allowed himself to imagine. He pictured his dad at work when his mom entered the store with him in the stroller. His dad plucked a lollypop off the stand on the counter and gave it to him. At that time, a local photographer was in the area and dad asked him to take the photo. But why wasn't mom included, the butcher thought. Could mom have taken the photo? But nobody had owned a personal camera. He looked closer at his father's facial expression. At only two, could I have made this man that unhappy, he thought.

He unbuttoned his shirt and rolled his shoulders, thinking deeply. "Father," he called out into the quiet, "Mother is now with you, I know." He unbuckled his blue jeans and stepped out of them. "Tell her how you necked with Abigail Stillman... She's got lots of things to share with you."

He paused and listed to his voice trail off in the silence. "I'll take care of what needs caring... Consequences," he whispered softly. "Consequences."

57

"We searched this whole damn town. It's like he's Houdini," Henderson griped and rolled the sleeves up on his policeman's uniform. "Where the hell is he?"

"Chief, you say something?" Tucker asked from the preparatory room. "You calling me, Chief?"

"Come to the rear," Henderson called out. "And be careful there's an oily puddle in the hallway."

Tucker started toward the chief. It was late afternoon, and they were rummaging through the butcher's shop, searching for anything that would lead them in the right direction, that would help them anticipate the man's next move. The sunlight that filled the front plate glass window helped illuminate the store and showcases, but in the back it wasn't dingy and cool. A string of dim bulbs was strung across the preparatory room. In the far corner was a door to the meat locker and a double basin sink next to it. They'd already propped open the rear door for sunlight and to cut the heavy smell of animal hide and chicken feathers.

"Chief?" Tucker said, entering an undersized room just prior to the rear door. Inside was a gray metal desk and a swivel chair crammed into a closet that had been converted to an office. The desk had neat piles of invoices and other paperwork, and a coffee can that contained pencils and a few pens and rubber bands. But that was it. A tiny fan sat on an empty bookshelf in a corner. Henderson's large frame consumed most of the room. He was fingering through a folder. "Step back outside into the hallway," Henderson said. "There has to be something. But the both of us can't fit."

"Did you call me for something?"

"Yes," Henderson handed him a stack of documents. "Look

through these."

"This guy has very few personal belongings," Tucker angled his hip to clear his holster and not rip his uniform on the door-frame. From the hallway, Tucker said: "Other than a basketball trophy and some athletic ribbons, his room was pretty sparse."

"So what's your point?" Henderson said. "Should every man have keepsakes?"

"No. But doesn't everybody have trinkets or something?"

"Look, the two of us can't fit in this damn room."

"I am in the hallway," Tucker said.

Henderson turned to Tucker. "It's so tight I thought you were on my back."

"Trying to figure this man out is not easy." Tucker fingered through the documents.

"Especially when your brain's all muddied up from working the overnight."

"Nights don't bother me," Tucker said. "Coffee fixes that."

A knock on the storefront window interrupted them. "See who that is," Henderson said. "If it's not Dankert, get rid of 'em."

Tucker passed the counter where the refrigerators sat humming. When Tucker was a kid in Colorado, he'd ridden his bicycle along the main street and into his local butcher's shop parking lot, where he watched the men heft large blocks of dry ice with a hook and noticed how they were covered in canvas and sawdust. The advent of electrical refrigeration had de-stroyed the ice trade. Electricity had also destroyed the candle maker.

It was Dankert rapping on the glass. "Let me in," he said in his policeman's uniform. On his breast was badge number three. On his hip was a revolver and a long wooden stick that looked like a small baseball bat ran down his powerful thigh. Behind him, parked on the street was the patrol car.

Tucker opened the door and greeted the big man. "You should've left the car across the street in front of headquarters."

"Why?"

"So he doesn't know we're here."

"What difference does that make?" Dankert said hastily.

"Less he knows, the better."

"Hopefully it'll lure him," Dankert snickered and stepped inside. "How is he?"He still angry?"

"Who?"

"President Roosevelt."

"Huh?"

"The Chief," Dankert shook his head. "Who else?"

"He's pissed off right now."

"Sounds about right," Dankert said.

"Yeah."

They headed back to the makeshift office, where Henderson was sitting behind the butcher's desk sifting through paperwork. At the doorway, Dankert tossed him a pack of smokes. "Here you go, Chief," he said.

Henderson caught the smokes, slipped them into his breast pocket, but said nothing.

Tucker handed Dankert the stack of documents, "Hold this a second," he said. "I want to check something."

Tucker went into the preparatory room and the men continued searching.

Twenty minutes later Henderson was still sifting through files when Tucker called from the preparatory room, "Chief! I found something."

58

When Henderson and Dankert hurried into the preparatory room, they found Tucker under a porcelain double sink from which blood had seeped into the oak cabinet below.

Tucker crawled deeper into the cabinet. "There's a box of some sort in a hole in the wall," he said. His voice was hollow. "It looks like a secret compartment."

"If you can't reach it, let Dankert give 'er a try," Henderson told him.

Tucker continued inching deeper in. All the others could see were his duty boots and the hems of his pants.

"Chief," said Dankert, "there ain't no way I can squeeze in there."

Henderson measured him with his eyes and then glanced down at the cabinet. "I guess not," he said.

"What's taking so long?" Dankert said.

"Give me a second. I almost got it," Tucker, who replied.

A dim yellowing bulb above cast a flat crimson light. Henderson rubbed the sink with his index and middle finger. "Hard to tell if all these stains are animal or what," he said to Dankert. "What's the difference between human and animal blood?"

"Nothing that the naked eye could see," Dankert replied, leaning against a thick butcher block that had a dimple in the middle where one would routinely cut. It was a short block fifteen inches thick with broad legs. "Them stains look like they've been there for a long time."

Henderson pondered that. "It could very well be old blood from when his father ran this shop."

"How long ago was that?" Tucker asked from below in a muffled voice.

"Years," said Henderson, rubbing his hand briskly over the surface. "It's deep-seated. This sink was probably bone white at one time."

"Kind of creepy," Dankert remarked, thinking of how much blood had washed down the drain over the years. "Even that oily floor drain behind you."

Henderson glanced at the drain and saw a small oily puddle over it and how the oil rainbowed in the light's reflection. He looked back at Dankert. "More than gets spilled on a battlefield, you can be damn sure."

Tucker slid out from under the sink with a smallish box. "What happened to his father? He still around? Perhaps we can go speak with him?"

"That ain't possible," Henderson muttered. "What's in that box?"

"But he may even be hiding out with him as we speak," Tucker said. "We could be wasting our time here and all along he's hiding with his father."

"You don't know what you're talking about," Henderson said. "Give me that box and shut up."

"Does he live in Palisades Park?"

"No," Henderson sneered. "He's dead."

"He die recently?"

"What difference does that make?"

"Makes some."

"No, it doesn't."

"Why's that?"

"Cause when you're dead, you're dead," Henderson said and retrieved the box from Tucker. "Move aside, Dankert," he added, and laid the box on the butcher's block. "Nothing matters when you're dead."

As they were standing there over the box, Tucker asked, "What could cause a man to snap like he did?"

"The million-dollar question," Henderson snickered.

"Coulda been anything," Dankert injected.

"But, Chief, you also said that you didn't think he was the type to kill somebody."

"And?" Henderson replied skeptically. "What is it you figure?"

"I'm just saying. A lot's not adding up."

Henderson curled his lip. "Not everything adds up in every

case. You should know that."

"Okay."

"Okay," Henderson said looking up from the box. He fished a black wallet and red leather handbag from it. "Looks like we got something here, fellers."

"There's also a corncob pipe with the initials carved into it," Tucker said.

"Where?" Henderson asked.

"In that hole under the sink."

"Well, go get it," Henderson said.

Tucker crawled back underneath the sink.

Henderson showed Dankert the tri-fold wallet that had a picture of the mayor and his wife and children folded into the billfold. There was also a photo of him posing with his arms crossed and the American flag draped behind him. Narcissistic bastard, Henderson thought. The mouth of the wallet contained his driver's license and identification from his job. There was no money. "Things adding up now, Tucker?" Henderson said sarcastically.

"Hang on. I can't hear you," Tucker's hollow call came from under the sink. "A couple inches more, and I can reach it."

Henderson dug into the red leather handbag. It was filled with tissues, one wrapped around a stale crumb cake that was blistering with mold and another around a rotting doughnut. There were three or four big combs and an oversized pair of reading glasses in a soft fabric case, some make-up, five different-color lipsticks—mostly deep reds—and a wide brown leather wallet with a gold clasp and a deep mouth that had two crusty pennies in it. There were no bills. Henderson examined it more closely and found an identification card for Abigail Stillman.

"Not surprised," he said.

Tucker, now on his feet, studied the corncob pipe in his hand. He could smell the burned tobacco and see residue around the rim. He noticed the wear marks on its shank, where its owner had pinched it between his fingers. The stem had tiny bites.

"You think they're still alive?" Dankert asked.

Henderson shook his head.

Tucker considered. "But if he tried to kidnap Emma and Damien, then maybe he didn't kill Stillman and the mayor. Maybe he's holding them hostage?"

"Impossible." Henderson's brows narrowed. "Why would he take hostages and kill my son, and Burgess and Dominic and Lillie?"

"Beats me." Tucker brushed the knees on his uniform pants with his free hand. "Here's that pipe."

Henderson retrieved it with shaking fingers. Thoughts of his son consumed him. He thought of how Freddy had lain dead on the ground and how he kissed him on the forehead but failed to protect his boy. It dug at him like a knife in his chest. He thought of how lately his beloved town had been driven so hard, he didn't hardly recognize it. "It's difficult to remember this town the way it was."

"Huh?" It was Tucker.

"It's gone to hell so fast, I can't remember the good days."

"You concern yourself a lot with what your town was at one time," Tucker said.

Henderson pressed the corncob pipe into his breast pocket, behind the pack of smokes. "There was a time I loved right here more than any other place on this earth."

"You still love it," Dankert suggested. "Or you would have abandoned it a long time ago."

"I should've," the Chief sighed. His cheeks grew a pinkish red and the veins in his neck were pronounced. "I should've done things differently, Tucker... should've known when to walk away."

"You can't say that, Chief. No regrets in this life."

"Forget the sentimental talk," Henderson said. "Keep looking around."

"Okay."

Dankert left the back room and shortly thereafter returned with a letter in his hand. "This was among that stack that you handed me. You must have missed it."

Henderson grabbed the sheet of cream-colored paper and read it. Tucker began reading it over his shoulder. It had been scribbled in blue ink, addressed to Michael, and dated December 24, 1932. It read:

Dearest Michael,

I know it's been a while since we've spoken, since we shared good times with each other. I'm wishing you a Merry Christmas and a Happy New Year, and respectfully request that you refrain from threatening me. If you continue, I will have no choice but to expose you to the authorities. You will leave me no other option. Please understand this. We can be civil with each other. I think it's best if you know the truth. I never did anything to you that you didn't want or enjoy. You shouldn't be bitter. I've done nothing that would constitute a violation of the law or a breach of morality. I loved your mother, and I loved you. Men can be intimate. There's nothing wrong with that. So please stop harassing me. It wasn't me who had your father killed. You know that. What you don't know is who did it. I'll tell you this, but you have to refrain from menacing me. I'm no longer in favorable health. It was Carter Henderson who killed your dad. I hope one day we can mend the fence.

Love always,

Charlie Burgess

Henderson swallowed, folded the letter, and stuffed it in his breast pocket behind the mayor's corncob pipe. "If he's not dead by tomorrow," he sneered, "I'll be damned."

59

"Glad to see you're home, honey," Emma said sheepishly. "It's been a long day for you."

"It's not our home, but it's something."

"Bless this Sinagra family," Emma said. "Are you okay?"

"I'm exhausted," Tucker mumbled. "I'm starting to see spots."

"Come into bed," Emma said. "It's warm in here."

Tucker strode over to the bed, twisting off the bronze and alabaster ball-shaped table lamp that held a cream shade finished with a contrast gold trim and scalloped edge with tassel trim. Tucker thought briefly about that shade and how he'd seen similar ones in the homes of modest families back in Colorado. How he longed to be back home. A wave of guilt swept over him. He blamed himself for their situation. Lots of questions raced through his mind. What if he'd found work in Colorado? What if they'd had children? Things would have been different? But it was late and Tucker shook off the guilt. It will be there in the morning, he reminded himself. So for now he'd straighten out his priorities. Sleep. Yes, sleep was at the top of his list.

Emma reached out her hand to feel her husband in the darkness. "I am waiting for you," she cooed.

Tucker softly grabbed her hand. "Yes, honey. Can you slide over a little?"

Tucker entered the bed and Emma dug her head into the crook of his shoulder. "He's still out there, huh?"

"Not for long," Tucker said as he pulled back the bedding and let out a long breath. It was after two in the morning. He knew, when the sun rose in a few hours, he'd be back to work. Digging. In the morning they planned to dig up whoever was buried in the butcher's backyard.

"Do you want to talk, honey?" she asked. "How was your

day?"

"You know I don't like talking about that."

"If you're worried about scaring me, don't. I'm involved in this too, and I think I need to know what's going on."

"Another time, honey. I'm so tired right now, I can't even form sentences."

He gave her an assuring hug in that bed in a small bedroom on the second floor of the Sinagras' home. With Dominic and Lillie murdered, they needed a place to stay. And since the Sinagras were protecting Emma while Tucker was out patrolling, Henderson had asked the boys if Tucker could stay too, and they'd welcomed the idea. The room was small and felt cramped, but safety was all that mattered. Tucker sensed Henderson was right. The Sinagra boys were more than able to protect Emma. They liked the idea they were being called upon in dangerous times.

The bedroom was painted a light blue, the color one would paint a boy's room. There was one double-hung window on the rear wall, framed by outmoded royal blue curtains that lent a somber ambiance during the day and pitch blackness at night. A faded crimson armchair sat tightly between the bed and the rear wall. There was no space for a dresser or any other furniture save for a small nightstand that had a New Haven mantle clock, with a cream face and gold hands, that sat on a wooden octagon and rectangular base. It read two twenty-two.

On the floor next to the armchair lay magazines and Robert Frost poetry books. Tucker tucked his gun under the bed, fully loaded and within quick reach.

"Can I ask one question?" Emma whispered. "Just one and then I'll go back to sleep."

"It's late, hon. How about in the morning. You can ask as many as you like then."

"Just one," she insisted. "It's been on my mind a lot lately and I need to ask you."

"Okay, honey. One question, one answer, then sleep."

"Okay," Emma said, then for a moment fell silent. She exhaled and as she was about to speak, she broke down into wracking sobs. Uncontrollably she wept into his shoulder.

"Let it all out. Being afraid is normal," Tucker reminded her.

"But," Emma said and fought the urge to continue sobbing.

"Fear always comes with uncertainty and the inability to control things. You have to trust me. I got this. I'm certain this will all end sooner than later."

"But that doesn't answer my question."

"Then what, Emma. What's on your mind?"

"Emma wiped the tears that were streaming her cheeks with the sheet. "What if he had kidnapped me that day," she coughed. "What would he have done to me then?"

Tucker swallowed the last bit of saliva that was in his dry mouth. "Nothing," he forced out. "I'd never let anything happen to you, hon. Like I said, trust me and you'll see. You're safe now."

Emma continued to sob into Tucker's shoulder and by the time the house had creaked enough to jog Tucker's nerves, Emma had already drifted back to sleep. He kissed her on the forehead. "Goodnight, honey," he whispered. "I love you."

60

Tucker had been asleep only twenty minutes when Emma shook him. "I keep hearing her scream," she whispered. "It's all I hear."

Tucker reached over to the table and twisted on the lamp. He rolled onto his left side and slid in closer to stare her in the eye. He brushed her hair lightly away from her face, registered the anxiety and concern.

"It's just a nightmare, honey... It'll pass."

"All I hear is Lillie screaming."

"It's normal," he swore. "It will heal in time."

"You keep saying everything is normal, Tucker. But what's normal about any of this? I don't know anybody who's gone through what we've gone through... Nobody."

"That may be true, hon. But life has a funny way of dealing the cards. Some people have it far worse than us."

"I don't know any of those people," Emma repeated. "Why us? Why do we have to live like this? I mean we're not even in our own home. We hardly know the Sinagras and here we are sleeping over like family."

"We'll get our own place again. This is all temporary. I promised you that."

"I know," Emma mumbled. "It was a nightmare and I guess I should be expecting them."

"No use worrying about the things you can't control."

"...Did you get nightmares after Tommy died?"

Tucker felt a lump in his throat. "I did, but when I woke up at night in panic, I forced myself to get back to bed. But—"

"It's late and you don't want to talk about it. I understand," she said, nodding. "Forget I mentioned him."

He kissed her tenderly on the cheek. "We got through the tough stuff—all those nightmares about your abusive ex husband. We'll get through this, too."

"Up until now, I thought that was the hardest part of my life," she said. "Having that man smack me and shove me to the ground, and when I got up he'd punch my face so hard, I'd rather've been dead than live another day with him."

"I know," Tucker said. "But calm down. Those days are behind us now. This too shall pass."

Emma rubbed the scarring on her arm. "I've got this scar to constantly remind me of my ex and yet when I'm with you, I never think about it."

"It'll all pass."

"I know," Emma said, then gasped, "Oh, no, Tucker! I just heard the scream again." She nervously looked up at the ceiling, then back at her husband. "I'm scared."

"Trust me, honey. You'll be fine."

In a nervous attempt, Emma pulled the bedding up to her neck and knotted her fists into the fabric. "What is it you did when you felt like this?"

Tucker moved in closer, his lips within inches of her lips. "I try my dang hardest," he whispered. "I try everything to avoid those thoughts, that's what."

"I know, but I've tried, and it's all I think about."

"Then change your thinking. That's what I do. It's all you can."

Her speckled brown eyes fluttered up from the pillow. She admired her husband, who was now softly rubbing her temples. "What do you think about?" she asked.

"When I'm feeling that deep despair, that bottomless hurt, I think about you."

"Me?"

"It works." He grinned. "It wipes out my sorrow every time. Like clockwork."

"What is it that you think about?"

"Well, take before for instance. We were looking through the butcher shop, and my mind started to fill with pity for Dominic and Lillie and for our situation. I felt like breaking down right there."

"You?" Emma asked softly. "You were crying?"

"I didn't say that, baby."

"But you felt it," she concluded, surprised. "You felt like crying?"

"It's normal to feel that way."

"Again with the normal theory... But it hurts badly," Emma shivered. "It's horrible."

"Yeah, and it cuts deep," Tucker said. "That's all to be expected. But the trick is not letting it get to that point."

A vision of Dominic and Lillie flashed through Emma's mind, and she heard Lillie's horrid scream. "Oh, my." She trembled. "I can't get it off my mind. What was it you thought of that helped?"

"That's what I'm getting at," Tucker continued, stroking her temples. "I pictured what our kids will look like, and how I hoped they'd get this pretty nose of yours." He touched her nose with his index finger. "Yesterday I envisioned you in the kitchen, and our unborn child pulling at your apron. How he'd call you Momma, and how you would pick him up and he'd smile."

Emma's left eye glittered with a tear. "In Buffalo. Is that where you dreamt it?"

"I don't know if I actually gave it that much thought." Tucker smiled. "It was a kitchen somewhere, and out the window was a rolling hill with green grass and some trees and lots of open space. If that's what Buffalo is like, then maybe that's it."

"Yes, that's it."

"Maybe unconsciously I was thinking of Buffalo." He winked. "But I've never been there. How would I know what it looked like?"

"Some things you just know." She returned the smile. "We need to leave."

"I know, Emma."

"Now."

"Huh?"

"Let's gather the little stuff we have and leave this town right now." There was excitement in her voice.

Tucker pointed to the window. "There's a cold moon and a dark gray sky out there now."

"So what?" Emma said nervously. "Let's leave. I just want

to get out of this town and move on with our lives. I want that child pulling on my apron. I can feel the weight of him in my arms and the softness of his skin. We'll name him 'Tucker.'"

"What's if he's a she?"

"Then we'll name her Rose, after my grandmother. If that's okay with you."

"Rose it is." Tucker wiped the tears from her cheeks. "That's a beautiful name."

"She's going to grow up to be somebody. I know it."

"If she's anything like her mother, she'll be perfect."

Emma kissed him and hugged him. In his ear she whispered, "So are we leaving now?"

"You know the answer to that."

"But...."

"We're leaving soon, and you're safe now. Henderson needs me. I can't run out on him."

"Okay," Emma said. "But promise me this—when we get to Buffalo, you find a different job. No more cop business."

"Why?"

"Because I worry too much about you."

"I couldn't promise you that, honey."

"It means that much to you, huh?" She pressed the palm of her hands against his cheeks and gazed deeply into his eyes. "Does it mean more to you than me?"

"Nothing in this world means more to me than you. You're safe here."

She fell silent.

"But I will say this, if it'll put your mind at ease. When we get to Buffalo, I'll look for carpentry work."

"Perfect," Emma exclaimed. "...And you were right."

"What?"

"Since my mind is occupied with you and me living in Buffalo and that beautiful face of our unborn child and our happy family, the screaming's stopped. I can't believe it stopped."

"See? Changing your thinking is all you ever need to do."

"I love you, Tucker."

"I love you, too." He leaned over and twisted the light off. The room grew dark, the only light now peering beneath the door from the hallway. Somebody had gotten up. "I've got to be up in a few hours. Tomorrow's going to be another busy day," he said, adjusting himself back into the bed. He pulled the bedding up to his neck and let his shoulders sink into the mattress. "If you need me, wake me up and we'll talk about it."

She spooned herself to him. "If I need you, I'll change my thinking."

61

Tucker, Henderson, and Dankert got to the butcher's house shortly after six in the morning. It was still dark. With only a few hours of sleep, Tucker was still rubbing his itching eyes. "I checked the house and everything surrounding it," he said. "He's not here."

The three men stood out front, exhausted. Henderson in a pair of blue jeans and red-and-black checkered button-down shirt rolled his sleeves up and ran the palm of his hand across his forehead. He felt the warmth of his skin and wondered if he was getting a fever. He'd known a shot of whiskey would knock out any cold, flu, or fever. But if his temperature climbed more by lunch time, he'd take an aspirin or some syrup. He was doing everything he could to stay away from the booze. When his hand trembled like a raging earthquake, he'd force his other hand to hold it steady. So what, he thought. If I catch a fever, it'll pass.

Henderson looked at his men. Dankert stood there towering in a pair of blue jeans and white shirt with the Palisades Park Arrows logo on the front. On the back was a big black number three. Tucker commented on it. "You play ball for that club?"

"I did," Dankert said. "I still do when they need somebody to fill in."

"Those digs are too big for you," Dankert noticed Tucker'd wrenched the belt around the waist to hold up his blue jeans; his forest green short sleeve shirt covered his elbow. "Where'd you find those?"

"Dominic," Tucker frowned.

"Let's not waste time," Henderson said. "In an hour, I want all patrols actively looking for him."

"Water, Chief?" Dankert said, stretching out his Thermos. "You want a drink before we start?"

Henderson shook his head. "Not water, Dankert. Hand me that other Thermos. The red one in that bucket."

Tucker brow's furrowed, but before he could speak, Henderson injected, "Coffee, Tucker. You want a sip of coffee?"

"Coffee?" Tucker asked.

"Yeah, coffee," Henderson repeated. "It'll give you a boost. And God knows we'll need all the energy we can muster up for the dig."

Thinking about how close he'd come to falsely accusing the chief of failing his sobriety, he smiled inwardly. "Okay, I'll have a sip of that."

Henderson spun out the Thermos plug and poured the fresh coffee into the lid. The smell of coffee permeated the thin crisp morning air. Two robins had flown through the yard and perched on the edge of the garage, looking down at the men like inspectors.

Henderson handed Tucker the lid full of lukewarm coffee. He sipped it and offered it to Dankert.

"Not me," Dankert shook his head. "I'm not in the mood for that shit."

"Suit yourself," Tucker muttered and in one long swallow, finished what was left in the lid, then affixed it back on the thermos and tossed it into Henderson's bucket that also held gardening hand trowels and hand cultivators.

"Hang on," Henderson said. "I'll have the neighbor sit on his front porch and if he sees anybody coming up the roadway, he'll blow this whistle." Henderson fished a chrome whistle from his front pocket. "Be right back."

Henderson slipped through an opening in the neighbor's fence.

"But wouldn't the neighbor be friends with the butcher?" Tucker asked Dankert. "Could he have some sort of twisted allegiance to him?"

"No way," Dankert assured. "Warren's a good man. He'll do as he's told."

Moments later, Henderson returned into the butcher's backyard. The sun had come up clear and hot when the men began shoveling the loose dirt to reveal whatever was buried in that crude grave. The land was quiet, save for the robins that were now perched along a brown tractor rusting away in a far corner. A few sparrows had come and were splashing around in the dirty water of an old white stone bird bath, too. A dilapidated garage that was leaning to the south had side planks missing where lots of rusted gardening tools hung above a ten-foot wooden ladder that lay fixed horizontally. In prior years, the garage had been a small barn used for stacking hay and feed; its original red paint, much faded, was still visible. The name Fitzgerald, painted in a dull white above the large double doors, was washed out too and barely legible.

Tucker dug the rounded edged steel shovel into the dirt and, forty minutes later, was waist deep in the hole when he came across the body. It was mushy when the shovel end cut into the fleshy thigh. "Hang on, Tucker," Dankert said to him. "Toss that shovel out. We need to finish carefully. Here take this hand cultivator."

Tucker retrieved the hand cultivator, and Dankert laid his shovel on the edge of the grave. They began gingerly scraping around the contour of the corpse. The body was lying supine, partially decayed, the flesh blue and green and black. Flies buzzed around the body, doing the work of the flies. The men swatted at them.

What struck Tucker was the face, turned a charcoal black, that had swelled to the size of a pumpkin. The maggots were swarming all over it, making it difficult to identify.

"We have to hurry with these damn flies and maggots," Tucker said. "I never cared for them during the war and don't care for em now."

Henderson and Dankert, too, had seen their share of maggots and flies. Whether down in Cuba during Henderson's time or far across the ocean in France where Dankert fought gallantly and thanked his lucky stars each day that he didn't come home in a box or with any of his limbs missing. They had known plenty of men who suffered that fate. Yep, all three of them had seen their share of maggots on dead comrades and enemies. And seeing those maggots on the corpse below their feet had churned up a lot of old memories. Memories of bolt-action rifles with bayonets and how many times it typically took to violently jab that bayonet into the enemy's trunk so that he'd stay down and couldn't reach for a gun and take your head off. Five. Five jabs usually did it.

Seeing those swarming maggots had brought on a somber silence.

In an effort to lighten up the mood, Dankert smirked, "If the little bit of money I've got grew at the exponential rate of these maggots, I'd be like one of those big steel Tycoons. In no time, I'd be richer than Andrew Carnegie ever was."

Neither Henderson nor Tucker responded.

"I get it," Dankert said aloud. "Forget my lousy attempt at a little humor. You guys are tighter than bark on a tree."

Henderson grew irritable. "The quicker we get this done, the faster we get the heck out of here," he said sternly.

The morning heat only made the smell worse. As they removed the dirt they noticed long, brittle hair. There were no noticeable wounds. There was dirt pressed between the slim fingers and fingernails still covered with a reddish nail polish that had lost its luster.

"Look at her neck," Dankert, now serious, said, pointing. "See that hand print? How the killer's fingers left an impression? He suffocated her to death."

"Good," Henderson said from above. "Let's get her on the board and close this hole up."

Tucker nodded; the police badge hanging from his neck was dripping sweat and the sun glittered from it. He shook his head to shake off the sweat that burned his eyes.

"Who's the bitch?" Henderson sneered. "It's hard to tell. Take this plywood, and let's hoist her ass out."

"Bitch?" Tucker considered.

"Cut the shit, Tucker. Take this plywood, and let's get out of here."

"Okay, wait. First I have to clear more dirt."

"The maggots ain't gonna wait for you," Henderson reminded him.

Tucker retrieved his shovel and began to open the excavation enough to allow for the board to be lowered into it.

He heard a thumping sound. He poked at it, and it thumped again with a hollow resonance. "Something here."

62

The horrid smell had become so potent that the neighbor's wife closed her rear door and the double hung windows. From an elevated view of the yard, the neighbor's wife observed the gravesite, the rotting body and gasped, covering her mouth with her hand. She hurried the curtains closed.

The men, drenched in sweat had realized the odor clung to them like an unwanted second skin. They'd have to wash before wearing their uniforms and starting patrol. The idea of sitting in those clothes in a hot car all day could make any man feel uneasy.

"What is it?" Dankert asked, wiping the sweat that was dripping from his forehead into his eyes. "Dig it out," he said.

Tucker clawed around the edges. "It's a wooden box of some sort. It's not that big."

"What's in it? Send that shit up," Henderson said from the grave's edge.

Tucker did so and climbed out of the grave. He brushed the dirt from his palms on his jeans and was about to wipe his forehead with his hand, but thought better and slid his chin into his collar and brushed back and forth to allow the cotton to absorb the sweat faster. But it was useless. His shirt was already drenched. The sweat formed a U pattern on the front and back that was slowly reaching the top of his pants.

"Well, open it up, son," Henderson said. "Go ahead."

Tucker broke the tarnished brass clasp and lifted the lid.

"Well what is it?" Henderson wanted to know.

With a suspicious look, Tucker offered, "It's bones of some sort."

"What?"

"Clean bones is all, Chief."

"Human bones?" Dankert lifted himself out of the hole. "What's it, a skull?"

Henderson had meanwhile taken the box from Tucker.

A whistle blasted and a vehicle clanged, and Tucker glanced out at the roadway. A white bread-delivery truck rushed passed, a tailwind of dust trailed it. Satisfied it was no threat, he resumed scrutinizing. "No," he said, "but whatever it is, it's been dead a while," he said.

"That's obvious, son," Henderson muttered, plucking a pair of spectacles from his breast pocket. He pressed them to the bridge of his nose and examined the bones. "Small dog, maybe?"

"Maybe a cat?" Dankert said.

"Possum?" Tucker suggested.

"Why would he bury a possum?" Dankert fished a pack of smokes from his dirty pants pockets. He lit the smoke and let out a slow drag. The cigarette smoke helped cut some of the horrid smell. Noticing that, he blew the smoke all around them.

"Beats me." Henderson swatted at the flies that continued swarming in drones over the grave.

"The more I look at it," Tucker said, "the more it looks like a cat or a small dog." He felt the loose teeth inside the tiny grayish jaw. The sharp point of the fangs made a dimple in his index finger. "Cat is what I say."

"He has enough compassion to bury a cat?" Dankert placed his hand on the chief's shoulder. "Why not just toss it in the garbage?"

Henderson closed the box and tossed it back into the grave. The lid popped off and the cat's bones spilled out. "Who gives a shit. The man's a loon."

"That's the truth," Dankert agreed. "Never know what goes on inside one's mind."

"And that ain't the half of it," Henderson said. "I think I still got the newspaper on my desk. It had the obituary in it."

"What obituary?" Tucker asked. "For the cat?"

"No, Tucker," Henderson smirked.

Tucker shook his head, embarrassed. "The heat must be getting to me."

"The dead woman." Henderson pointed to the corpse.

"This is his mother."

With a confused look, Tucker said: "How can you be certain?"

Henderson nodded. "I thought it was old lady Stillman, but nope, it's his mother."

"How are you sure?"

"Call it lots of investigative experience."

"But, Chief," Tucker allowed. "The face is rotted away. It—it could be anybody."

"It's his mother."

"It's the long hair, huh?"

"Nope." Henderson repositioned the long piece of narrow plywood in the grave. "Get back in there, fellers."

Tucker and Dankert did so.

"What makes you so certain?" Tucker called up to Henderson.

"The obituary was for his mother, and it was two months ago."

Tucker angled the plywood along the corpse. "She ain't been dead that long."

Dankert interrupted. "I read the paper every day, and I haven't seen that obituary for Mrs. Fitzgerald."

"It wasn't in our paper," Henderson spat. "News of our troubled town got around and a resident from the Poconos mailed me this obituary. It was in the Pocono Daily. The resident found it odd, because she'd received a birthday card from the dead woman. It was postmarked a month after she was supposedly dead. The resident sent another letter and never got a response, so she mailed me the obituary. I received it yesterday."

"And how does the butcher's mom know this Pennsylvania woman?"

"The Fitzgeralds own a house up there. Apparently Mrs. Fitzgerald and this woman are friends."

Feeling a chill in his belly, Tucker said: "It's all premeditated, huh?"

"Something is," Henderson muttered.

Tucker positioned the corpse's neck and shoulders on

the plywood. So close to the body the smell was thicker, and when the old lady's blotchy leg brushed against his forearm, a squirmy feeling raced through him. He quickly scrubbed his arms on his jeans. "Any other people show up in the paper you can't confirm died?"

Henderson thumbed his chin. "Not that I can recall off the top of my head."

"Nothing," Tucker asked.

"Nothing," Henderson repeated.

"How about that date? The one he wrote on the wall in blood. That has something to do with all this."

"I still haven't figured the connection for that," Henderson lied.

"Well," Tucker said.

"Well what?" Henderson scoffed.

Tucker lifted both ankles and moved the lower portion of the corpse onto the plywood. The flies were biting at his skin. He wanted to ask Henderson why, if it was true, he was concealing that he had killed the butcher's father. Tucker and Dankert had both read the same letter he did from Burgess to the butcher and it clearly claimed Henderson had done it. But why? Tucker thought. Why not discuss that accusation? Why not fess up? But something about Henderson being the chief and he a patrolman kept him quiet at that moment. Instead he said, "I'm working up an appetite."

Henderson bent down from above and stretched out his hands. "Come on. We don't have all day."

"Let's send a letter to the papers and find out if they have anything for that date," Tucker suggested.

"I've already done that," Henderson lied again. "I called a friend of mine who works for *The Times*. He couldn't find any significance involving that date."

Tucker fell silent.

"Okay, Chief," Dankert said. "We're ready."

Henderson reached further down and clamped his massive fingers on the plywood. "On the count of three," he said.

Forty minutes later, the butcher's mother and her cat were reburied.

63

The shadows were growing long when Tucker shut off the cruiser and entered the police station. It had been an uneventful afternoon. Not a single call, other than from the Hackensack Police who reported that a colored man had stolen the purse of a woman and was last seen boarding a trolley headed for Palisades Park. Hackensack police said it was possible he was heading for Edgewater to board the 125th Street Ferry to New York City. Tucker had checked the Morsemere section of the town and a few passing trolleys before phoning Hackensack and letting them know the man was not found. What would he have done if he found and arrested him? A woman would get her purse back while the butcher killed somebody? It just didn't add up. Tucker was glad he hadn't seen even a single colored man fitting the description.

In the hallway, Dankert was approaching. He tossed him the car keys. "Tank's full... How'd you sleep this afternoon?"

"Got four hours after lunch... Four solid hours."

"I bet you had a decent bath and that helped. I've been itching all day from those damn flies and maggots."

"You didn't wash?" Dankert asked astonished.

"I did but a smell that bad needs a longer bath and a lot more scrubbing. I was too much in a hurry."

"Oh," Dankert curled his lip. "Now you're making me itch."

"Hackensack was looking for a colored man earlier who stole a woman's purse. They said he was six foot tall with a medium build, black pants and white shirt, last seen boarding a trolley destined for Pal. Park."

"I could give a shit," Dankert said. He put the keys in his pants pocket; the silver buttons on his shirt were polished and gleaming brightly. His uniform was pressed and heavily starched. The big man looked good in it. His large frame and rounded chest were authoritative all by themselves, even without the gun on his hip. Tucker thought back to when he had been a cop in Colorado, and of a shorter cop named Macom who was famous for saying, "Size doesn't matter." He'd insist that not everybody respected the badge, but everyone respected the gun.

Dankert was holding his policeman's hat in his left hand. Tucker noticed a photo tucked into the inner rim. "Picture of the wife and kids, huh?"

"What?"

"In your hat. Picture of your wife and kids?"

"Oh, that." Dankert held up the hat. "They're everything to me."

"I know the feeling," Tucker said.

Dankert nodded.

"Aren't you concerned the butcher will do something to your family while you're working?"

"What for?" Dankert asked. "We don't know him like that."

"But you're helping us hunt him down and maybe in a sick sort of way he's got an ax to grind with you for that."

"I doubt it," Dankert responded. "But to play it safe, my brother and my brother-in-law are home the wife and kids."

"Smart move."

"Anything else going on around here?"

"Been a long day since we dug out the butcher's mother," Tucker said. "I checked his house and store at least forty times. Walked the property and noticed those orange Do Not Enter signs we glued in the door jambs. They're sealed tightly. No sign anybody was tampering with 'em. Even the hasps and padlocks appeared not to've been tampered with."

"Remind me," Dankert said. "Are you or the chief relieving me in the morning?"

"Me. I'll be back early."

"Good. Let the chief do what he needs to. He's been so irritated lately, it's hard to be in the same room with him."

"It's to be expected," Tucker nodded. "Say, did you ever work with his son, Freddy? I heard he wasn't a cop that long when he was killed."

"Long?" Dankert raised a brow. "Poor kid was still wet behind the ears. It was only a few weeks. Maybe a month tops."

The hallway shrank from the size of them. Tucker placed his policeman's bag on the floor along his right foot. "Was he a friendly kid or more like his old man?"

"You mean could the kid be nasty and callous like the chief?"

"You know what I mean," Tucker said. "Were they similar?"

"Well as they say the apple don't fall far from the tree. Only difference I could tell was that the kid was a bit naïve. But then again maybe all kids are like that when they're fresh out of high school."

"True, but life hardens everybody up at some point. Some younger than others."

"Poor kid didn't have enough time to get to that point. All he thought about was chasing that girl whose ex-boyfriend set himself on fire."

"Veronica, right?" Tucker offered. "The one chief met over at the doctor's office and then beat the dickens out of Doctor Anderson?"

"Yeah, her."

Tucker nodded. "Well, anyway, I'm beat."

"Go home and put your feet up. And get some rest—that is if you keep your hands off your bride," Dankert joked.

"I'm going to pass out as soon as I finish dinner. But hey a little romance is sometimes as good as a full night's rest," he winked.

Dankert headed for the door. He paused and glanced around. "If he's around here, I'm going to put him down before he gets a chance at us," he said in a low voice. "Give the bastard what he deserves."

"Just make sure it's legal. No need to deal with all that."

"Oh, I know what that's all about."

"I know," Tucker muttered. "Have you killed anybody since the war?"

"No."

"Lucky you," Tucker said.

"Why, you have?"

"Botched robbery," Tucker said in a low tone. "And the guy

tried to kill me."

"He gave you no choice, huh?"

"That's right."

Dankert winked. "I'll make sure he'll give me no choice too."

Tucker returned the wink. "Have a good night, bud."

"You, too," Dankert said and disappeared out the front doorway. Tucker picked up his policeman's bag and let out a long breath. He thought back to the day he'd shot the robber in Colorado. It was windy and the rain was slanting on him. His uniform was soaked, his brows drenched. He wiped away the rain from his face and demanded the man drop the gun. But the man hadn't and by the time he would have gotten off a shot, Tucker fired twice in rapid succession and dropped him into a shallow puddle. Tucker recalled how the man's blood seeped into the puddle and mixed with the oil from the roadway. In his mind's eye, he envisioned the man's long mustache and how the rain dripped from its tip and onto his shirt collar. Had Tucker's reflexes been a second slower, he'd've been the one dying in the puddle.

Tucker heard the door on the patrol car slam and then the engine crank. He shook off the reflection and headed for his locker. It was a long day and he craved a hot meal and the softness of Emma.

64

Tucker opened his locker, tossed his policeman's bag into it, and began undressing, hanging his tie from the edge of the door and his uniform shirt from a hanger on the wall. The locker was thin and not big enough to hold all his gear, so he used the wooden hooks fixed to the wall, and a coat-tree where a raincoat was hanging. They were all sharing the raincoat. Below the coat tree stood a large pair of fireman's boots for heavy storms and blizzards. There were also three heavy pairs of leather work gloves.

After changing, he brushed his hair back with the comb he kept in the rear pocket of his blue jeans. There was an old mirror on the wall next to the coat tree. It was foggy, dusty, and the corners were tarnished, but it was still good enough to see in. What he saw wasn't the reflection he was familiar with. He adjusted the collar on his white cotton undershirt and noticed the creases across his forehead, and how his hair had receded a bit; some grays seemed to have sprung up overnight. Years of stress that weren't evident from all the days he had fought in the Argonne had worn heavy on him. He looked closer, at the corners of his mouth and how they dipped into his chin, the sharp jaw line that was more pronounced since he lost weight. He was tired, the hours he had put in on the case taking their toll. He wondered why the locals hadn't stepped up. Other than Dankert and the Sinagras, people had their heads buried in the sand.

The office door with the frosted glass and the gold foil etching that read Chief of Police was creaked open. "Is that you, Tucker?" Henderson called into the hallway.

There was a fresh smell of coffee brewing.

Appearing in the doorway, Tucker said, "Yes, sir. I'm all finished for the day."

"Well, get in here and have a seat."

Tucker pushed the door open and sat in the chair across from the chief's desk. He leaned back and crossed his right leg over his left, feeling his hamstrings and lower back stretch. It was a feeling he wanted. He tapped his fingers on his leg and saw how the stacks of paper were piling higher as the days went by. A mug with steaming hot coffee sat on the desk next to tall stack of paper held down by a rock. As the fan swept a warm breeze over the stack, the papers buzzed lightly. It swept the aroma of coffee across the room. "Yes, Chief?"

"You want a mug of crushed beans? I just brewed 'em."

"No thank you."

"It'll make a man out of you."

"What's that supposed to mean?"

Henderson coughed on a mouthful of hot coffee. "I've been drinking it since I was a kid. It's the drink of the Gods."

"Coffee?" Tucker asked. "Now the Gods like coffee?"

"Yeah and it's good for you."

"No thanks," Tucker waived his hand dismissively. "I'm ready for bed and sometimes those beans get me jumping."

"Not me," Henderson countered. "I could pour it over ice, take it down in one swallow and fall asleep like a baby."

"Well, that's good, I guess. Considering you do drink a lot of it." Tucker wondered if he'd always been a high consumer of coffee or was it because he didn't have the booze and the coffee had a way of balancing his nerves. Tucker believed the latter.

Henderson began to read a document on his desk.

Sensing himself falling asleep, Tucker interrupted, "Chief, I know you didn't call me in her to talk about coffee. What's on your mind?"

Henderson removed his spectacles from his face and began toying with them in his fingers. "I think we've got something."

Tucker noticed the spectacles shaking excessively, the man's fingers trembling. When Henderson laced them behind his head, Tucker was surprised to see half moons of sweat under his armpits. He had thought that man was as cool as a block of pond ice.

"Everything okay, Chief?"

Henderson leaned in and placed his big elbows onto the desk. "If you must know, I'm shaking because I need a drink. My nerves are shot, and the nightmares are daunting."

"Maybe it's all that coffee you drink. Too much of anything is no good."

"It's the booze," Henderson assured. "Or lack of it that's causing all these crazy nightmares. Like take for example earlier. I fell asleep briefly and dreamt of a gray housecat the size of a mountain lion. It hurdled a fence and was striding toward me, digging its claws into the cobblestone, when I pulled out my gun and shot it, the damn cat broke up into a million pieces and disappeared into rays of white light. Next thing I knew I jolted out of this chair and almost lost a finger or two to the fan's blade."

"Maybe you dreamt that because of that cat we found buried earlier?"

"Not sure," Henderson said. "Very strange."

"I know the feeling, Chief. I've had a few menacing ones myself."

"It's different. For whatever reason, when you quit drinking cold turkey you get these uncontrollable nightmares. I don't know why it happens, but it does."

"Beats me," Tucker said.

"Okay forget my crazy dreams for now," Henderson shook his head thinking back to his dream. "I still can't believe the size of that house cat. What a sight."

"So what is you want to discuss, boss?"

Henderson picked up a cream-colored envelope with writing on it in black ink and placed it on the desk. "Before we discuss this, I've been meaning to ask you about the wife. Is she starting to feel better?" There was genuine concern in his voice.

"Time is healing some things. But she's still frightened to death. I was lying next to her last night, and all she kept mumbling was how she'd heard Lillie scream and how she'd barely escaped."

"That's a lot to deal with."

"Yeah, it seems that every waking second she keeps asking me the same question."

"What's that?" Henderson asked.

"Wants to know when we're leaving," Tucker sighed.

"You running out early on me, or what?"

"No, sir."

"Then I've got a better idea," Henderson said, putting the end of the ear stem of his spectacles to his lips. "This should help calm the old lady down a bit. You and Emma come live with me for a little while."

"We couldn't possibly impose."

"You're not... When I'm not home, you can watch 'em, and when I am, I'll watch 'em."

"...That's a safe idea."

"Well?"

Tucker thought for a second. "Okay," he said.

"And," Henderson said, and slid the envelope across the desk to Tucker. This here address is in Dingman's Ferry, Pennsylvania."

"Where's that?"

"It's where we're heading if I don't get answers."

"Is it far?"

"Far enough," Henderson said, and sipped his coffee. "First thing tomorrow. I'll put a call into the Pennsylvania State Police. I found the butcher's address. I need them to check."

65

The following day, the butcher awoke at four in the morning, way before the sun rose, and padded to his kitchen. He was enjoying the silence of the Pennsylvania countryside. He brewed a pot of coffee and soon found himself sitting at his desk in the large room with a blank piece of paper and pencil, sipping his coffee. Each day began sketching different ideas and scenarios. They all ended with Henderson lying dead on the ground and the butcher spitting on his remains. He wanted him dead. Badly. But it was the scenario he had written out the night before he liked the most. It included Emma, and it couldn't wait. He'd have to return to Palisades Park and do it that day.

Along the way down Route 15 through Sussex County, the butcher watched the sun rise from behind a long rolling hill where cows typically grazed. He saw men working in the sparse cornfields while the field boss, dressed in a red-and-black shirt and blue overalls, with a pot belly and a straggly beard, held the water can. He was well fed, and the butcher knew why. He wasn't like the men who lumbered to the tractor with their baskets of corn. Those men weren't men of conviction, weren't the type to throw down their baskets and cut their own way through life. It took a certain kind to be a field boss, especially if he was his own boss.

The butcher thought of Emma and grinned, both rows of teeth showing.

Around Lafayette, a small cowpoke township in western Jersey, he came to an intersection where a diminutive restaurant sat; ahead lay the Lafayette Post Office. He wheeled into the dirt parking lot and got out. Standing before the drop box, he kissed the envelope and tossed it in. In a few days, it should reach its addressee. As he was reentering the roadway, a man with a big green John Deer tractor chugged past towing a load of hay, the suspension creaking. The butcher nodded, and the man tipped his Stetson. There still are places of morals and values, he muttered to himself. It's the simple life that pays the most dividends.

The sun was higher, lighting the land with subtle hints of yellow and orange and blue, as he continued his journey. The crisp air had that fresh feeling. The early autumn leaves were already turning shades of yellow, orange, and brown.

An hour or so later, he passed Broad and West Kinney Street in Newark, and his face twisted into a grimace. So they're still holding up shop, the butcher muttered, looking at the Federal Enforcement agency that was too minuscule to handle the bootlegging problem but still felt they needed to maintain a presence. The butcher considered America's prohibition. The cops would arrest a bootlegger in the morning and he'd still have enough time to be back at work that night. The punishments were laughable when compared to the profits. Booze runners who got caught didn't seem to care. Once a man's criminal record was established, then what's the point in trying to keep it clean. They'd known the judges drank the illegal booze. The cops charged with arresting the bootleggers sipped from the same well of impurity. The problem was bigger than any agency of morality could ever fix. People wanted their booze and their disdain for the hypocrisy was apparent. Prohibition had done more for organized crime and men like the butcher looking to make a fast buck running the illegal booze, then any righteousness it sought. What a waste of money and effort, the butcher thought. All that money could have been spent to feed the poor, before they stood famished along the soup lines.

It was a little before eight in the morning; children were walking on the sidewalks with knapsacks on their backs, and in their arms some held books bound in leather straps. The city was bustling as commuters began their daily trek. He watched a colored man walking a menacing looking hound dog, beige with crimson spots. He knew why that man was on the corner. He was the lookout. The butcher motored past him through the Weequahic-Clinton area of the city. There were lots of residential houses behind whose doors were hidden inconspicuous boozeries and whoopee parlors. He glanced at a big red house with white shutters and recalled the young girl, a blotto blonde with curly locks who hung around the brew houses. When he'd had time to burn, he'd slip her a few drinks, get her juiced up, and take her for a short ride to the closest hotel for some romance. Hard and fast was what she liked. He considered knocking on the door and seeing if she was home. But he thought better of that idea and decided not to make too much noise. The fewer people who saw him, the better.

The home on Lehigh Avenue was surrounded by similar ones that all were involved with illegal booze. The owners were bootleggers who colored and bottled the alcohol in their residences. It was very different from the commercial loading docks, where he purchased the illegal booze on his runs. It was where the man he was paying a visit lived. He checked the block twice. No spotters or lookouts. No cops either.

He angled his vehicle next to the curb, killed the engine, and climbed out. His towering frame dwarfed the hood of the vehicle as he walked around it and rang the bell. He heard the chime and the faint echo it made in the hallway beyond the door. A boy raced by on a yellow bicycle with school books in a front basket fastened to the handlebars. A man in a suit with a black attaché case was kissing his wife, and an elderly woman was pushing a wired cart filled with produce. Save for them, the block was relatively quiet at that hour of the morning.

"Yes, sir, can I help you?" A woman in a beige nightgown had appeared in the door.

"Of course, ma'am." He smiled with a trusting smile. "Carlos asked that I drop him off some paper."

She rubbed her eyes and brushed the brown hair that had fallen over her forehead. "He works nights, and he's sleeping. Are you sure he's expecting you?"

"It's eight in the morning, and he asked that I be here with what he's expecting. I don't want to disappoint him, ma'am. We all know how temperamental he can get when somebody disobeys." He patted his breast pocket. "He's expecting this."

The woman gestured with her index finger. "Okay, let me

wake him. Give me a minute." She slipped back into the house.

The butcher whistled tonelessly, tapping his foot, and waited.

When the door creaked open again, a big Hispanic man was squinting in the sunlight, wiping the sleep from his eye. "Who the heck are you?" he spat.

"You asked me to come here, and then you play like you don't know me?"

The man was bigger than the butcher and had sharp features that were cold and hard. There was a tattoo that showed from the front collar on his white cotton shirt. He had big muscles and a neck as wide as telephone pole. He was built solid, the mob's hard-boiled torpedo. "Big Los," they called him. "I asked you a question," he said. "Who are you?"

Looking up from the bottom of the three concrete cement steps that made the man seem taller and bigger, the butcher said, "I'm nobody." He pressed a cigarette to his lips, reached into his breast pocket, and pulled out his revolver, firing two quick shots in rapid succession. The man's eyes flared wide as the slugs struck him in both knee caps and the dark blood started seeping through his pants. He tried to hold onto the door jamb, then felt the holes in his knees, saw the blood on his fingertips, and gasped. His face went pale and he fell face first down the steps, like a tall pine, to the butcher's feet.

"You frigging knee-capped me, asshole," the man seethed trying to reach for the butcher.

"Who am I," the butcher said sneering. "I'm a friend of Roger. Maybe you know him... You should. You've cost me a lot of money." He noticed the man grit his teeth and try to stand to lunge at him. But the bullets had taken out his legs and he fell back onto the sidewalk. "Next time you go breaking somebody's legs, asshole, make sure he ain't got a friend like me," the butcher struck a match on the bricks of a small neighboring wall that separated the street from the front garden. He lit his cigarette and took a long drag. He exhaled into the morning air. "Enjoy your wheelchair."

66

The butcher left Newark and, later that afternoon, drove into Palisades Park. He slanted his car facing north at the intersection of First Street and Central Boulevard. There was a huge church on the corner and a school directly across from it. The school bell rang loudly and it brought the butcher's attention to it. He cranked down the window and angled himself out the driver's window. He glanced up at his old school, three stories tall and two buildings wide. Central Boulevard School is what they called it. He was staring at the top floor of the second building, now built over thirty years prior. All those hot days he baked inside Mrs. Brown's classroom, longing for summer recess, longing for time on the diamond.

He briefly thought back to the summer after finishing fifth grade. He'd practice at the baseball field from sunup to sundown. Working on his pitching and batting form. Getting whatever advice he could from the local men who played for the Palisades Park Arrows. He'd serve as their batboy, water-boy, and scorekeeper. Whatever it took to stay involved. To be a part of something.

The distant sound of a train's whistle shook him from his reverie. Then he recalled something recent. He grinned when he thought about a memorable day a few years ago when his small town found notoriety for their semiprofessional sports teams. Truth be told, that special day came one afternoon at the baseball fiedl when Columbia University graduate and later Yankee star Lou Gehrig hammered a majestic shot over the centerfield as a member of Everett Millet's All-Collegians against those same Palisades Park Arrows who taught the butcher how to respect the game.

The sky went from a dull white like the blindness in a man's eyes, to a savage red, like the blood of a man's body to eventually a soft pink and then to dark purple, like a priest's robes. It was hot and the long drought was starving the earth and the sky. The crisp air he earlier enjoyed in the mountains of Pennsylvania had become a distant memory.

As the sky grew darker, Tucker could see the clouds moving quickly and the sun light slanting through in the distance. It wouldn't be too long before the sun baked the land again.

The butcher readjusted himself in the driver's seat and stared over the steering wheel. There was determination on his expression. He watched down the roadway toward the main avenue. From that position, he could see Henderson's police cruiser, and when he caught him wheeling out he'd be able to follow without being detected. He sat there sucking on a tooth. Patience, he reminded himself.

He was yawning when, nearly twenty minutes later, Henderson appeared outside the police station and mounted his vehicle. The butcher slid slowly away from the curb. From his position, he'd have to go around the block to follow his prey—the only problem being, if Henderson was traveling in his direction, he might spot him. So he paused like a cheetah in the brush stalking the unsuspecting gazelle drinking from the watering hole, and when Henderson went down the hill toward the railroad, he reversed and, from a comfortable distance, paced him. He followed him past the Heisenbuttle Hotel and to the train depot, which was a thirty foot A-framed roof that covered half the platform and had an office where tickets could be purchased. On top of the train depot was small steeple with a weather-vane. Older billboards for real estate developers and special events were hung on the exterior walls. Henderson parked his cruiser by the platform and got out with a hammer in one hand and small piece of plywood tucked under his arm.

Fearing he'd be detected, Michael hid his vehicle at the rear of an industrial building. He slithered out and sought cover behind a shed along the tracks that the post office used to store mail. He was close, well within earshot of Henderson, and his heart began racing. He heard the smacking of the hammer as Henderson continued nailing the board into the side of the train depot. The train whistle blasted, and it became visible in the distance, the chattering and clanging of the rails and the squeal of brakes breaking the early-afternoon stillness.

Henderson drew the sea of people who disembarked from the train. "Gather round, folks," he called to them. "I have a matter of great importance to discuss with you."

They began to congregate in a half circle around Henderson's posting. They were covered by the roof of the train depot. A man was pulling at the leash on his dog, who'd dug his paws into the dirt and made it difficult for the man to drag him closer. "He's shy around people," the man said. "He's still a puppy."

A teenage boy in blue overalls glanced down at the dog and smiled. "Golden Labs are cute," he said.

"Yes, Chief," the man dragging his dog said. "What is that you're posting?"

"You see here?" Henderson said. "This is Michael Fitzgerald." He placed his finger on the poster, tracing the word WANTED. "He owns the butcher shop on Broad Avenue by the Betty Lee."

"I know who he is," said a woman in red slip dress.

"That's cause you used to neck with him, Becca," a man in suspenders snickered.

"It's not true," the woman said. "I know which men to stay away from around here, and you Allen, you're on that list."

Henderson nodded. "Yes, some of you may know him. But hear me now, and hear me good. This man is a sick man who's killed innocent people. A coward."

"Is he still around?" an elderly man wanted to know. "I haven't seen him in a while. The window sill at his shop has a layer of dust at least an inch or so thick. He's always been meticulous about cleaning."

"I haven't seen him either, sir. But that's what I need from you. If anybody sees him, you report to me right away."

The congregation began chattering. "Is it true, Chief? Did he kill Dominic and Lillie Garrett?" asked the woman in the red slip dress. "...Are we safe?"

Henderson nodded. "You're safe, Becca. But I'd be lying if I told you he didn't kill those nice folks."

The woman shook her head. "When you get him, you see to it he's put to death."

Henderson nodded gravely.

The train embarked north along the rails. A stray brown dog approached. An elderly woman with graying hair began gently petting him. "Easy, boy," she whispered.

"Thank you," Henderson said, tipping his hat to the crowd. "You see him, you call right away now, you hear? Time is always of the essence."

With his back against the white wooden paneling on the mail shed, the butcher became enraged. Coward, huh? He heard the word again in his mind and clenched a fist. "I'll show him coward, he whispered softly. "We'll see if that word crosses those lying lips when I'm done with him... And what's with Becca? I give it to her all good like the way she likes it and now she wants me put to death. We'll see about that."

67

"With all that's going on," Tucker said to Henderson, "I need a couple hours with the wife to vent."

"Have fun, kids," Henderson said winking. "Don't be night owls, now. I expect you home before ten."

Tucker grinned. "Sure, Dad," he said, smiling. "Thanks again for allowing us to stay with you." He closed Henderson's house door. Tucker glanced out at the street and saw the spot where the butcher had parked that night he tried to kidnap the chief's son. He saw how the reeds and bulrushes and the creek were in the distance across the street. And it reminded him of how close he had come to getting him. He felt the guilt of his failure and knew that the only way for him to overcome that feeling was to put the man away for good. They stood on the porch and let the evening air fill their lungs. It was breezier than usual and the September sun had scorched them earlier in the day. It was setting now and offering some mercy. It was still hot, but far from unforgiving hot.

Tucker and Emma paused briefly and saw north down the roadway how the shell of a barn lay wasted with rotting farm equipment in a lengthy tract of land that stretched as far wide as the eye could see. The land forgotten like the farmers and tradesman that once flourished. Palisades Park was changing. There were taller structures farther ahead where the train depot sat among them. They were in the immediate area of King's Highway, now called Grand Avenue, a roadway that spawned the settlement along it. But tonight they were headed to the Park Lane Theatre located east up the hill in the developing section of the town.

"They've been very good to us," Emma said gratefully. "Who knew the cop we saw choking that guy on the street on the first day we got here could be like this?"

"Yeah, he's got a good side to him." Tucker held Emma's

hand. "You looking forward to the movie, honey?"

"You don't have to do this, Tucker. I know you're busy with work, and I don't want to be in the way."

"Nonsense, honey. I suggested a few hours of escape to the chief, and he welcomed the idea."

They walked out of Henderson's yard and passed the row of hedges that trimmed his sidewalk.

"If it's okay with the chief," Emma said, "then we better take advantage of the recess."

Dankert was motoring north on Grand Avenue when Tucker and Emma crossed the street. He tooted the horn on the police cruiser, and they exchanged a wave. Tucker appreciated the extra help Dankert's re-employment allowed.

If not for him, Tucker would have been out there patrolling. But the moment wasn't about the police department or the tragedy that'd plagued the small town. That's right: It was about her. It was to help relieve her mind. To show her that even with all the hurt, they could still have good times.

She clenched his hand tightly. "Remember back home when we went out one Saturday night and stopped in a roadhouse along that barren roadway deep in the Colorado countryside?"

"Which time was that?"

"You know."

"I don't recall."

"It'll come to you."

"I am not sure, Emma. My mind is slow processing memory lately," Tucker smiled.

"Come on," Emma lightly elbowed him in the bicep. "Remember the night we were minding our business when that man with that hot-tempered Indian blood challenged you to a game of pool?"

"Yeah," Tucker recalled. "The big Indian—how could I forget? With those deep, dark features, and that long ponytail. He slid a dollar onto our pool table and said, 'Challenge.' I threw down another two bucks and said, 'Best of three.'"

Emma grinned. "You should've seen his expression when you took his mark and upped the ante. He swallowed a glass of moonshine and was measuring you. But you weren't even the slightest bit nervous. That's one of the things I love about you."

"How about my skills? My game? Remember how, during that first match, I fudged a few balls, threw out those curious faces, and over-measured each shot, making it look like I had beginner's luck? It came down to a single shot, which I missed and let him win."

"Of course," Emma said. "But it's not the game I'm talking about."

"Well, anyway, that Indian thought he had me. He walked around the table, planted the butt of his stick in front of me, and said, 'Let's double the money, and whaddaya say the winner gets the lady?'"

"Yes, that's what I'm getting at, honey... He curled a finger to an attractive woman sitting on a corner stool. She sidled over in that tight pink dress, curves as sharp as a razor's edge, and the Indian wanted to trade her for me if he won. And when you hit him in the mouth, I knew then and there that I'd made the right choice marrying you."

"Nobody's going to suggest anything like that about you to me."

"That's what made the rest of our date so memorable. It was the passion and intensity that followed that I remember mostly. You remember how we slept that night under the big sky and bright stars, kissing and doing what lovers do on that blanket?"

"How could I forget?" he said somberly. "It was the night we conceived... well, I guess there's no need to discuss that."

"No, honey, don't get grieved about that," Emma insisted. "If God wanted us to have that child, I wouldn't've had that miscarriage."

"But—"

"No, Tucker, I won't allow any sulking from you. Not tonight. Not when the first night alone with you has me this excited." She kissed him on the lips. "Maybe we can find a comfy place along the Overpeck later."

"You? You'll go to the bank of the creek during darkness?"

"I'd go anywhere with you."

68

A block away from the theatre, they saw how the building dominated the landscape ahead. The sun was casting a low orange glow as it sank into the earth. Ten minutes or so and the squirrels and birds would trade places with the raccoons and opossums. It'd become time for the night critters to ravage through the residential garbage cans and piles of waste the restaurants tossed out back in the alley.

A housewife with a blue apron with white trim and a cautious smile, exited her front door and twisted on a lamp on the porch. Its bulb was barely luminous in the twilight.

"To think just over ten years ago and these people didn't even have a police force to protect them."

Emma thought about that. "They'd have to protect themselves, right?"

"Yeah but they'd already forgotten how," Tucker said. "Now they expect the police for everything."

Emma raised a brow. "The more I learn about this town, I'm starting to think in some way or another everybody's related."

"Chief said all those Italians on the hill are all related."

"Small towns," Emma smirked. "I hope Buffalo is big enough for some anonymity."

"Me too," Tucker said thinking about the prospect of an intimate night with his wife, Tucker looked her up and down. "Those glad rags fit fine," he suggested, feeling the fabric on the green dress she wore. It was tight and Emma's long, sleek gams were exposed. "Honey." He kissed her on the cheek as they stood outside the Park Lane Theatre, which was featuring Today We Live, with actor Gary Cooper and actress Joan Crawford.

"This picture is about the war?" Emma asked.

"I think it's a wartime romance. You should like it."

"I know you'll like it."

"Why's that?"

"You like all of Gary Cooper's pictures."

"He's good at what he does," Tucker assured. "Nobody can argue that."

There was a small crowd in the hallway as they entered and purchased their tickets. Typically, smaller crowds foretold the quality of the picture. But this wasn't the case. A year prior on a night like tonight, the Park Lane Theatre sold about four hundred tickets and lots of confections, but the impoverished state of the economy coupled with the frightened townspeople, had quelled the business. Half the seats would fill up with penurious people who avoided the concession stand. The smell of popcorn lay heavy in the air. It wasn't the ambiance that had them beaming. It was the love they shared and how it went a long way after all the heartache.

He approached the concession counter still holding Emma's hand. "A bucket of kernels and two pops," he told the attendant, and grabbed a fistful of napkins from a chrome holder. "Nice when there's no line."

The attendant handed them their popcorn, and Emma sprinkled extra salt on it. "Makes it tastier," she said.

"Sure does." They entered the theatre and found seats in the center about midway down. "We need more nights like this," he whispered in the darkness. "More nights of just us."

The lights soon dimmed, and the picture started. She rubbed his thigh.

Tucker glanced down and saw how the light shining from overhead and behind him was highlighting her legs in the bunched-up dress. It reminded him of the first day he laid eyes on her. And how he loved those long legs and soft facial features and brown speckled eyes that spoke volumes. Why would any man want to hurt a woman as sweet and beautiful as Emma? He was lucky her ex-husband and the last man she'd been with hadn't appreciated her. If they'd only seen what he had, they'd've never laid a hand on her or given up someone so precious.

"You're off tomorrow morning, right?" she whispered.

"Yes."

"Swell," she cooed. "Because you ain't sleeping tonight."

"No?"

"Not if I get my way," She winked. "Not for a second."

When the movie let out, they went for a stroll. And once they settled into the flat area in the reeds and cattails that skirted the bank of the Overpeck Creek, they kissed, raising a certain urgency in Tucker, a deep, deep desire to have her, and she willingly lay back and let him kiss her and run his hands lovingly over her, feeling the strength of them through the fabric of her clothes, her own passion as great as his.

"Do you think someone will see us?" she asked at one point, half sitting up, her arms crossed over her breasts that were now exposed.

"No," he said. "Let's not concern ourselves out here in the middle of nowhere. Let's turn this night into a memorable one, huh?"

As he entered her, he felt whole again, like a man who'd never seen death, and whatever demons he'd had to deal with until that moment were gone from him, and they were as Adam and Eve in the Garden and made the sweetest love.

"So this is where you almost got him?" she whispered.

"A little more north... by where that dock I took you to is."

"Oh," Emma said. "Where all those men fish and crab?"

"Yes, right about there. Where those old tires are pressed into the mushy bank."

"I know exactly where that is," she winked. "But let's not think about that."

"Think about what?"

"Exactly."

69

"Chief! Chief!" A neighbor was banging on Henderson's front door. "Chief!"

Henderson swung open the door. "What is it, Thomas?"

"Granado's house is on fire!" the man gasped. "His daughter's trapped on the second floor. We can't get to her!"

"Molly." Henderson shouted into the house. "Come lock the door. I got an emergency."

She rushed to the front vestibule in her white nightgown and slippers. "Oh, my God," she cried. "What's going on?"

Henderson was hurrying into his boots. "Peter Granado's house is burning. I'll be back soon." He looped his belt, holster, and gun around his waist. "You can smell it."

She sniffed the air. "My God, that's right behind our house. Be careful, honey," she pleaded. "Be careful."

The man who had banged on Henderson's door was rushing away. Henderson hurried after him. As he drew closer, he smelled the wood burning and saw the thick, heavy gray smoke filling the neighborhood, and how flames were spilling from the front windows and licking up toward the second floor, burning the beige clapboard. He saw the yellow, orange, red, and blue flames dance from the windows and beads of moisture streaming down the darkened glass and into the frame. The house was breathing.

There was chaos. A man screamed from an upstairs window. "Help, we can't get down the stairs. My daughter! Help!"

"Peter," Henderson shouted. "Hang in there. I'm on my way."

Tires screeched as a police cruiser came to a skidding stop. Dankert jumped out and began charging the front of the house. "Chief," he shouted. "You can't go in there. It's too dangerous."

The flames were spilling out a front window and the thundering black smoke was choking the man calling from the window. He held his hand over his mouth and slipped back inside.

"Baloney," Henderson countered. "Peter and his daughter are up there. We've got to get to them."

"But, Chief," Dankert said, "let's go through the back. There's less fire."

"No!"

A girl was now screaming from a second-floor window, "Help! Help! Somebody help. Daddy!"

"Frank has a ladder next door," Dankert suggested. "Help me lift it to window and we'll get in that way."

"No."

"I'm getting the ladder, Chief. Don't go in there."

Henderson cupped his hand over his mouth and charged the door, shouldering it and falling into the vestibule. Knowing the layout, he entered the front parlor—the fire room—and felt the heat, felt his ears warm as if they were melting, and his eyes were welling up with uncontrollable tears. His skin was pinching and itchy, his heart pumping in panic. He dropped to the floor and began crawling. He was choking in the pitch blackness but spotted flames highlighting the stairway to the second floor. He jumped through the flames and ran his hands along his legs to see if he was on fire. It hadn't caught his clothes and he charged up the stairs and crept low, on his hands and knees, toward a bedroom with a closed door. "I'm coming," he shouted into the darkness. "Hang in there!"

What he felt next on the floor outside the door caused him to nearly vomit. It was his friend Peter, who lay there breathing, though barely. He confirmed it by feeling the face on the body and stroking the long beard. "Peter," he shrieked. "Are you alive?"

There was no response.

The body was warm and hadn't burned yet. Feeling for a pulse, he pressed his shaking index and middle fingers against his neck. He felt a faint pulse and placed his cheek to the man's mouth and felt his exhale. Smoke inhalation most likely had him unconscious. Henderson coughed, spewing phlegm, and knew he couldn't spend another second in that blistering hot hallway or he'd find himself lying next to the homeowner. He climbed over him and reached for the closed bedroom door.

When he plunged into the bedroom, he fell on his wrist and let out a grunt. The smoke began to fill the room. He dragged the homeowner in the room, and quickly closed the door. He heard the girl panicking uncontrollably. She was ten years old and had her body halfway out the window. "I can't breathe," she was shouting. "I can't breathe!"

"I'm here," he shrieked, grasping the window sill and pulling himself up into the frame. There was loud popping sounds and what sounded like wind whirling. Henderson pinched his nose and felt the grit that stuffed it. He was sweating profusely. He struggled to fit through that window with the screaming girl and was finally able to draw a breath of fresh air. The firemen were spraying water on the window below them and it had turned the direction of the smoke. He draped the girl's arms around his shoulders. "Hold on, young lady," he gasped. "We're gonna charge back down them stairs, and we'll be safe."

The girl was crying. "Daddy. Where's daddy?"

Henderson began to get very fuzzy. He looked into the girl's eyes, saw the fear mounting her face, her tears, and how her lips quivered. She continued screaming for her father. He tore off his shirt and wrapped it around the girl's mouth. He was searching for something to cover his but his eyes were burning and stinging so badly he couldn't see. He started to slip back into the window. He was growing dizzier and, through a haze of spiraling shades of gray and black and white, he saw his dead son. He tried to shake it off, searching below he felt the window sill with his free hand. He tried to concentrate and consider his next move. It was either they did like he had originally wanted and charged down the stairs, or they'd jump from the second story of the home. Henderson's mind was slowing and his body began convulsing. His breathing became more sporadic, the phlegm thick in his throat. He spit it out and his eyes went wide when through the smoke and flickering of the flames, he again saw his dead son. Was it a ghost? Was he being called home to be with his son?

70

Hiding behind a parked vehicle across the street from Henderson's house, the butcher had watched the neighbor bang on Henderson's door, watched the chief answer with great concern and rush toward the burning house: like luring a kid with a lollypop.

When he could no longer see Henderson, he had fished a smoke from his breast pocket and pressed it to his lips. Sitting with his back to the parked auto, he had let the smoke fill his lungs, held it briefly, and felt the spinning, buzzy feeling he liked so much, the brief numbness that was so alluring. He glanced at the cherry end on the cigarette and considered his plan. Liberating, he thought. Cathartic.

He'd already seen Tucker and Emma whisked away earlier, both smiling, and had spat on the ground and considered charging up and putting a bullet straight in the man's head.

He snuffed out his cigarette on the curb and started for the house. When he was on the front porch, he noticed the large and gnarled old elm tree that cast a long shadow over the deck. He smelled the fire and heard firemen shouting orders and the sounds of broken glass. The burning house was within a hundred feet of the Henderson's. But that wouldn't have mattered anyway. A hundred feet or one hundred miles, neither would matter, the butcher knew. Henderson was consumed in his duties.

He fished a big flat-head screwdriver from his jeans pocket, pressed it to the jamb, and within seconds had compromised the door. It swung open quietly, like a church door. He entered the house. Looking up at him was a young boy with eyes as blue as the ocean. "Damien," the butcher said softly. "You remember me?"

71

Tucker, lying on his back with his elbows dug into the ground, leaned forward to kiss his wife on the lips. She melted into him, and they continued kissing. There was a loud chirping of insects and a light autumn breeze that made a vibrating, sweeping sound through the reeds. The moon shined in the vastness, highlighting the stars like diamonds strewn across a black canvas.

"Should we sleep out here tonight," Emma asked.

"You'll stay out here until the sun rises?"

"Yeah," Emma embraced her husband. "Whenever we wake up, we'll head back."

"Is this not the same place that you refused? You did choose that abandoned store over this fresh air, right?"

"You know I hate night critters and such, but tonight, I don't care what's out here. As long as I'm with you, I'm not gonna let a little raccoon or an opossum ruin our evening."

"You forgot muskrats and foxes," Tucker smiled, playfully. "Last week on the overnight my headlights caught the glare of two sets of eyes and when I got out and inspected them, there were two red foxes right out in the open."

"Nothing," Emma said finally. "Nothing's gonna dissuade me."

Tucker laced his hands behind his head and felt the tiny pebbles press into his back. It had a therapeutic effect, loosening up his tight back muscles. "I know I promised you I'd find work as a carpenter in Buffalo, and come to think of it, I actually enjoyed all those days I spent working with Dominic. It made me feel like I accomplished something, seeing that house come together the way it did."

"If we fall into some money, you can build our house," Emma whispered into his chest. "Three bedrooms on the second floor and a large kitchen and parlor on the main."

"We don't need something that big, hon."

"Extra rooms always come in handy."

"Either way, I'm going to build a decent-sized two-car garage, if we ever fall into money, that is. Then I'm gonna buy us something fast and smooth. Something comfortable for travel and fast enough to get us places quicker than that damn flivver."

"That car was junk from the start," Emma said. "So many problems. We should have known it wouldn't make it across country."

"It did make it all the way to New Jersey," Tucker said somewhat proudly. "That's the best we could get out of it. But maybe we can stay here a little longer, hon? Work like this is hard to come by."

"You love being a cop that much, huh."

"We'll save this conversation for later," he said.

Emma fell silent.

Shortly thereafter, they dressed again and lay there in the cover of the reeds—the only light coming from the moon—until they smelled something burning.

"What is that?" he asked.

She glanced along the bank. "You think the brush is burning?"

He rushed her to her feet. "I don't want to find out in here." They moved quickly, Emma adjusting her dress back down below her waist and Tucker his blue jeans so the gun fit comfortably around his waist.

They rushed through the reeds when Tucker called out: "Wait. I just stepped on something mushy."

Emma stopped and when she saw what lay before her, she screamed. "Oh my God! Tucker! What is it?"

"Easy, hon."

"Who is it?" Emma asked, frantically. "Another dead person. This damn town is cursed."

Tucker examined the remains. He saw how the skin had blackened and was greenish in some areas and how he could see spots where the flesh was clean to the bone, he knew from being eaten away by the animals. Then he observed the long silver hair, that was strewn over the hollowed out face that spilled along the neck and torso. Tucker could see deep caverns where the eyes had once sat. A closer inspection showed vertebrae visible in the neck. The bosoms were missing.

"It's old lady Stillman," Tucker considered. "Who else could it be?"

"We'll let's get out of here. If these reeds are on fire, we'll be trapped."

"Remember this spot. I'll be back later to examine it further."

"You don't need to come back here," Emma claimed. "We're getting the heck outta this damned town."

"I know, honey. Come on."

They hurried away and when they slipped out of the tall reeds, Emma gasped. "Over there!" She pointed. "There's a massive fire."

They saw how the smoke funneled into the dark sky and grayed and dispersed, stretching like a raincloud over the town. Fragments of ash were falling from the sky, and Tucker felt an unease in his stomach. It was a hundred yards away but a fire that big felt like they were sitting barefoot in front of a fireplace. They could see the crackling of the burning wood and how it speckled into the sky like sparks from a welder soldering. They heard the popping sounds. Heard the men shouting. The wailing of sirens in the distance got louder as the racing fire truck sped down the hill. Tucker clenched Emma's hand and they began running toward it. "I hope it's not Henderson's house."

72

The boy was shaking his head when the butcher bent before him in the front vestibule of the Henderson's home. "Surely you remember me," he said politely.

The boy bit his top lip. "I ain't sure," he said.

"You're Damien, right? I taught you how to ride your bike. Remember? The more you pedal, the easier to balance?"

"Ugh, I—I don't have no bike. Daddy said Santa's bringing it this year."

The butcher chuckled; it echoed in the quiet home. "Ah, yes, Santa. He's coming early this year. What else is he bringing?"

"My... my daddy says not to talk to people I dunno."

"But you do know me, Damien. I taught you how to hit a baseball. And throw that fastball. Remember where your fingers go on the laces?"

"Daddy said he'd teach me when I get older. We're working on hitting." Then in a burst of courage he said, "I bet you can't strike me out, mister."

"I bet I can't," said the butcher. "Say, are those your toys, lad?"

When he turned, the butcher clamped his steel-like hands around the boy's body, one tightly around his mouth, the other on his throat, and dragged him inside the kitchen, where his mother was rushing toward the commotion. She shouted, "Get your hands off him!"

He did, and turned to her, his gun drawn, the hammer back. "Stand back, Molly."

Her eyes dilated with fear. "Leave my boy alone, Michael. Take your hands off him," she said. Then she realized he was the demon who had terrified everybody. Oh, God, she thought. With shaking hands she managed to mumble, "Please, Michael. It doesn't have to be like this."

"Everybody says that."

"It doesn't," Molly insisted.

"Okay," he said. "Maybe you're right."

She stood frozen in the silence that followed and stared into his cold and distant eyes.

"I just have a question, Molly. It won't take long. Have a seat."

She was shaking as she tried to sit down on a dining chair but slipped and fell to the floor. She kept eyeing the chair as if she wanted to hit him with it.

But she didn't.

Her arms were trembling. She tried to drag herself up. "Wh-what do you want, Mike?"

"I never thought you'd ask. I was sent here by your husband."

"That's nonsense."

"Nonsense?" he retorted.

"You've destroyed this town," she spat. "You've killed people senselessly."

"It's your husband, Molly. Can't you see that?"

"It's not my husband," Molly said. "It's you. Everything is about you."

With a confused look on his face, he said, "How can you not see it? He did this to you."

"He's done nothing to me, Michael."

"He should've known better," he said, squinting and aiming his pistol. She had the same look of fear in her eyes, the same horror, the impossible idea on that frantic September night that life would soon be over. "Had you ever thought it would end like this?"

"Oh, God, no. You couldn't possibly. We've done nothing to you. What have we done to you?"

"Actually, you're wrong," he said, curling his lip. "Your husband killed my father. He destroyed my life."

"That's ridiculous."

"What's ridiculous?"

"This whole thing," Molly said.

"Were you ever so destitute you had to sell yourself?"

"You're talking gibberish."

"Call it what you want, Molly. I call it the truth."

"What does this have to do with me or my son?" she shouted. "Carter's in the back room."

The butcher laughed. There was an intonation in his voice when he said, "Now, is it polite to lie to someone? You think I didn't just watch him rush away to the fire?"

When Molly said nothing, he nodded. "Duh. Of course I started that fire."

"W-what do you want?" she murmured again. "Leave my boy alone. Leave him alone!"

"You're pushy too, huh," the butcher said. "Is this how you treat all your guests?"

"Just leave us alone," she muttered, eyes welling with tears.

He angled his gun to the center of her chest. Her heart was pumping wildly. "Did you? Did you ever think it'd end this way? That I'd walk in here and decided when you die?"

"Carter! Come quick!" she called over her shoulder.

"What'd I tell you about lying?" he said.

"He's sleeping, I can assure you."

"Then I guess I won't shoot you," he said, and pulled the trigger. The muzzle sparked. She fell to the floor with a loud thump.

He looked down at her. Her body shook and twitched briefly before it went still. "Don't take it personal." He closed her eyelids with his index finger. "Why don't you rest a while. I'll be right back."

73

The ladder smacked hard against the building. "Grab it!" Dankert screamed from bellow. "Grab it, Chief, and get down here now."

Henderson could barely see the rungs. He shook off as much of the pain as he could and seized the rung with his left hand. The girl clinging tightly to his neck, positioned like a chimp on the back of its mother. Henderson next dug his boots into the rungs. He was moving purely on adrenaline. He clambered shakily down the ladder, back straining and arms stiff. He felt the wobble in his ankles and arms as he tried to steady himself. He was huffing and desperately trying to get fresh air. His eyes were bloodshot and stung with a burning sensation that was so fierce it caused him to scream.

Halfway down, he felt a hand grab at his boot. "Stop, Chief." Dankert ordered. "I'll take the girl."

She was petrified as he transferred her to Dankert's hefty arms and descended the rest of the ladder.

He exhaled a long breath and wiped the tears from his right eye with his blacked hands. It left a mark across his cheek, as if he had swiped a piece of charcoal across it. The sweat was pouring from him, his clothes soaked. When his foot touched the grass, he collapsed to the ground. "Dankert," he muttered. "Peter's dying in the same room upstairs. Somebody get to him quickly."

The fire chief overheard Henderson and ordered his men up the ladder and into the window from which Henderson had descended.

The world was spinning above Henderson, and the abyss drew him in.

Two neighbors raced to the girl and whisked her off. They rushed her into a vehicle and sped down the roadway straight for Englewood Hospital.

"Chief." Dankert shook Henderson. "Wake up, Chief."

Henderson opened his eyes and, with a confused look, said, "Where am I?"

"You're going to be okay," Dankert said kneeling over Henderson. "There you go. Come back to your senses."

A man rushed a bucket of water into Dankert's hand and he splashed it over Henderson's face. The water washed down his very red skin.

Within seconds the firemen had Peter and were descending the ladder. "He's still breathing," a firefighter called out.

Dankert tossed him his shirt. "Put it on. She's okay now. It'll cool your skin."

Henderson sat up and got into his uniform shirt. Then he heard the sound of gunfire over the roaring fire. "Oh, God." He panicked. "Oh, God."

74

"Hurry, Emma!" Tucker exclaimed with her in tow. He was clutching her hand and rushing toward the fire. "It's not Henderson's house. But it's close."

"I can't move this fast in these shoes," she replied. "Slow down."

He glanced back at her, turned, and tripped over his own feet. He fell to the ground, and she followed. On her backside, she said, "I told you."

He got to his feet and helped her to hers, brushed himself off, and ran toward the house. "We're almost there, Emma. Come on."

As they rounded the corner, they could taste the smoke, heard the commotion, and saw local men rushing toward the fire. "It's the neighbor's house," Emma said, panting. "I can't run anymore."

Henderson's son Damien was ahead, screaming as he raced toward the fire. "Damien," Tucker called out, but the boy kept running and screaming in panic. "Hold on, Emma," Tucker said. "Something's not right."

They slowed down and began to catch their breaths. They were within fifteen feet of Henderson's house, skirting—as the butcher appeared on Henderson's front porch—a tall, thick hedgerow that hid them from him. "Damien." the butcher called out. "Oh, sweet boy, come here."

"Quiet," Tucker whispered to Emma. They halted under the hedgerow and Tucker drew his gun. They crept low. He pressed his lips against her ear. "Slowly back up, and hide in that garage on the corner. Take cover, and don't move. Do this as quietly as you possibly can. We don't want to give up our cover."

"Please, Tucker," she pleaded. "Come with me."

"Shh. You hide in that garage until I come and get you."

Her eyes flared, and she began to tear. "Please, Tucker," she said, her voice barely audible. "Come back with me."

He held his index finger to his lips and then motioned her on. She did as she was told.

"Remember to wait there for me," he reminded her.

She looked over her shoulder and saw him angling himself from the corner of the hedges, his gun held out to his side. An additional fire truck raced past with men standing on the sideboards. When it stopped at the corner, they grabbed hoses and ladders and dashed toward the fire. There was an elderly lady with a cane ambling toward the commotion when Emma grabbed her by the arm. "Turn around," she said. "It's too dangerous."

When the old lady saw the tears in Emma eyes and the expression on her face, she gasped. "Oh, dear, is anybody hurt?"

"No," Emma said. "But it's too dangerous. Come with me."

The old lady didn't respond but turned and allowed Emma to help her retreat.

Tucker could see the butcher through the hedge and, when he started for the sidewalk, Tucker exploded into his path. "Put the gun down, or I'll shoot you!"

The butcher held his hands up. "Oh, how nice of you," he snickered.

"Drop the weapon."

The butcher smirked. "Here I was looking for Damien, and how pleasant of you to show."

"Drop the gun, you sonofabitch," Tucker sneered, "or I'm gonna shoot you."

"Why?"

"Cause you tried to kidnap my wife."

"Let's be fair," the butcher said. "Had I wanted her that day, I could've easily done that."

"Drop the gun. You're under arrest."

The butcher cautiously stepped backwards. "Did you figure it out yet?"

Stiffing his grip on his revolver and sighting the butcher's chest in his sights, Tucker said, "Figured what out? How you killed innocent people over nothing."

The butcher shook his head, "You couldn't be that foolish."

Tucker narrowed his gaze. "Drop the gun, asshole."

"July 28, 1903. Make any sense, huh?"

"I don't care to figure nothing out."

"Well, you should."

Tucker kept the gun trained on him, thumbing the hammer to make certain it was back.

"Henderson's the killer around here," the butcher said as if he was exposing the biggest secret in town. "I bet he never explained that to you."

"Put the gun down, Mike," Tucker repeated. "The game's over."

"You're willing to die for a killer, huh?"

Tucker spat and crept closer, the gun in his hands stretched out in a triangle before him. "If you don't put it down now, I'm gonna fire."

"Henderson's the one you need to arrest, Officer." The butcher raised his hands higher in the sky. "Can I ask a question?"

"Drop it, Mike."

"You the hero type?"

"Put it—"

"All right, I'll put it down."

"Nice and slowly."

The butcher got down on one knee and, in an exaggerated fashion, brought the weapon to the grass. As he placed it on the ground, he managed to get off a shot, striking Tucker in the left shoulder. The butcher tumbled on the grass and fired again. The round hit Tucker in the collarbone.

That's when Tucker heard the screaming, an ungodly sound as piercing as a hawk's. Through the pain and the intense heat, he fired and struck the butcher clearly in the torso. He fired again and dropped him to the grass. The butcher landed with a loud thud. Lying on his back, he angled his gun at Tucker, fired, and Tucker collapsed to the sidewalk, rolled around, his fingers cold, left eye was twitching. He felt the blood from his shoulder and realized he had been hit. But he couldn't feel much of it. Pressing his fingers into the hole in his collarbone, he forced himself to stand and charge the butcher, who was bellowing in pain when Tucker pounced on top of him and punched him in the face with the butt of his gun, turned the muzzle, and fired again, but the gun jammed. There was great heat and pain blazing inside him. He managed to retrieve the butcher's gun and stuffed it into his waistband before he fell backwards.

In the silence that followed, Tucker realized where the screaming was coming from. It was Emma. Through hazy eyes that were now projecting spiraling images in gray and black, he could make out Emma standing over him, terrified and sobbing uncontrollably. "Oh, my God, Tucker!" she screeched. "Nooooo!"

The moon was full and bright in the smoky sky that made the gray smoke seem fuller. Tucker tried to stand and made it to his knees; half bent over, Emma slid an arm under his shoulder and endeavored to carry him into the cover of the hedges. She glanced at the butcher. He was on his hands and knees, getting to his feet. He screamed through his teeth, "Emma, get over here!"

She never heard him call. She did, however, sense he was lumbering toward them and, with all her might, continued to heft her husband away. She managed to get him behind the hedgerows before he collapsed again. She tried to help him to his feet but couldn't. "Please, Tucker," she cried. "God, please."

The butcher was gaining on them. "Emma, get over here, dear." he called out. "Get here now."

When he was within ten feet, Emma searched frantically for her husband's gun. From the corner of her eye, she saw one protruding from Tucker's waistband. She grabbed it and, as if by magic, it appeared before her. As the butcher leaped for her, she fired two shots in rapid succession, and he fell to the ground. He continued screaming for Emma, but he wasn't able to get back up.

Tucker was coughing up blood as Emma stroked at his face. She gripped his hand but felt little strength. His hands were ice cold. "I love you," he whispered, his voice erratic, a thin line of blood streamed from his mouth. He was choking. The smoke lay heavy in the air, the wind whipping it through the hedges and over them.

She cried, "I love you," and tried to stop the bleeding, panting, her breaths faster and shorter. But when Tucker's hand went slack, horror consumed her.

Henderson appeared and dashed toward them. A quick search of the butcher proved he had no weapon. Henderson kicked him in the face and then applied his boot to his face. "What have you done," he shrieked. "What have you done?"

Dankert appeared and wrapped his hand tightly around the butcher's neck. "Check on Tucker, Chief. I got him."

"Somebody, help!" Emma cried out. "Help!"

Suddenly, the Sinagra men appeared and they trained weapons on the butcher while one stood with his back to the commotion and scanned the area. Dankert continued to hold him down as the butcher squirmed with all his might. There were three firemen who dashed up the sidewalk with a ladder. A 1925 America La France fire truck came wailing down the roadway from Grand Avenue. Its siren commanding over the commotion, its headlights beaming cones through the smoke. Through the haze appeared leather helmets and black coats and the ringing of a bell aggressively as the fire truck skid to a stop and the men pulled hoses and raced toward the fire.

Henderson rushed for Emma and saw lots of blood, quickly got on his knees, and assessed the young man's injuries. His worst nightmare had come true: He briefly thought of the day he had pinned that badge on him and how he had been the one to get him into this.

Emma was murmuring like a baby. Henderson felt for a pulse on Tucker's neck. There was none. "Bastard." Henderson screamed and flew back to the butcher. "Step back, Dankert," he shouted.

The butcher looked up at Henderson with fearless eyes. "You killed him," the chief said. "He'd done nothing to you."

"It should have been you," the butcher gargled on the blood that had pooled in his mouth. He pushed his tongue forward and the blood seeped out of his mouth. "You killed my father," he said.

"Bullshit," Henderson sneered. "Your old man was drunk,

and when he attacked me, he fell on his own gun and it went off."

Dankert kept his gun trained on the butcher. Henderson motioned for him to step back. The Sinagra men kept close watch.

Henderson crinkled his nose. He pressed his gun against the butcher's forehead. In his mind's eye he flashed images of a day he rolled on the green grass with an eight year old Freddy and how they'd smiled and hugged and laughed while, Molly looked on with wonderment. He pressed the muzzle of the revolver firmer into the butcher's forehead, dipping it deeper into his skin, he felt the butcher's skull through the weapon. The wind picked up, and he felt his index finger stop shaking as it lay softly on the trigger. He felt a calming sensation, as if his spirit had been freed and the abyss no longer drew him in.

But he hadn't had to pull the trigger. The bullets Emma had pumped into the man had done their job.

Epilogue

Three months had passed, and Christmas was two weeks away; Henderson was sitting behind his desk in the police station. It was mid-morning. Over Henderson's right shoulder, the snow was accumulating on the windowsill. The glass had begun to frost and a blistering chill racked through the corners of the windowpane. Henderson had his son Damien on his knee. "Daddy, it's cold in here," the boy said. "Can somebody get frozen like ice?"

"No, son, that ain't gonna happen," Henderson assured him, rubbing the boy's red wool hat that Molly had made for him. "As long as your head's warm, you're body's warm."

The boy wrapped his arms around his father and placed his head against his chest. "Am I getting a bicycle from Santa?"

"Yes, son," Henderson replied softly. "The nicest bicycle his elves can make will be reserved for you."

The boy relished the promise. "Would I be able to ride my bike in the snow?"

"You'll slip all over the place," Henderson said. "And you need to watch out for the handlebar. I saw a kid one time fall off his bike and it went straight into his biceps."

"What's a biceps, Daddy?"

"Never mind," Henderson said, then touched the boy's right bicep. "It's this muscle that helps you move your arm."

The boy looked at his biceps then glanced out the window and watched the snow fall. He knew kids would be sleigh riding soon and he thought about his sled and how one day he'd try to ride his bike in the snow.

Henderson lifted the paper that he had refused to read since Dankert nervously pointed out what he had discovered two days after Molly's death. He turned the page, and his eyes dwelled on the obituary the butcher had submitted to the paper:

> Carter Henderson, Chief of the Palisades Park Police Department, sadly announces the untimely death of his wife Molly Henderson and their son Damien. Mrs. Henderson was a mother of two boys, Frederick (deceased) and Damien. She was a parishioner at the First Presbyterian Church and a member of the American Legion Auxiliary, where she was instrumental in the planning and organizing events for disabled veterans. A private service was held, and the burial took place at the Hackensack Cemetery. Chief Henderson would like to thank all of his friends for their thoughts and prayers during this trying time and respectfully requests a period of privacy to allow for healing.

"Daddy, don't cry," Damien said. "I know what else could keep somebody from freezing."

Henderson craned his neck downward. "What's that, son?"

"You, Daddy," he smiled. "You're warm, and you ain't got a hat on."

Henderson smiled and, through his son's eyes, saw a future. He'd live solely for the boy now. Solely to see him grow up without all the horrors of his early childhood, without worrying about what was behind him and focusing on what he'd become in life. Henderson would be damned if Damien followed in his footsteps. His boy was going to be somebody.

The chief rose and wrapped his big arm around Damien's bottom, turned off the desk light and slid the large stack of papers into the garbage can. He took his policeman's hat from its usual peg and tossed it in with the papers. He let out a relaxing sigh, dug deeply into his pocket, fished out his badge and the medal he'd gotten for fighting the war down in Cuba. He stuffed the medal into his pocket and flung his badge in the garbage.

Just then, Dankert walked in. "So today's the day, huh?"

"What do you got there?"

Dankert showed him the bronze plaque he was holding for honorable service as chief of police. "Feel the weight on this."

Henderson took a step back. "What do you plan to do with that?"

"I'm going to hang it on the wall right there, so the new guys we hired will know who you were and what you done for this department."

Henderson seized the plaque and tossed it in the garbage, too. "You want to memorialize a hero, then nail something about Tucker on that wall... or my son Freddy. But don't you ever hang me from any wall in this place."

Dankert swallowed. "Is that an order?" His brow furrowed.

Henderson nodded and walked out the door, down the corridor, and out onto Broad Avenue. Large white snowflakes were floating to ground. It was quiet, save for a maroon Model A's rear slipping as it rounded the corner onto Broad Avenue. The vehicle slid into the curb as the driver spun the wheel frantically to avoid it. Within seconds the vehicle was able to regain traction and continued wobbling down Broad Avenue. The sun was casting light brightly from the east that made the snow sparkle as it floated softly to the pavement.

"Daddy," Damien said. "You're breathing like a dragon."

Henderson let out a long exhale and it smoked in the cold air.

"Daddy," Damien again said, smiling in his father's arms, "Christmas is almost here."

Two hours later, there was a foot of powdery snow on the ground when Henderson found Emma outside the train depot. Two men in business attire with hats and long wool coats spoke as they waited for the train to arrive. Behind them stood Emma. Henderson approached cautiously as Damien sat in the car wiping at the fog on the windows to watch as the train approached. Henderson hadn't made eye contact with her and the red scarf she wore around her face concealed most of her identity. But he was certain it was her. He could tell from her stature and her beige coat with the brown collar. It was Molly's coat and he had given it to her saying that it'd belonged to Molly's sister so she wouldn't have felt funny about wearing it. She held a small bag with her belongings.

Henderson paused briefly and recalled Tucker's burial out at the Hackensack Cemetery. The United States Army had come and given Emma an American flag as she had sat there sobbing along the side of the grave. She had wept throughout the whole ceremony. A preacher had intoned the solemn opening words of the Episcopal burial service: "I am the resurrection and the life, saith the Lord; he that believeth in me, though he were dead, yet shall he live; and whosoever liveth and believeth in me shall never die." When the preacher had finished speaking, he'd closed the Bible, the graveyard men lowered the ropes, and Tucker's coffin sank into the earth. Lots of cops had come from far and wide to pay their respects to the man who had fought the man they all feared, a monster who didn't value human life or authority and could easily have put any one of them in the grave. Guilt washed over Henderson. He felt responsible for Tucker's, Molly's, and Freddy's deaths. Deep down he felt he could have prevented it. Over the past three months, many scenarios had played routinely in his mind. It was the obvious that bothered him mostly. The obvious he had not seen. They say hindsight is 20/20, and it was weighing heavily on him.

The train whistle blasted in the distance as it chugged toward Henderson and Emma. They could hear the squealing of brakes and see the tailwind of smoke streaming across the frosted window as it came to a halt. The train's engine clanged as the exhaust huffed out densely, spiraling like a rooster tail in the thick cold air. "All aboard," the conductor shouted. "We'll be leaving momentarily."

"Emma," Henderson called out.

Emma turned slightly and saw it was Henderson. She took off her scarf and revealed her pinkish cheeks and eyes welling with tears. She stuffed her scarf into the top of her coat. She was about to speak but didn't.

"Thank you," Henderson said.

Emma nodded and covered her mouth with her hand. She was holding back a sob.

A cold wind picked up, and the snow on the ground was

accumulating quickly, especially since the train had pushed it from the tracks and directly onto her boots.

"I've got to go to Buffalo," she said. "It's what Tucker would want for me."

Henderson paused briefly then said: "At least your sister and her husband can look after you. And you can spend some time caring for her kids."

Emma bowed her head and she broke down, sobbing. The brown collar on her coat was wet with frozen tears. There were fingernail markings on her neck and chin where she scratched at the stinging frost.

Henderson embraced her. "Your husband was a good man. A hero," he said softly.

"But," she cried, and rubbed her belly with her left hand. "It's not showing much. But it will soon. Doctor Anderson said I am three months." There was a brief pause; then she said. "His child will grow up without him."

Henderson thought about Dr. Anderson and how much he despised the man. He was about to ask her if he had suggested she abort the child, but thought better of asking. As Henderson stood there hugging her, he felt her sorrow and her uncertainty over what lay ahead, felt her loss. At that point, he did the only thing he could think of doing—he continued to hug her. "Be strong," he said.

The conductor shouted, "Train's leaving."

Emma pulled away from him, nodded, and wiped the cold tears that were streaming down her cheeks. She mounted the carriage stairs. At the top, she stopped and turned to him. "I'll be back every now and then to sit a while with Tucker. And to bring his child to meet him."

Henderson tipped his cap. "Be well, Emma," he said.

The engine cranked, and, moments later, the steel wheels slowly began to move.

Later that afternoon, Henderson found Veronica under the maple tree in the Graystone courtyard. She was sitting with her back to him as he approached. She was wearing a dark blue jacket, black slacks, boots, and a blue wool hat. Next to her sat an old suitcase tied with cord. There was lots of snow on the ground, and he could see the tracks she had taken to get to the place she had found was the most tranquil. The trees were bare and the flower beds scarcely visible in the drifts that had settled in the open courtyard. The sun was shining brightly above, and the sparkling snow seemed as polished as glass.

"Veronica," Henderson said calmly.

She didn't turn her head.

There was a little wind, and Henderson wasn't sure if she had heard his call, but something told him she had. He decided not to call again.

As he got closer, his boots crunched in the snow, collapsing the thin sheet of ice on the top of it.

At that point she turned to him. "I'm nervous," she said. "I don't think I could live in Palisades Park again. It'd bring back too many bad memories."

"We're not," he told her. "Where we're going, it doesn't snow, and the sun always shines."

She smiled. "Are we really?"

"I wouldn't lie to you," he said.

"But your son Freddy's baby," she frowned. "How could you forgive me for what I've done?"

"Forgiveness is all I got left."

"But I can't forgive myself. How can you forgive me?"

Henderson could see her yellowing teeth and how they contrasted against the very white landscape behind her, could see the tall wrought iron fence that surrounded the institution's courtyard, and how the place, although serene in some respects, was nothing more than a compound to house mentally fragile people until they died. A month before, when he approached Veronica with the idea of freeing her from that, she had welcomed it wholeheartedly. A few weeks of pulling strings and calling in a favor to an old politician who had known his father, had her released into his custody.

They climbed into his vehicle and drove down the Graystone driveway and onto the snowy road. He exchanged a short wave with the guard. The car was slipping a bit, but the tires still maintained contact with the road thanks to the sun, which was melting and clearing some of it. He'd take it slow to avoid anything foolish. No sense hurrying.

As he spun the wheel around a corner, all he could do was think. He stole a glance at Veronica, her face beaming with frosty red cheeks. He felt her peace and happiness. It was a warming sensation. In the rearview mirror, he could see Damien glancing out the side window and the questions in his expression. He thought of Freddy and of how much he had loved his dear boy and wished he was sitting next to Damien.

And about Molly: He smiled, recalling the dream he'd had of her the night before. She had been stretched out, basking on a sugar-white beach with the endless blue ocean at her toes and the golden sun showering down, and seagulls squawking and sailboats floating by. He could smell the salt water. When he approached her, she had smiled and brought her sunglasses down the bridge of her nose, revealing her beautiful blue eyes. He had settled down next to her, and they'd held hands. Recalling the dream brought him comfort.

"Hello," Damien said from the back seat. "Are you coming with us too, ma'am?"

The windshield wipers slugged a heavy sheet of snow that had slid forward from the roof. It left a glaring film. "Yes," Veronica replied, half turning her head to the boy and self-consciously covering the scars on her wrists.

"Don't worry about that, Veronica," Henderson said. "The Florida sun will blend it all in."

Made in the USA
Lexington, KY
23 August 2014